P9-BZN-365

3 4604 9107 1 4020

Mystery Rus
Russell, Kirk, 1954-
Redback ': a John Marquez crime
novel

WITHDRAWN

REDBACK

The John Marquez series by Kirk Russell

SHELL GAMES
NIGHT GAMES
DEADGAME
REDBACK*

available from Severn House

REDBACK

Kirk Russell

SALINE DISTRICT LIBRARY
555 N. Maple Road
Saline, MI 48176

JAN - - 2011

Severn
House

This first world edition published 2010
in Great Britain and in 2011 in the USA by
SEVERN HOUSE PUBLISHERS LTD of
9–15 High Street, Sutton, Surrey, England, SM1 1DF.
Trade paperback edition first published
in Great Britain and the USA 2011 by
SEVERN HOUSE PUBLISHERS LTD.

Copyright © 2010 by Kirk Russell.

All rights reserved.
The moral right of the author has been asserted.

British Library Cataloguing in Publication Data

Russell, Kirk, 1954–
  Redback.
  1. Marquez, John (Fictitious character) – Fiction.
  2. California. Dept. of Fish and Game – Employees –
  Fiction. 3. Government investigators – California –
  Fiction. 4. Drug dealers – Mexico – Fiction. 5. Wildlife
  smuggling – Fiction. 6. Detective and mystery stories.
  I. Title
  813.6-dc22

ISBN-13: 978-0-7278-6965-4 (cased)
ISBN-13: 978-1-84751-294-9 (trade paper)

Except where actual historical events and characters are being
described for the storyline of this novel, all situations in this
publication are fictitious and any resemblance to living persons
is purely coincidental.

All Severn House titles are printed on acid-free paper.

Severn House Publishers support The Forest Stewardship Council [FSC],
the leading international forest certification organisation. All our titles that
are printed on Greenpeace-approved FSC-certified paper carry the FSC logo.

 **Mixed Sources**
Product group from well-managed
forests and other controlled sources
www.fsc.org Cert no. SA-COC-1565
© 1996 Forest Stewardship Council

Typeset by Palimpsest Book Production Ltd.,
Falkirk, Stirlingshire.
Printed and bound in Great Britain by the
MPG Books Group, Bodmin, Cornwall.

For Judy

ACKNOWLEDGMENTS

As with the first three Marquez novels many thanks go to Nancy Foley, Chief of Patrol, head of the law enforcement branch of California Fish and Game, and Kathy Ponting, the real-life Marquez, patrol lieutenant of the Special Operations Unit, the SOU. And thanks as well to George Fong, former FBI Assistant Inspector at FBI Headquarters. Without George's help Marquez never would have made it on to a task force and out into the broader world. Though he appears in the book climbing mountains, Adrian Muller did more than that to help this book along. Finally, and once again, many thanks to my agent, the indomitable Philip Spitzer.

I
Group 5
(June 1989)

ONE

Baja California, Mexico

In the summer heat, glare, and dust of Tijuana, Marquez picked up their informant, Billy Takado, and drove east across the desert plain toward the dry folds of the Sierra de Juarez and a meeting with the most violent cartel in Mexico. On a pass high in the Juarez he pulled over. He retrieved the satellite phone from the trunk and as he waited for it to connect studied the thin road below where it left the mountains and ran through the pueblo, and out through fields of alfalfa and pale green maize to the abandoned bull ring across the valley. The bull ring was a dark ellipse in after-noon shadow. The bull ring was where the meeting would go down.

When one of his squad, Sheryl Javits, answered, Marquez said, 'We're close. Tell them we'll come through the pueblo in about twenty minutes.'

Mexican Federal Judicial Police, the Mex Feds, were backing them up today. From her desk at the Drug Enforcement Administration Field Office in Los Angeles, Sheryl was coor-dinating. Marquez stowed the phone and tried to get Billy talking again as he got back in the car. Somewhere along the climb up the pass Takado had gone quiet.

They drove the potholed road through the pueblo past a whitewashed church and cinderblock buildings with corru-gated tin roofs, and on through air rich with the sweet heavy smell of alfalfa. When they reached the bull ring two armed cartel guards waited beside a jeep parked near rusted entry gates. The guards watched the Cadillac, with its show pipes, candy paint, and trick wheels, roll through the dust and stop.

Marquez got out first. He wore snakeskin boots, black jeans, and a white linen shirt with gold-colored threads woven through it. The back of the shirt was damp with sweat after the long drive. He wore a heavy Rolex and wrap-around

Ray-Bans. Billy wore clothes the Salazar brothers knew him by, Hawaiian shirt, gray cotton slacks, and sandals.

As the guards approached, Billy said quietly, 'I know the one on the right. He's a cop in Tijuana.'

That was who patted them down, jabbing fingers hard into armpits and groin before leading them into the bull ring where Marquez took in a thousand splintered and sun-silvered wood seats and ground hard as stone. He watched the guards take up positions and then looked past them to the rim of the arena and the bright blue sky over the mountains. When he heard a car he looked back at the gates. A black Mercedes sedan with tinted windows pulled up. Dust cleared and as the right rear door opened, Marquez felt both fear and exhilaration.

Special Agent John Marquez was thirty-one with eight years in at the DEA. He was young to be supervisor of a squad, but his career so far was a string of successes. His squad, Group 5, worked Baja traffic. In the last six months they'd focused strictly on the Tijuana-based Salazar Cartel. A week ago things started coming together and now were moving so fast Marquez didn't feel enough in control. Yet he wanted to keep it happening. In just a few days they had bumped up from the low level management to this meeting.

His hope was that Luis, the younger Salazar brother, would get out of the car. Luis was the one to connect with. The older brother, Miguel, was an unstable sociopath, and Luis's ambitions were more than enough. Luis wanted to wipe out the competitors, control Baja, and then keep expanding Salazar business in the US. He wanted the great cocaine cities of the east coast, New York, Miami, Washington, and Boston.

Neither brother got out of the car. Instead, it was someone Marquez had never seen before, a tall man, tanned and sure of himself. Looked like he was early forties, dark-haired, possibly European, possibly Spanish, and with a posture and stride Marquez knew he would remember. This could be the money man they'd heard whispers about, the financier. He wore a coat in the heat and made eye contact with Marquez as he walked toward them. But it didn't feel right, and when he reached them he shook Marquez's hand without giving his name. He stared at Billy as he pulled papers from his coat.

He handed the papers to Marquez, saying, 'You're going to carry a message back to the DEA from the Salazars.' As Marquez read the papers the man turned to Takado and asked in a quiet almost gentle voice, 'Did you really think I'd forget?'

The papers were copies of Federal personnel forms, the individual 52s for Jim Osiers, Brian Hidalgo, Sheryl Javits, Ramon Green, and himself, his squad, Group 5. Marquez shuffled through them as he tried to figure a way out of this.

'Tell them this, anyone who works against the Salazars is in danger. So are their families. We will kill your girlfriends, your wives, your children. Do you understand?'

That was it, meeting blown, meeting over, and with Billy walking stiffly just ahead of Marquez they headed toward the car. They were nearly to the Cadillac when a door of the Mercedes opened behind them. Marquez heard the door fall shut, the footsteps coming and knew from the footfall that whoever it was would catch them.

He said quietly to Billy, 'Don't look back. Don't look up. Just get in the car. We're out of here.'

Marquez slid the key into the ignition before Miguel Salazar rapped on the driver's window with a gun. Marquez started the engine anyway. That angered Miguel and when Marquez lowered the window Miguel shoved the gun against his temple.

With the barrel digging into his scalp, Marquez said, 'Look, I get it; I'm taking the message back.'

'*Llaves.*'

Marquez turned the car off. He handed Miguel the keys, put his hands on the wheel as ordered, and then watched Miguel walk around the front of the car with the gun's aim moving from him to Billy. Now Miguel was at Billy's window cursing, calling Billy a traitor, calling him the shit of a whore as Marquez tried to shut it down, speaking to Miguel in rapid Spanish.

'Not his fault, Miguel. Not his fault. We put him up to it. We forced him. We didn't leave him any other out.'

But that was just more bullshit to Miguel Salazar. He looked from Billy to Marquez, eyes bright with hate for this mixed-blood gringo agent and hate for all gringo agents and all people who would get in the way of his family. And maybe it was something he saw in Marquez's eyes, or respect he didn't see. Or maybe this was the way it was planned.

He pushed the barrel of the gun into Billy's forehead, forcing his head back so Billy had to look up at him. Billy was two-faced, a snitch, a *chismoso*. He was nothing. He was a mistake.

Miguel looked at Marquez, wanted Marquez to understand in a way that he would never forget, that he was powerless, that he could do nothing, that the gringo DEA, the United States of America, the Mexican government, the judicial police, could do nothing. He pulled the trigger and Billy's head jumped as blood and brains spattered on to the backseats. Before walking away Miguel threw the keys at Marquez and said, 'Next time you.'

TWO

B efore the pueblo, Marquez braked hard and got his gun and the satellite phone out of the trunk. His hands were shaking when he pulled over in front of the adobe church in the pueblo. Billy's mouth was open, his head slumped against the passenger window, the seat behind him glistening with blood. His bowels had released. Marquez checked the street, rear view mirror, the wooden church door just barely opening, now shutting again. He didn't know if he was waiting for Mex Feds, or not. But as the church door closed, he pulled away from the curb, deciding the Mex Feds weren't going to show themselves. They'd have some explanation later.

He lowered his window, wiped Billy's blood off the side of his face, his mind racing, his ears still ringing from the gunshot. With the gun in his lap he turned back toward the bull ring. He got halfway there before doing another U-turn and driving into the mountains. At the pass he pulled over where he'd called in last and asked for Sheryl Javits.

'Miguel Salazar shot Billy. He's in the passenger seat next to me. He's dead.'

'John, where are you?'

'Off the side of the road up in the Juarez.'

'Takado is dead?'

She didn't seem to get it. Marquez stared at a car approaching and reached for the gun. The car passed as Sheryl went on about the Mex Feds, repeating that she had talked to them all day.

'They picked you up when you crossed the border. They tracked you the whole way. They had officers at the bull ring.

Just stay where you are,' she said. 'I'll call you back. I've got to talk to Boyer.'

Marquez knew what Boyer, their ASAC, the Assistant Special Agent-in-Charge, would do. He'd kick the decision upstairs to the SAC, Special Agent-in-Charge, Jay Holsten, who ran the LA Field Office, and Marquez could guess Holsten's reaction.

After hanging up with Sheryl, he worked the seatbelt so Billy's body wouldn't slide down anymore. He made sure Billy's door was locked and then stood outside in the late sunlight looking in at Billy as he waited for her call back. He'd pushed Billy to make the meeting happen. Billy had reservations. Billy worried on the ride over.

'Holsten does not want you to move the body. That's an order, John. You're to wait there. The Mex Feds are on the way.'

'Tell Boyer and Holsten I'm headed to Tijuana. Ask our agents in Tijuana to drive toward me. I want witnesses when I turn over the car and Billy's body.'

'You're going to make it worse.'

He looked at Billy. Takado just wanted to live his life. He didn't want to go to jail again. He overplayed his connections with the Salazars and I knew, Marquez thought. I should have seen. I'm sorry, Billy. I'm so sorry.

'You need to stay where you are.'

Marquez registered that and answered, 'Tell Holsten that I said it was too dangerous to wait.'

'John, listen to me, you've got to stay there. You can't move the body. The Mex Feds want you to stay where you are.'

The fuck if he was going to sit here and wait for the guys who'd already burned them once today. He broke the connection and as he pulled back on to the road Billy slid down in the seat. Marquez turned the air conditioner on full and lowered the rear windows halfway.

Billy Takado lived alone. He didn't have any children. He didn't have anybody. He was the son of a Japanese father who'd immigrated to the US and a Mexican mother who lived just long enough to see her son do a five-spot for cocaine trafficking. She missed the next bust and Billy cutting a deal with the DEA.

When Marquez came out of the mountains he killed the air conditioner and drove with all of the windows down. The wind carried away the smells. It carried dry mesquite, creosote, and sun-baked desert rock. He kept checking the rear view mirror and up ahead the sky purpled with dusk. He ignored the satellite phone's ring and kept going until he ran into a Mex Fed roadblock. They pointed their guns and when he resisted handcuffs they got angry.

But they were angry anyway. The big gringo didn't know what they were up against or what it was to fight the *narco trafficantes*. Americans only cared about Americans and no one liked the Drug Enforcement Administration with its attitude and agents who couldn't even speak Spanish and came from a country full of drug users yet complained about drugs.

The Mex Feds locked him in the back of a car, and then went through the Cadillac. In Tijuana they interrogated him until 3:00 in the morning and barred anyone from the Tijuana DEA office from seeing him. Tonight, on principle, he was a suspect caught trying to escape with a body, presumably to dispose of it, presumably because he worked for the Salazar Cartel. The officers who questioned him promised that whether or not he killed Takado he would do prison time in Mexico for moving Takado's body. That much was a certainty, and when they became confident that his Spanish was fluent they worked another more elaborate theory.

At dawn they let him use a toilet and then a sink to wash Billy's blood off his arms. They returned his badge and gun, but couldn't find his Rolex or sunglasses, although the captain in charge promised to get them back to him. The captain carefully copied down an address to mail them to. By mid morning the issue between the DEA and the Mexican Federal Judicial Police was reduced to one of miscommunication, a natural problem of working together under difficult conditions.

That said, the Mex Feds voiced doubt about Agent Marquez's judgment. Fleeing with Takado's body suggested a lack of operational capacity. They speculated that Marquez's general decision making had compromised the undercover operation. It was understood that Marquez was unwelcome now in Mexico as a DEA agent. Additionally, it was agreed that Marquez might need to be questioned again as the Mex Fed investigation progressed. They asked that Agent Sheryl Javits also be reprimanded for accusations she made yesterday and Jay Holsten, head of the LA DEA Field Office, agreed to that, though he wouldn't think of doing that to her. Nor would he ever send Marquez back to Tijuana. They could bring their questions here.

A Mex Fed captain explained the conditions of release to Marquez. As he finished, the captain added that the Cadillac would get returned after the Mexican Federal Judicial Police concluded their investigation. They drove Marquez to the San Ysidro Puerta and he walked to US Customs with the copies of the 52s because he had never told them how they came into his possession.

Two of his squad, Ramon Green and Brian Hidalgo, were waiting at Customs. Like Marquez they were fully engaged in the drug war and on the drive back to LA Marquez recounted how it went down. After listening, Green and Hidalgo rationalized Billy Takado's death, guessing that Takado's nervousness was because he knew the man who delivered the papers to Marquez might be present. Point being, that Billy Takado like many snitches may have tried to play both sides. Marquez didn't see it that way and said so as they drove north in traffic. This was on a bright clear June morning in 1989, the same day the world watched a student in China face down a tank in Tiananmen Square.

THREE

Marquez's SAC, Holsten, had the nickname 'Lockjaw' for the way he worked his facial muscles when he was angry but restraining himself. Right now, he looked like he was chewing gum as he waited for an answer.

'Agent Javits relayed the order for you to park and wait for the Mex Feds, but you didn't do that. You ignored the calls made to you and drove nearly all the way back to Tijuana. Is that correct?'

'Yes, sir.'

'Don't keep giving me this short answer wounded hero crap, Marquez. You're feeling sorry for yourself, but what happened is you screwed up and I want to know why.'

Holsten paused.

'What I should do is suspend you. You gave the Mex Feds

a way to paint you into the picture and an excuse not to inves-
tigate. They're telling us they don't want you in the country
again in an undercover capacity, so you tell me how you'll
ever run your squad again if you can't operate undercover in
Mexico. Have you got an answer for that?'

Marquez was quiet a moment, then said, 'The Mex Feds sent
the message yesterday that the Salazar brothers carry more
weight with them than we do. They signed off on killing Billy
Takado so long as the DEA agent didn't go down as well.'

'If the newsflash is there's corruption in Mexican law enforcement, that doesn't come close to explaining what happened.
Where did they get the personnel forms they handed you? Why
did you disobey an order? Do you want to know what the Mex
Feds think? They think you didn't stop and wait because you're
on the Salazars' payroll and you were driving Takado's body
back to Tijuana so it could be thrown in a vat of acid.'

'Bullshit.'

'It's what they're saying. They believe you had the Fifty-
twos, the personnel forms, with you and nothing was given
to you in the bull ring.'

'Where were they?'

'They claim they had two officers there who witnessed the
shooting but didn't see anyone hand you papers. They saw
Miguel Salazar shoot Takado and then you drove off. When
they called us we told them you'd reported in and would wait
on a pass in the Juarez. But you didn't wait and we couldn't
get a hold of you, and that doesn't work in this department.'

Holsten paused, drew a breath and said, 'Here's what I want
today. I want the name of everyone who knew about this bull
ring meeting, and I want everyone on your squad to voluntarily
take a lie detector test over at the FBI office this afternoon. When
you get there, ask for Ted Desault. He knows you're coming.'

'Why is the rest of my squad getting hooked up to a lie
box and why at the FBI?'

Holsten picked up the copies of the 52s off his desk and
shook them.

'There's a leak and we're going to find out where it is and
I don't give a damn whose feelings get hurt in the process.
Javits has already tested. I'm sending her tomorrow to back
up Osiers. Since you won't be visiting Mexico you'll work
leads here while I figure out what to do with your squad.

You shouldn't have driven on with the goddamned body, John, and you should have answered the phone and called in from the village, not the pass. What did I tell you was the most important thing when I hired you?'

Holsten did his riff on chain-of-command, the glue speech, and it occurred to Marquez that Holsten always referred to Mexican pueblos as villages. Maybe that was about Vietnam where Holsten did three tours. Holsten stood up as he finished, adding, 'I want the Group Five analyst tested along with the rest of you. I've forgotten her name. What's her name?'

'Rachel Smith.'

'And when you leave the FBI office you come back here and sit with a sketch artist. I want something we can work with on the man in the bull ring.' Holsten's tone changed slightly as he asked, 'Where do you think he's from? Could he be South African?'

'Could be.'

'Educated?'

'Yes.'

Marquez sat with the artist late in the day. He had a very good memory for faces and the artist was quite intuitive. With the second sketch she got the man and that sketch faxed east before Marquez left for home.

Two days later, a Kerry Anderson from the Intelligence Division out of headquarters in Virginia showed up to interview Marquez. They sat down in a conference room. Anderson had the faxed sketch with him and a name for the man, Emrahain Stoval. He also had photos but he didn't show those yet. He pulled them from a manila file and laid them facedown on the table. He wanted Marquez's eyes drawn to the packet of photos. Wants to control the conversation, Marquez thought.

'Stoval is a money man and a connector who sits in the background and helps organize and fund various criminal enterprises. He supplies both long and short term loans. If you've already got a track record and you need five million dollars to buy cocaine you'll sell to distributors in the States, you might go to him for a three-week loan. In some cartel operations we believe he gets a percentage of everything. He's woven in, but at your level you won't necessarily see him. I don't mean that derogatorily. I don't mean any offense.'

'None taken.'

Marquez took in Anderson's look, the coat, the starched shirt, receding red hair, bony face, a freckled scalp he touched periodically.

'He also deals in arms and maintains direct links to hit squads. He's got a reputation as ruthless in the way that defines the meaning of the word.'

'Why hit squads if his business is loaning money?'

'Think about the people he loans to. They aren't always the most honorable. We think he wants his clients to remember he's dangerous.'

'Who's the "we" you're talking about?'

Anderson shrugged. 'I think,' he answered. 'I'm the Stoval expert.'

'Did you fly out here just for this interview?'

'No, but I would have.' Anderson flipped over the stack of photos now. 'Take a look. Some are of poor quality.'

Marquez flipped through twenty or more and returned to one of the early ones, a grainy profile shot at a distance of a man looking at monkeys in bamboo cages. He flipped through them all again before going back to the monkey photo, telling Anderson, 'Only this one.'

Marquez slid the photo over and watched Anderson slowly nod.

'Very good,' Anderson said. 'That was taken at an animal market in Indonesia. He's a passionate big game trophy hunter and a constant wing hunter. He'll travel all over the world to hunt. He also traffics in animal parts.'

'What doesn't he do?'

Anderson smiled at that.

'Who took that photo?' Marquez asked, and reached for it.

He studied the small dark shape of the monkey behind the bamboo slats. Wildlife had its back to the wall. We treat the earth like we own it, but why would the DEA follow Stoval to an animal market in Indonesia? They wouldn't.

He slid the photo back and Anderson said, 'It's a CIA photo.'

'What are you doing with it?'

'Sometimes if it's in their interest they share with us. Not often, but sometimes. Stoval has provided information to them. They won't tell me exactly what, but I gather in Mexico it's been about the Salinas government. The CIA considers Stoval an intelligence asset.'

'Great.'

'He gets unobstructed passage in and out of the United States, and knowing what I know about him, that turns my stomach.'

Anderson put his glasses back on. He seemed agitated. He tapped the photo forcibly and his voice rose with emotion, something Marquez didn't see often from an analyst.

'Do you know what this is a photo of?' Anderson asked, and then answered his own question. 'This is what the devil looks like in the twentieth century. You've never met anyone like him.'

When Marquez didn't respond fast enough Anderson gathered up the photos and snapped his briefcase shut. He handed Marquez a card.

'We'll talk more and I'm going to warn you, there's probably a reason he made contact with you. It's not chance that he was there in the bull ring. With him, there's always a reason.' He tapped his briefcase. 'Always.'

FOUR

For one hundred thirty years Loreto was the Spanish capital of Baja. Now it was a fishing and tourist town with an airport eight hundred miles from LA. After landing it was fifteen minutes from the airport to the DEA safehouse. The dry spine of the Sierra La Giganta rose behind Loreto and the highway and on the other side where the safehouse was, long beaches faced the Sea of Cortez. Sheryl Javits didn't know if it was true or what it really meant, but Marquez told her that this part of the Sea of Cortez had more biodiversity than anywhere else on earth. She loved coming here. She called it her vacation assignment. She liked to watch the whales and the birds in the early morning. The flight wasn't long and the house the DEA leased was simple, small, and on the beach. Weather was usually good.

The problem was Jim Osiers. Osiers pretended he was glad to see her, but he was obviously disturbed Holsten sent her to back him up. Ten minutes after she arrived, he told her he didn't need her and then acted like he owned the house, like she was some sort of uninvited guest. He didn't loosen up until she helped him catch up on overdue paperwork. She was killer on paperwork and now they were outside with cold Pacifico beers in their hands, sitting in the lawn chairs, bug zapper on, the night warm and soft, and the only light on the Sea of Cortez starlight. They drank and speculated as they had all evening about Billy Takado's murder and what had happened to Marquez. She never liked Takado but knew that Marquez did, that he and Billy became friends, so when Osiers said Marquez got too close, she nodded.

'Never get close to a confidential informant,' Osiers said, repeating the axiom.

But both of them knew Marquez had a way with people that neither of them had. People like Billy Takado wanted to trust Marquez. Sheryl trusted him and liked working under him. So did Osiers. She took a pull of her beer and thought about her feelings for Marquez. Complicated and private, but with a couple of beers in her and this far away from LA she didn't have any problem asserting, 'If the brass blames John, I'll quit. I've never worked under anyone as good as him.'

'You're not going to quit.'

'The fuck I won't.'

'And then do what?'

When she didn't answer, Osiers rolled his eyes. Sheryl went inside to use the bathroom. She left the bath door ajar as she sat down to pee. She felt the beer, her head swimmy, the last few days catching up to her. On her way back out, the phone rang.

A voice said, '*Hola, chica,*' and Sheryl, who never forgot the voice of an asshole, said, 'What's going on, Rayman?'

'Something is going down tonight.'

'What's that?'

She waited. She listened and part of her turned alert. Baja was one happening place. The sleepy sun-drenched peninsula was very busy and the DEA often worked joint operations with both the ATF, Alcohol, Tobacco, and Firearms, and the Mex Feds. Sometimes the US military kicked in and helped track a large transport boat clearing Colombian waters. The Sea of Cortez, the water between the Baja peninsula and the mainland, was the big cocaine pipeline between Colombia and the United States.

The latest thing was a phosphorescent chemical called NK-19 that smugglers used to mark the water for plane drops. They put a big X on the water and a transport boat or a plane dumped a load. Tricked-out speed boats or fastboats picked it up and moved it north. Tonight, at dusk the Sea of Cortez had been smooth as polished glass. Thousands of birds gathered to feed on a school of fish. Carmen Island was a brown line hovering at horizon, and then the darkness came and night was when it happened around here.

Rayman was Raymond Mendoza. More and more the cartels were picking up kids who already held an American passport and spoke Spanish and could move at will back and forth over the border. Rayman grew up in Santa Monica and attended UCLA where he got most of an undergrad degree in economics before he got bored and quit. Now he was low level inside the Salazar Cartel and either he wasn't sure about his career choice or the Salazars were behind Rayman contacting them. For her money, it was the latter. Twice they'd given Rayman tip money, but the drops he'd tipped them to were shipments of rivals of the Salazar brothers, meaning so far his tips only hurt the Salazars' competitors. Still, as long as he delivered they'd keep dancing with him.

'The shipment coming in tonight is going to get taken,' Rayman said. 'It's big, as big as me, *chica*.'

'You're such a geek. Is it coke?'

'Yes.'

'What time and where?'

'You're going to take care of me?'

'Of course.'

Sheryl wrote down the name of the beach, went over it again with him, hung up, grabbed the map and walked outside. Osiers had opened two more beers. Hers was sitting on the patio concrete next to a leg of her chair. He pointed it out so she wouldn't knock it over and at first he didn't ask who called. But when he saw the map he put his beer down.

'Rayman says there's a load coming in tonight that will get ripped off by the Salazars.'

Osiers frowned and leaned over the map as Sheryl ran her finger up the road from Loreto. She tapped the spot.

'Looks like that beach at the hook in the road, the one that has the bar and kayak rentals.'

'Whose drop is it?'

'Some other Sinaloans, some enemy, some rival, not a name I recognize. I wrote it down. I'll go get it. He claims it's going to happen right around midnight.'

'There have been a couple like that, lately. How did he sound?'

'I don't know, like an asshole, like he always sounds.'

'What do you think?'

'I just got here. You're the Baja guy, what do you think?'

'You should have put me on the phone with him.'

'You heard it ring. You heard me talking. Why didn't you get up?'

Osiers picked up his beer again. He took a small sip and then set it on the table as if he was done with it.

'He told you the Salazars are going to steal the load?'

She nodded.

'Then that's the first time he's given us anything where the Salazars are in action.'

Sheryl got it. She didn't need it typed out for her. If the Salazars were standing behind Rayman as he talked to her, then the plan wasn't to let the DEA follow a load they were stealing. Start with that and you could go a bunch of places with it. You could even start believing Rayman. Or you could go really dark and guess that the Salazars knew the standing order right now in the DEA Baja operations was to minimize contact with the Mex Feds until everything got sorted out. Without the Mex Feds they could only follow the stolen load so far. Or even darker, all of the above was true and Rayman was calling to lure them into some plot the Salazars cooked up. Play with that in your head and you have to think about the threat made to Marquez.

'Should we call home?' she asked.

'Call who?'

Osiers knew full well she meant Marquez. This was just male pride, but if she said Marquez's name now Osiers would scoff.

'No, we gear up and go,' Osiers said. 'That's what we're here for.'

An hour later they were in the car driving slowly through little Loreto, then out on to the highway and north into the night.

FIVE

The moon threw just enough light to follow the dirt road without headlights. They parked and then for hours watched the ocean and the waves breaking on the crescent of beach below. The dark shapes of moored fishing boats rocked gently. The beach bar with its blue neon sign and rose-colored lights leaked music. Two vehicles sat out front of the bar, a battered Toyota pickup and a light-colored minivan. Javits studied each again. Nothing had changed and she was tired and doubting Rayman's tip.

But she did not doubt that Rayman knew she was in Baja before he made the phone call tonight. She brought it up again.

'Who passed the word that I was coming down here to double up with you?'

'You're paranoid because of what happened to Marquez.'

Osiers was weary of talking about it but she kept worrying away at it, trying to get at what she was missing, and they kept watching the dark sea with the arrow of moonlight across it. Her thoughts jumped to John driving back to Tijuana with Takado's body in the seat next to him.

'Hear that?' Osiers asked.

At first she only heard the music and the waves breaking, but now heard the low thrum of a plane, a vibration as much as a sound. Osiers pulled on the night vision goggles, plastic straps snapping against his skin. Whatever was out there was flying without lights. The sound grew closer.

'Got it,' Osiers said. 'I see it.'

Sheryl heard the plane's engines working as it made the drop and pulled up. Boat engines kicked in and sounded like mosquitoes at this distance. Boats must have been sitting out there waiting in the dark. Now, below them a truck turned off the highway and started along the road toward the beach and the bar. Headlights traced the road. It passed the bar, continued on toward the dock and the beach. A jeep followed a few minutes later and Osiers called it out.

'I count four in the jeep.'

He pulled the goggles off and asked, 'Hear the bigger boat, that droning? That's the ambush coming.'

She saw the lights of the smaller boats way out there. They had found the load and were probably winching it up and now were very scared as the fastboat's engines rose in pitch and closed in. The fishermen picking up the load were more than likely locals with families here. They were out there making extra money. The *narco trafficantes* arriving in a fastboat were coming in without lights, closing for the capture and kill.

From up here she and Osiers watched it like a play, a bit episode in centuries of smuggling. They saw the flash of gunfire, heard the shooting, the pip, pip, pip loud enough to be real and far away enough not to be.

'They're dying out there,' Javits said softly.

On the beach the panel truck backed up to the dock and men got out of the jeep with weapons. The bar lights went out. Shooting out on the water stopped and very faintly the scream of a woman carried on the wind and made Javits shudder. Made her wish she was a thousand miles away living a whole different life.

But it was only that one scream and then a brighter light shone out on the sea. That had to be the big offshore boat using a searchlight. There was no more shooting, so they must be getting their pilots on to the fishing boats and starting the boats this way, she guessed. The searchlight went out. The fastboat's engines droned loud again as it ran south into the night, and the convoy of fishing boats moved slowly this way, their lights rising and falling, their owners left somewhere back in the dark sea.

As they watched the boats come in and off-loading start, Osiers said matter-of-factly, 'I'm going down to those trees where the beach road hits the highway. Do you know where I'm talking about?'

'Right where the beach road meets the highway?'

'Yeah, right there, and I'll wait in the trees and try to get some plate numbers. Stay here until they pull out and we know what direction they're going. I'll radio you to come get me and we'll call the Mex Feds if we get license plate numbers.' He paused. 'You got that?'

'They could have someone down there watching the road.'

'No, I watched both vehicles pull in, neither slowed or stopped, and if we don't get plates and makes on the vehicles, the Mex Feds aren't going to do shit. I know how they work around here.'

He left before they could argue about it, and she watched him as far as she could. Ten minutes later her radio squawked as he reached the trees.

'I'm here.'

Javits watched the Jeep and the panel truck leave the beach and start up the road toward the highway. She glanced back toward the beach. Bar lights remained off, same two vehicles still parked in front. The panel truck and Jeep drove out the beach road and slowed where the road met the highway near the trees where Jim was waiting. When the vehicles turned north and disappeared she started down. As she reached the highway she expected Osiers to radio and she paused there, and then drove slowly down the highway. When she neared the stand of trees and the beach road entrance, the Toyota pickup that had been parked in front of the bar pulled out on to the highway, accelerated and passed her going north. So the pickup hadn't just been left there for the night. That bothered her and when Osiers didn't answer the radio she got worried.

She drove down around the curve in the highway and then came back slowly, expecting him to walk out on to the highway shoulder. She cued the radio repeatedly and now turned down the road to the beach, stopped at the trees, and got out. She called, 'Jim.' She used her headlights and then a flashlight, and then hurried back to the car.

She drove slowly forward trying the radio. Twenty minutes later she fought to keep her voice calm as she used the satellite phone to call Marquez. Her heart hammered. The phone rang. Come on, John, pick up, please pick up, and then he did.

SIX

After Sheryl's call, Marquez drove to the Field Office. At dawn he tried again to convince Holsten.

'You're not going,' Holsten said. 'Hundreds of *federales* are already looking for him and Highway 1 is shut down both directions. The Mexicans put up roadblocks at

Santa Rosalia and outside Lazaro Cardenas last night. They're
stopping vehicles in and out of Ensenada this morning.
They're stopping boats. There's nothing you're going to bring
to the equation and you're needed here.'

Just before noon Sheryl called from Loreto, her voice flat
and dead as she reported, 'Jim had a girlfriend in Loreto named
Alicia Guayas. She's nineteen and pregnant. The Mex Feds
just took me to meet her. She says it's his baby and they also
claim he has a bank account in La Paz under a false name.
The girlfriend told them that Jim is leaving his wife for her.
They're trying to tell me Jim staged his disappearance so he
could run off with her.'

'Did you get to talk to her?'

'Yes, but with the locals watching over my shoulder, but
she's either a great actress or really is scared that something
has happened to him. I'm going back this afternoon to interview her, but don't tell Holsten or Boyer that I told you that.
I'm not supposed to tell anyone.'

Marquez understood. Earlier, he'd seen Boyer, Group 5's
ASAC, in a conference room with Holsten and a translator.
Neither Holsten nor Boyer would talk about it when they
came out.

'Did you know about a girlfriend?' Sheryl asked.

'No.'

'The girlfriend says he pays for her house.'

'What's her name again?'

'Alicia Guayas. She has photos with her and Jim.'

'How do you read her?'

Sheryl hesitated. She sighed.

'I don't know.'

Marquez wrote the name Alicia Guayas on a pad. From
his desk Marquez could easily see Jim Osiers' desk and the
framed family photos. He could see Jim's marriage hitting
a hard spot, but not Jim abandoning it or taking bribe money.

'What about Rayman?' he asked.

'No word.' There was static and then she said, 'The Mex
Feds claim they have people in Loreto who've known about
the girlfriend and say it's been going on for awhile. In one
photo he's got an arm around her and he's leaning over as
if he's going to kiss her.' Marquez was more worried about
the false bank account. He heard voices in the background

and Sheryl said, 'I'm going to have to call you back.'

Jim Osiers had three sons and a wife in the Inland Empire. He bitched about his salary and commute, but who didn't? Even with locality pay it was tough to make it in LA on a DEA salary, and Marquez had always gotten the feeling Osiers savored the break in Loreto just to get away from the grind of the commute and trying to raise three sons on his salary. Marquez lived in Hermosa Beach out in South Bay like a lot of the single agents, but he'd always thought Osiers lucky to have a family to come home to at night. The drug war was a soul destroyer. It ate you from the inside out and you needed ways to counter that.

Marquez walked out of the Field Office in the late afternoon looking for food. The afternoon was smoggy and hot, the sky white with no depth. On the sidewalk two construction workers talked loudly about a truck parked in their restricted zone as if the owner would overhear and move it before they had it towed. Marquez glanced at the panel truck as he passed, rust-stained, chalky white paint, *Perez Cabinets* stenciled on the sides in black letters. It had two front tires bald in a way you could only get away with in a part of the country where it didn't rain much. More than likely, the Perez Cabinet guys were working nearby and saw a chance to steal free parking.

He bought a black coffee and a tuna sandwich, and when he walked back the construction superintendent and other worker were gone. In the Field Office a TV played and he ate the sandwich and watched a CNN report with shots of the Sea of Cortez and Highway 1 in Baja. Competitors called CNN crisis news, but at least they were there. No one else was covering.

A flyover search for bodies in the Sea of Cortez had yielded two local fishermen and they were looking for four others in what CNN called cartel infighting. There was nothing new on Jim Osiers and it was too late for good news. Marquez stayed at the office until 8:00 that night and then went home to the apartment, frustrated that Holsten wouldn't let him go to Baja, but also very disturbed by what Sheryl had learned.

Marquez lived in a one-bedroom on the second floor of a three-story stucco apartment building with a Spanish motif. The apartment had oak flooring and a concrete deck with black iron railing, the deck with a view of the ocean. At night after the traffic died, he could hear the waves breaking.

Sometimes he'd sleep with the sliding door open just so he could hear that.

Marquez had drifted into his early thirties living alone. Ask him why and he'd shrug off the question, though he knew the answer was his wife's murder in Africa. 'Wife' was an impersonal word for Julie, and really, married barely fit them. They married young, most would say way too young, and maybe time would have done to them what it did to other people, but Marquez still let himself believe otherwise. He allowed himself that. He didn't indulge grief and make a touchstone out of sorrow. He didn't sit at a bar, drink with you, and then wait for the chance to tell you about his sadness. But he did live alone.

He'd gone out with plenty of women in the last five or six years. He wasn't a loner. He liked to laugh and have fun. He got a beer from the refrigerator now and opened it. Summer dusk was settling in. Jim Osiers was missing and he couldn't picture Osiers staging his disappearance. The girlfriend, OK, maybe, but Rayman making the call after Sheryl arrived, the late night tip, the bank account revealed before mid morning the next day, no way. It all felt a little too organized. He needed to go there and find out.

He finished the beer and then stacked some charcoal in the Hibachi and lit it. Smoke curled in from the deck through the open slider. The sailboat of an ex-cop named Dunfield slowly passed out beyond the surf, ghostly in the twilight. The boat's name was *Blow Me* and for that Dunfield, who was retired, had become a minor celebrity with the local teens. Dunfield was often in shorts, sandals, a T-shirt, and a cap. He was getting by on not much more than his pension money, but seemed happy.

Marquez opened another beer and then grilled a chicken breast and corn. He was eating when his sister, Darcey, called.

'Nathan left last night,' she said, meaning her husband. 'He's going back to New York and leaving me the boat and the restaurant.'

She sounded defeated and he was sorry for her but it didn't surprise him. This had been coming for awhile. It was a long way from New York to Seward, Alaska, and owning a restaurant that made its money on tourists in a season that wasn't much more than five months. Darcey loved it there, but Nathan had threatened to leave more than a few times.

'I'm sorry, Darcey.'

'I'm not. I'm glad it's over.'

Marquez didn't know what to say to that. She was hurting. That's why she was calling. He wished they talked more. He wished she lived closer and was happy. He listened and tried to forget about Osiers as he talked with her.

He hung up remembering a foggy night when he was fifteen and crossing the Golden Gate Bridge in his grandmother's old Chevrolet Impala desperate to find her. He didn't have a driver's license yet, just a permit, and was afraid the bridge toll-taker would see it in his eyes, call the cops, and they'd stop him from driving into San Francisco to the Tenderloin where one of Darcey's stoner friends had told him she'd gone after running away from home.

That night he had a photo of her lying on the passenger seat, a blowup of her high school yearbook picture, though she'd stopped looking like her photo months ago. Heroin made her rail thin, her hair stringy, and her face dull and gaunt. He found the address in the Tenderloin and then a building with a stairwell stinking of urine and littered with trash. On the fourth floor pale yellow light came out from under the door and when he knocked, the man who opened the door said, 'Go home.'

'I'm looking for my sister.'

'I don't care if you're looking for God. Get the fuck out of here before I kick your ass down the stairs.'

Marquez had pushed his way in and the guy punched him, but Marquez was already six foot one and strong. He hit back and hard, but the fight like all fist fights was a mess. When he left the man on the floor and staggered down a hallway and pushed into a bedroom he found a doped-up Darcey, maybe not even aware what the fat guy on top of her was doing. It was that hard and that long ago. He had carried her out wrapped in a blanket smelling of sex and sweat.

On the sidewalk a big guy pulled a knife and said, 'I own the bitch.'

Marquez still believed the guy would have stabbed him if a police cruiser hadn't rounded the corner. The police didn't hesitate and in that moment his view of the police changed permanently. He'd run wild as a kid, wandered the forests of Humboldt County, and listened to his parents' friends talk about their pot fields and getting ripped off by cops. The family had lived for two years in a tent with a dirt floor and later in San Francisco they'd lived out of a VW van. The cops were always rousting them. He'd been a truant before he was seven years old and was taught to look at the police as enemy. But not after that night, not after those cops got out and helped him. That night changed everything.

SEVEN

A t sunrise the Perez Cabinets truck was still on East Temple, though now a bad smell leached into the soft early light. Blow flies crawled across the rear rolling door toward a crack, and Marquez watched them and then crossed the street and called LAPD from downstairs in the DEA building. He got transferred to a Detective Broward.

'Have you run the plates?' Broward asked.

'Not yet.'

'Give them to me.'

He read them off and said, 'Why don't you get a patrol car out here and I'll meet the officer.'

'Are you that sure?'

'Yes.'

'Have you been around this before?'

'I have.'

Broward thought about that for a few moments and said, 'I'll need you to wait there.'

A handful of construction workers gathered to watch the lock on the roll-up door torn off as a pry bar lifted the door. Tortured metal wrenched and snapped and as the door went up the heavy smell of death rolled out like a breaking wave. When the detective saw the body he started clearing everyone.

But Marquez didn't leave. He backed up and then remained where he had a view of a male body lying on its side with its back to them. He studied the pants, shirt, short brown hair, and the shoulders. When he turned, he saw two reporters who'd been hanging around the Field Office waiting for word on Osiers cross the street as they saw crime tape strung.

Detective Broward walked over to Marquez, put a hand on

his shoulder, said, 'Thanks, but I need you to step outside the perimeter now.'

'When will you turn the body over?'

'When we're ready.'

'Call me when you do.'

'Why?'

Before the call came Marquez let his squad know that the body in the truck looked too familiar. Hidalgo and Green came with him as he went back out. The truck's bed was almost waist high and the police had placed a stepladder there. He followed the detective up into the truck and stood where he was told to. He heard the detective ask him, but for a few moments Marquez felt like he was outside his body looking at Jim Osiers. He leaned and looked at the face again, made himself do it, the eye socket, the blood that had run down to his collar. He saw the bruising and where a piece of Osiers' skull had erupted through his scalp. He saw Jim had bled, so had been alive when it happened. Rage and deep sorrow rose in him and pushed away the shock and disbelief.

'This is our missing agent, Jim Osiers. He was on my squad. We started at the DEA the same year. We came in together. He's the agent missing in Baja.'

Marquez was aware that the detective already knew who it was and that he'd only confirmed it for him. He heard Detective Broward say he was sorry, but it didn't really matter who was sorry. It was the scale of the thing they were up against. The money was too large, the demand for drugs too big, and it seemed to him that the world was different than it had been when he'd started at the DEA. The violence had been there, but it was more accepted now, just as it was accepted as normal that more people had guns that spit more bullets faster. He turned to Broward.

'His wife is going to insist on seeing him, but she shouldn't see him like this.'

'We'll take care of her.'

Broward managed to say it like he meant it, though of course no one could take care of her or the kids, or protect them from the other stories that would come out now. From behind him, Hidalgo asked, 'Is it Jim?' When Marquez didn't turn, he called again, 'John, is it him?'

EIGHT

Three days later, Marquez picked up Sheryl at LAX as she returned home. 'John,' was all she said as she got into the car. As he pulled away from the curb and threaded into traffic she pressed her palms flat on her thighs and stared through the windshield. Her dark hair was parted in the middle and cut at an angle that fell across her cheeks. She closed her eyes as a car somewhere behind them honked.

'Are you OK?' he asked.

'I've been better. I went back and talked again to Alicia, the girlfriend, and she showed me things Jim had written her. Not long love letters or anything but notes, and it's his handwriting. She showed me jewelry he gave her. They've talked about names for the baby. I don't know what he was planning, but he wasn't denying it was his baby, and one of the names they were kicking around was his middle name. He told her he was going to move to Baja. He didn't say how he'd make a living.' She exhaled and leaned back. 'He was out of here, John.'

'How was he when you were there?'

'Tense, but I always think he's tense, especially when he says he's relaxed. He had five beers in him when we went out that night. I had three.' Sheryl turned and looked at him for the first time since getting in the car. When their eyes met she said, 'Here's what I know. He had a girlfriend. That's confirmed, and I can tell you she's pregnant and grieving. Even if the Salazars or somebody made her get involved with Jim, she's in shock. And there was a bank account in La Paz. I drove down there and the bank manager took me through it.'

'How much money went through it?'

'Three hundred sixty-three thousand dollars in six and a half months, but maybe he got a pay raise I didn't hear about.' She reached over and touched his arm. 'I didn't tell you that, OK. Let Holsten tell you.'

'Does Holsten know you went to La Paz?'

'He sent me. Everything I've done in Baja he's directing. You don't know that either, but that's not about you, John.

It's about the leak. He said he won't trust anyone until we know how the Salazars got the identities of our squad.'

'It may not have been the Salazars.'

'Same point.'

'OK, what else did you learn in Baja?'

'I've got to say this first, I've let myself start believing things about Jim I couldn't have imagined two days ago. When he disappeared I said bullshit, bullshit, bullshit to what the Mex Feds were telling me. Now, I believe it's all possible, and it's making me question everything. I don't know what to do with that.'

'Don't do anything with it yet.'

'All right, I'm trying not to, but Pete Phelps showed up with more evidence. The ATF was already on Jim.'

'That's according to Phelps?'

'Pete is one of the good guys.'

If you say so, Marquez thought, and then lined up in traffic getting on to the 405. It was going to take a while to get Sheryl home. He turned over the idea of Pete Phelps showing up and the ATF watching Osiers.

'Were you really the one to ID his body?' she asked.

'I think LAPD figured it out first and I confirmed it.'

'Holsten wants me to look at the panel truck. He thinks it might be the one Jim and I saw at the beach. What did they do to Jim?'

'Crushed his skull.'

'Oh, God.' For several minutes she didn't say anything and then, 'The ATF thinks Jim was trying to squeeze too much money out of the Salazars and they got tired of it.'

'Is that a Phelps opinion or an ATF conclusion?'

'Pete is actually OK, John.'

She didn't talk after that but she was right, he didn't trust much of anything Pete Phelps said. They drove in silence most of the rest of the way to her house where Marquez said, 'I'll call you tomorrow and let's get lunch. I've got a meeting with Holsten in the early morning. I'll call you after that.'

'I'd like that. I need to talk.'

'So do I. See you tomorrow.'

NINE

Saturday morning early the Field Office was quiet. Holsten had stopped on the way in at the day-old bakery he frequented. Croissants, muffins, and cookies sat on a white paper plate. Next to the plate was an unopened quart of orange juice and paper cups. It was much more than the two of them would eat and Holsten explained before Marquez asked.

'Agents Javits and Steiner are on their way here. We're going to reorganize this morning. I've got to go get something out of my car. Tell them the food is for everybody if they get here before I get back.'

When Sheryl walked in she said, 'He called me late last night and said be here at 8:00.'

Steiner, it turned out, thought he was going to be promoted, not transferred to the one squad that was falling apart. He looked angry as Holsten delivered the news. Boyer, Group 5's ASAC, was home sick with the flu, but Holsten made it clear the changes weren't Boyer's anyway.

'They're mine,' he said. 'Agent Marquez you're relieved of your supervision duties. Agent Javits you'll work with your ASAC and eventually be squad leader. Marquez you'll work undercover locally with Agent Steiner.' He nodded toward Steiner. 'Tom is an old friend of mine. We started at the DEA together. We go back that far. He's transferring to your squad as of this morning.'

Nobody said anything and Holsten stared at Marquez.

'Agent Marquez, we're going to send a strong message, starting with the hippie tour boat operators you're already watching. Monday morning I want to know how we're going to bust them.' He paused. 'What do you call them, again?'

When Marquez didn't answer, Sheryl volunteered, 'The Fab Four, but it's a joke.'

'We'll call this Operation Fab Four. This is where we start to rebuild Group Five.'

The meeting ended twenty minutes later. That afternoon

Marquez bought flowers from a florist near his apartment and
then drove to the Osiers' house with the big vase and lilies
filling his car with fragrance. Last night he'd written a letter
that he now gave to Jim's oldest son, telling the boy that the
letter was for his mother and for himself and his two brothers.
He came home to his empty apartment and the Saturday mail
that included a small package with two micro-cassettes and
a one-phrase note in Billy Takado's handwriting on a piece
of lined paper.

'In case something happens to me. Billy.'

For a minute Marquez didn't move and then dug in his gear
bag for his recorder. He locked the door and closed the slider
to the deck, then put the tape labeled #1 in and stood the little
recorder on a kitchen counter.

*'I'm making these tapes and giving them to a friend to mail
to you. There's a guy named Emrahain Stoval. I saw him
yesterday. He was with the Salazars at that restaurant I told
you about in Tijuana and he didn't see me, but if he does I'm
dead.*

*'In 1971 I was a twenty-two year old hunting guide with
a small business in San Fernando, Mexico. Mostly, I guided
dove hunts. Some of my clients were Mexicans and some came
down from Brownsville. My father was Japanese, my mother
Mexican, maybe I told you that once. My mother came from
San Fernando and there was a lot of white-wing dove in that
area. Flying knuckleballs is what they got called and you
could shoot what you wanted, so it drew plenty of hunters. I
had a good business and I was in love and engaged to get
married. Her name was Rosalina and she was everything
to me.*

*'One day Stoval showed up. He was a big wing hunter and
we got to be friends and he had a lot of money and pretty
soon he was taking me places I could never have gone on my
own. He had all kinds of money and liked to hunt with me,
so we went all over the world. Africa, Asia, everywhere. We
left for Canada and a bear hunt the day Rosalina disappeared.
I was one of the last people to see her alive. Her body turned
up on a dirt road out near a farm in Tamaulipas and that's
pretty much where my life ended. She'd been raped and stran-
gled and the* federales *didn't have any suspects so started
looking at me. They thought I killed her before I left.*

'*They would have charged me, but Stoval backed them off. He hired a good lawyer. He knew the right people to call and he even paid for a beautiful headstone. He was my only real friend and he got me back to work guiding again. He'd come into town and check on me every month or two, or he'd call me. He invested money in my business and I hired other guides and Stoval was my silent partner. That's how he works. He's like a disease you get and the symptoms show up gradually.*

'*One morning we were sitting in a duck blind and I told him we needed more money to start bringing in richer clients. I wanted to build cottages and a hunter's bar and restaurant.*'

Billy coughed. A glass touched a counter and Marquez heard Billy swear as something spilled. No doubt a drink from his slowed voice.

'*He listened to me and said we could do it, but it was a lot of money and it was going to change our relationship. He'd become the real owner. I'd still have a share and I'd make a much better living, but I'd be working for him. Man, I was just a kid and trying to get over Rosalina and I trusted him – I wasn't always the mess I am now. We made the deal and bought a new bus to bring rich Texans down. They liked the idea of being able to drink on the bus and not have to drive in Mexico. We got the bus and built the cottages and the restaurant and by then I knew what he was doing with me. It was what he'd been doing from the start and I hadn't realized it. He broke me down a little at a time until I was just a servant to him. He started talking to me like he owned me. Once after a hunt he had me wait outside with the dogs.*

'*The bus got a special compartment so it could carry cocaine under the bed. He showed that to me after he got me hooked on coke. My job was to take the bus to a mechanic's shop on every run north. They'd unload it there. We went three or four years that way, but I got myself off coke and I watched how people he didn't like disappeared. I started making a plan and one day after dropping the bus at the mechanic's, I walked out and didn't stop until I got to California.*

'*I heard later that he put out a contract on me so I hid for a long time, and eventually enough years went by that I stopped worrying. But it's not like I ever stopped watching. When I saw him yesterday I knew he'd still kill me if he could because*

I've told people he killed Rosalina. I never had any proof. I just knew.

'I'm going ahead with the meeting at the bull ring with you because that's the deal, and he won't be there. But the brothers know him, so I've got to take off, man. I've got to go a long way away. You're getting these tapes so you know nothing bad happened to me. I left these with a friend and asked her to mail them. I'll get back in touch with you sometime, but it might be a while. You always treated me fair and never made me feel like something that should be wiped off a shoe. You take care, John. Sorry to skip out on you.'

Marquez clicked off the recorder, opened a beer, sat out on the deck and thought it over. By the time he called Kerry Anderson's home number it was 2:10 in the morning on the east coast and he woke Anderson up. But Anderson didn't mind and even thanked him. He said, 'I need you to send me those tapes.'

TEN

Marquez and Steiner watched the tour boat through a chain link fence from the corner of a port parking lot. Steiner was gray at the temples, fit though nearing fifty, too old to be sitting in a car watching a boat, and he was having trouble with it.

'Holsten called me Friday afternoon,' he said. 'He wouldn't say what the Saturday meeting would be about but I was sure it was good news. My wife went out and bought a good bottle of champagne and steaks to celebrate. Ninety-five bucks for the champagne – I thought for sure it was a promotion.'

'Did you drink the champagne?'

'We drank it Friday night. I should have known better.'

'He said you're old friends. You started at the DEA together.'

'Oh, he was everybody's friend, you know what I mean. He was climbing the first day he got here. You know why I'm here, right?'

'Sure.'

One of the rumors swirling was that all of Group 5 was dirty. Osiers took money and it was going to turn out all of them were in on it. When Marquez walked through the squad room yesterday his presence hung like second hand smoke, and that was very hard on his pride. He felt an untethering from what he'd been so loyal to and anger moving around inside him like something alive.

He lifted binoculars and scanned the white-painted hull now, nervous energy billowing in him. Four foot high blue and red lettering read *Captain Jack's Sea Tours*. For seventy-five bucks you got a bumpy sea cruise that might include whale and dolphin sightings and lunch. If you wanted a beer with your lunch you paid at the bar where the Fab Four featured Pacifico, Bohemia, and Corona smuggled in from Ensenada. They bought caseloads of beer and avoided duties and taxes by selling it for cash on the boat. In the tour schedule were gaps where Group 5 had figured out the runs to Ensenada got made. The boat was just back from one of those. They should have drugs to move but whether it would be today was anybody's guess.

But now all that changed. The captain of the boat, Tony Marten, appeared and as Marquez focused the binoculars, Marten wheeled a large suitcase down the gangway on to the dock. Within minutes the other three followed also pulling black suitcases. It was improbable and comic and he understood Steiner's chuckle, but it was also disturbing in a way Marquez couldn't name yet. Maybe because the Fab Four were older and obviously awkward and uncomfortable in this role, Keystone Kops of crime. More than that, he thought, their actions looked forced, unplanned. It felt wrong.

They rolled the suitcases out to an old diesel Mercedes and a maroon Chrysler LeBaron in the same lot Steiner and Marquez were in. Two suitcases went into each trunk and as they drove east out of the LA basin they separated by more than a mile and then traded off the lead.

Watching them switch the lead car again, Marquez guessed, 'This part they've done before. We've been looking for a place they call the ranch. Maybe that's where they're headed.'

Marquez felt the change. He radioed Hidalgo and Green and gave them their position.

On the road to Palmdale the Mercedes and LeBaron were

half a mile apart. The Mercedes turned off first and tracked down a dirt road running a straight half mile to a rundown ranch complex. A rooster tail of dust rose behind it, and the LeBaron came behind it a few minutes later. Marquez watched a man open sliding barn doors and both cars drive in. He brought the glasses back to the sagging ridgeline of the two-story house and told Steiner, 'I'm going to call for more help in case we end up going in.'

For an hour nothing more happened and then a white refrigerated truck drove out of the barn and bumped down the dirt road to the highway. Marquez radioed Brian Hidalgo.

'OK, now we've got a refrigerated truck with two Hispanic males leaving the ranch and turning south on to the highway. The name Campania Poultry is painted on the side. We're going with it; stay with the ranch.'

An hour and a half later, south of LA, the refrigerated truck exited and drove past a new strip mall and subdivision and five miles out into dry hills. Marquez and Steiner hung back as it climbed into low hills and disappeared over a crest down into a valley. There, another vehicle, a black BMW four-door, waited on a dirt turnout. Beyond the vehicles the road dead-ended, so they'd have to come back out this way. The BMW driver got out and opened his trunk. The driver of the refrigerated truck and his companion were also out of their vehicles. One man relieved himself on the side of the road and Marquez didn't see the suitcases. The men looked around and watched the road their direction, but he didn't get the feeling this was a drug transfer.

'If that poultry truck has the suitcases in it, he's only going to be able to carry two of them,' Steiner said. 'He'll have to put the other two in the backseat.'

'Yeah, I don't know what they're doing here.'

'They're up to something.'

Marquez agreed. He just wasn't sure what it was yet. When the BMW driver pulled two orange plastic gas containers from the trunk another thought hit him and he touched Steiner on the shoulder and said, 'I'm going to radio for county backup.' Now he hustled back to where they left the car and radioed for help. Then he pulled the car forward to where the men below could not see it and leaned on the horn. Sound carried out over the valley, but only briefly.

The low heavy *whumph* of the gas igniting drowned the horn. An orange-yellow ball of fire enveloped the poultry truck and the BMW was already accelerating their way.

'Get in the car,' Marquez yelled to Steiner, as the Beemer climbed toward them.

Now the BMW driver rode his horn and their bumper, and then tapped them hard as Marquez drove slowly and blocked them from passing. As the Beemer hit them, the car fishtailed and Marquez fought for control. He straightened it out. He swung over to the right and the Beemer roared up alongside with the front passenger window lowering. Marquez hammered the accelerator, turned into them and rode the BMW right off the road. It plowed down the embankment, making terrible metal ripping sounds as the rocks and brush tore its guts out. At the bottom it spun sideways. It slammed into a tree.

'You're fucking crazy, Marquez. We need to call an ambulance.'

'Call it in.'

Marquez started down with his gun out, Steiner at the edge of the road on the radio. One man made it out a window before he got there, but that guy had a big bump on his forehead and a confused stare. Marquez walked them all back up the slope and with Steiner handcuffed the biggest and put restraints on the other. County backup arrived within minutes and the men went into county cars.

At the bottom of the hill the poultry truck still radiated heat, though a fire crew had sprayed foam and then cooled it with water. The stench was acrid, burned rubber and plastics. Part of the rear door had melted and after he got inside the county detective waved everybody back and then talked to Marquez.

'I'm going to ask you to take a look and tell me what you can,' he said. 'There are four of them but it's not pretty. You OK getting in there?'

Seeing the charred bodies of the Fab Four left Marquez quiet and he was only able to ID two of them. They'd need dental records for the other two. When he left there with Steiner they drove back toward Palmdale. A SWAT team moved in before they got there and Hidalgo radioed, 'We're in the barn with four suitcases packed with coke and we've made one arrest, a Jose Pinza, but I don't think he knows much more than he's supposed to guard these suitcases. Someone else took off on a dirt bike as we were coming in. We're trying to find him, but he may have gotten away. Why did they kill those guys?'

'That's what we need to figure out and we're not coming to you anymore, we're heading back to the harbor.'

Marquez and Steiner put on tactical vests and DEA jackets in preparation for boarding and literally ran into a man leaving the boat with a duffel bag. The man dropped the bag and took off running. They lost him but got the duffel bag and as Harbor Police searched for him, Marquez and Steiner went through the bag. It held business records. Five minutes more and the man he'd chased would have gotten away with it.

Marquez locked the bag in their trunk and then boarded the boat with Steiner and two local officers. In the main cabin were benches with red cushions and a vending machine for coffee drinks and cocoa. There was a bar. You could whale watch from the bar. Below were sleeping quarters, a bathroom, and a tiny galley. They ran crime tape but they didn't find anything.

When they got back to the Field Office the green duffel bag was checked in as evidence and inventoried. Marquez checked it out again immediately and took it upstairs. He spread everything out on a table and started going through it as he waited for Hidalgo and Green to make it back from the ranch. With Steiner he made one pass through all the documents in the duffel bag, and in the early evening after Steiner went home, he worked his way slowly back through the leather bound account books. Accounting wasn't his deal. He wasn't any good at it and it took him hours to figure out how they were coding things.

Hidalgo and Green picked up some food on their way in and brought him a burger and fries. When they walked in he said, 'Look at this. There's a plane in San Diego and this almond grower out in the valley. This could be how the Salazars move much bigger loads.'

They looked over his shoulder but they were done for the day. For Hidalgo and Green it could wait until tomorrow.

'Try the burger,' Green said. 'It was good.'

But Marquez was just getting to his point. He looked at Hidalgo, and then Green.

'The Salazars knew we were going after the tour boat. These guys died because they knew too much and we had them targeted. They lured them out to that ranch house and then sent someone to clean documents off the boat.'

'Osiers,' Green said, and Marquez didn't answer because that didn't explain it. He looked at Green, then Hidalgo, and said, 'Let's find this almond orchard and the pilot in San Diego.'

ELEVEN

B efore dawn Marquez retrieved his copy of the *LA Times*. When he slipped the rubber band off he found a sealed envelope with his name on it taped to the front page. In the envelope was a sheet of paper with typed excerpts of an autopsy report that could only have come from the LAPD detective, Ed Broward, though Broward didn't sign it.

He read and then laid the sheet of paper on the newspaper. The skin of his face felt as if he had just walked into a very hot wind. When he picked up the autopsy report again, his hand trembled with anger and visions of revenge surged in him.

'Severe skull fracture as a result of cranialencephalic trauma . . . No contrecoup-type injuries were found but severe contusions occurred most likely a result of bone fragmentation and subsequent impact of brain surface . . . Injuries indicate the victim's head was in a fixed position . . . hemorrhaging and contusions indicate victim was alive . . .'

He reread the paragraph. Osiers was alive for hours as his skull was mechanically crushed. They drew it out. Marquez stared at the words and then made a decision that he tried to tell himself wasn't impulsive and fueled by anger. He refilled his coffee, gassed up the car at the corner Chevron and rolled south with the dawn traffic, running in a stream of lights toward San Diego.

From the San Diego Airport he phoned Sheryl and left the message that he was checking out the pilot of the Sherpa aircraft whose name they found in the tour boat documents.

When she called back he didn't take the call. He let it go to voice mail, as he did with all calls he received that morning. He located the Sherpa, a boxy former Coast Guard transport plane, sitting on a runway, gray and cool in the early light. He copied down the tail numbers and took photos, and then drove south toward the border, toward the San Ysidro Gate and Mexico, and crossed to Tijuana, fully aware of what he was doing.

He drove the main drag past the discount everything stores, the instant auto-body repair shops, the massage parlors, the few remaining *floristas*, and then left La Revo and worked north until he found the restaurant Takado showed him, a place where the narco-juniors, the wannabes, gathered and hung with Miguel Salazar.

He parked, went in, asked for a table in a corner just inside the back patio, knowing that he was going to do something he might later regret. He told himself he'd already known Osiers' skull had been crushed, but that didn't change him. Morning sunlight fell through the leaves of a jacaranda tree and the shadows of the leaves flickered over his wrists and hands as he rested them on the table. The waiter came and he ordered *huevas a la Mexicana*, eggs scrambled with chili, onion, and tomato, and drank coffee and watched the iron gate at the back of the patio garden.

Just before 9:00 a.m. a white Porsche parked across the street near his car and two young and well-dressed men entered the restaurant. They walked toward the patio, shoes clicking on the tile, hard stares searching for anything and finding Marquez, as he knew they would, as he willed them to. He lifted his coffee cup in a mocking salute as they passed by, his eyes answering their promise of violence.

Out on the patio an old waiter took their orders, but they were agitated. Marquez had violated their morning, their sense of themselves, and he continued to stare at them as one lit a cigarette and cocked his head toward him. It wouldn't be long now and for Marquez time slowed. He saw it all as one scene, a painting with the doors to the patio garden, the waiter in black, the soul-poisoned sadism of Miguel Salazar, the fountain bubbling in the shade of a loquat tree and the young disciples of cartel money and power gathering themselves at the table, readying for their ascendancy. Hibiscus and calla and blue tile of the patio and sunlight reflected off the white tablecloth, all of it bright, vivid, and inevitable.

It's a new world, he thought. Instead of dealing in millions of dollars, the larger cartels dealt in billions. They buy banks and bankers. They buy the fastest boats, the best planes. They buy judges, prosecutors, police, and politicians, and the kid who got up from the table now, who held his eye and came toward him, swaggered with certainty. The patio door swung open. The young man stepped in and stopped at Marquez's table. He slid his coat back to show a gun and spoke in English.

'This place is not for gringos.'

'Who is it for?'

'Get up.'

Marquez picked up his coffee cup and turned toward the garden. He was aware but not watching directly as the boy who would be a man brought his gun across in a hard sweeping motion and shattered the cup, drenching Marquez's clothes and splattering the tablecloth and floor. The blow left three fingers on Marquez's left hand stinging and numb, but before the kid could bring his arm back, Marquez swept his legs out from under him and his rage at everything that had happened fed the next minutes.

Now he was outside, his shirt torn, lower lip leaking blood. Inside, the old waiter helped one of the men to a sitting position. The other lay curled on his side and would need an ambulance. Marquez had left money for the damage, but the trip here was a bad mistake. He was leaving when Miguel Salazar drove around the corner.

Even then he should have walked away. Instead, he waited and when the chance came closed the gap before Miguel reached the back patio gate.

'Miguel, I'm here to see you. *Que tal?*'

Salazar went for his gun, but Marquez gripped his collar and jerked him so hard he could barely get the gun free before it was knocked from his hand. Then it was all he could do not to fall as he stutter-stepped backwards, Marquez dragging him at almost a run and turning him as he reached Miguel's car, then slamming his face down hard. Marquez heard Miguel's nose give, the cartilage grinding like a footstep in gravel, and lifted his head and slammed it again. He threw him down on the sidewalk, drove the air out of him with a knee, ground the side of his face into the concrete and put his full weight onto Miguel's skull as Miguel fought back.

'You're going to have to watch everywhere all of the time and we're going to lean on them to take you down, so you're going to have to pay more. Eventually, you'll become too much of a problem, then what do you think will happen?'

Marquez punched him hard, watched him go slack, and then took his weight off him. When he got in his car and started driving he shook from adrenaline. He drove back to San Diego and the airport and parked for an hour before returning Sheryl's calls, and then talked normally, relating what he learned about the Sherpa pilot, Del Weaver, from the Federal Aviation Administration

'I'll see what more I can learn. I've already talked to the FAA. Weaver routinely flies to Calexico and then north into the Central Valley to a private landing field, some almond grower named KZ Nuts. Weaver's business is as a short haul pilot. He's got a reconstructed Sherpa, a C-23 rebuilt after the Coast Guard auctioned it off.'

She listened and then asked, 'Where have you been? I called six times. Billy Takado's body has disappeared. They're saying it may have been accidentally cremated. We got a call from the Mex Feds this morning. Until it's found again the investigation into his death is on hold.'

'It won't get found.'

That night he was swept by remorse and disappointment in himself. His hands were bruised and swollen. When he washed them in the bathroom and looked in the mirror he saw yet another cop unable to deal with the job and lashing out at the enemy, inviting retaliation. But there was something worse than that, a sensation as though he was unraveling as he was drawn in, as if anything could happen and he didn't know himself anymore.

He took a late night call from Sheryl who asked near the end of their conversation, 'What happened today, John? Did something happen? You don't sound like you.'

'Something did happen.'

'What?'

'I can't tell you.'

'If you change your mind, I'm here.'

TWELVE

After the memorial service for Jim Osiers, Sheryl asked if he wanted to come back to her house. Marquez went home first. Then he drove over to Sheryl's and they sat in lawn chairs under the big oak in her backyard. But even in the shade it was hot. You couldn't see anything in LA Basin other than yellow-white haze and he couldn't lose the image of Jim's sons standing alongside their mother, the youngest crying, the oldest trying to stand tall in a way his father might be proud of. What would happen when he got older and learned more about his father? Would he be able to forgive him?

Dusk came and Sheryl invited him to stay for dinner. They moved into the kitchen and she leaned against him as pasta boiled. She was a little drunk now, alcoholic heat radiating off her and him. A light sweat shone on her forehead and her eyes carried both challenge and sadness. They ate outside and drank more wine, but the wine didn't do anything at all for him tonight. He thought about Miguel Salazar lying on the sidewalk with his nose broken and bleeding, and of the investigation of Jim Osiers that had begun and would touch all of his squad and likely linger with them the rest of their careers.

What he'd done to Miguel Salazar in Tijuana needed to come out. He couldn't hold it secret and no question they would come for him. They'd come in waves if the first didn't get him.

Sheryl put her hand on his and said, 'Don't go quiet on me. Let's keep talking. I need to talk.'

'I'm here. I'm listening and I'm thinking about what we got off that boat. I'm going to chase this Sherpa pilot lead. Holsten and Boyer are going to take apart Group Five, but I'm going to chase this wherever it goes first. We know the Sherpa pilot flies to Calexico regularly and we've got enough on him and the almond grower to start looking at both more closely. I'm betting the pilot, Weaver, moves drugs for the Salazars.'

'Former military pilot?'

'Yeah, but it's going to be the same old thing.' It's always the money. 'I'll get them all,' he said, and didn't sound much like himself.

'Do you want to bust them or do you want something else?'

'I'm fine.'

'No, you're not.'

'Jim got framed.'

'He didn't get framed about the girlfriend. Her baby is due in mid November.'

He'd go to Calexico in the early morning. He'd keep pushing. Sheryl went back inside and got a bottle of brandy. She put two glasses on the picnic table, handed him the bottle, and Marquez opened and poured. He came close to telling her what he'd done with Miguel. They drank. They moved back inside. She looked at his hands. She touched his swollen knuckles.

'I'll call you from Calexico,' he said.

'No.'

She hooked his belt with her hand, put her arms around him and said, 'Don't go yet.' She pulled his shirt out, slid her hand up his back. 'Stay. You should have stayed a long time ago.'

She pressed tight against him, dropped her hands, fumbled with his belt buckle, and then he was taking her clothes off. It was the line they'd never crossed and he wasn't sure why it was happening now, but he was aroused and a little drunk and they were alive. That was the unspoken thing. Her skin was very smooth and warm and her mouth tasted like brandy. She wrapped her legs around him and stopped talking and let her heels fall to the soft covers of the bed. She was not in any hurry and slowed him and whispered, 'Only this once,' as a moan started from low in her chest. She was trying to tell him something else that night, but he was still too young, too caught up in the events of the week and the thing they were doing.

He was at Sheryl's when Anderson called. His half-ass mobile phone rang and woke both of them at a little after 4:00 in the morning. Marquez found his shorts and the phone and answered as he walked out of the bedroom.

'Sorry to call so early.'

'That's OK, Kerry, what's up?'

'I sent you copies of files on Stoval. The package should arrive addressed to you at your office this morning. There's also a file in there on a man named Kline that we can link to Stoval.'

'What about the stuff I called you about?'

Sheryl padded into the room. She was naked and he watched the refrigerator light silhouette her body as she opened the door just far enough to reach for a pitcher of water. Then she stood in the quasi-darkness listening to his conversation.

'I checked with Customs,' Marquez said, 'and they tell me Stoval has been in and out of the country eight times in the last three years.'

'More than eight,' Anderson answered, 'but the point is he's protected. That's what I told you the first time we met. Remember? And you won't get anywhere trying to talk to the CIA. They'll obfuscate and wear you down. That's how they work. But I didn't call about them. I'm only calling about the package I sent you, and I can't talk long. I've got to catch a flight.'

When he hung with Anderson, Sheryl asked, 'What package?'

'Files from Anderson for me.'

'Stoval files?'

'Yeah, and if I'm in Calexico will you catch them for me when they come in?'

Sheryl did more than that. She caught the package as it arrived and then opened it and went through the files. That surprised him. But maybe it shouldn't have.

THIRTEEN

C alexico is in California's Imperial Valley just over the border from Mexico. Human mules routinely crossed here. Marquez had once seen a bust where cocaine got baked into plastic animal carriers that were then shipped with dogs in them. At the time, US Customs avoided bringing their drug-sniffing dogs around other dogs, so the carriers passed through with little scrutiny. Once through, the dog carriers got dissolved in vats of chemicals, the cocaine extracted and the waste poured out into the ground behind a warehouse.

There were DEA agents stationed in Calexico, but Marquez didn't check in with anybody. He drove to the little International Airport and parked in the bright sun near the tarmac. Then his car phone rang and a retired newspaper editor in San Fernando, Mexico introduced himself.

'Thanks for returning my call,' Marquez said.

'Oh, I'm happy to talk about him. I liked him a lot.'

Marquez listened to the quaver and enthusiasm in the old man's voice as he remembered Billy. He thought about how differently the same human being was talked about at the DEA.

'I knew his mother too. He was like her. He could make you smile just by walking into a room. He had a business of taking hunters out for bird hunts. He used to bring me birds. He'd come right into the newspaper office with them and put them on my desk.'

'Were you in San Fernando when his fiancée got killed?'

The old man coughed. His voice quieted. For whatever reason, he didn't want to talk about that.

'It was very sad.'

'Who killed her?'

'It was never solved.'

'Was Billy accused?'

'Yes, the police were very stupid.'

'Who did you suspect?'

'Oh, it's so long ago. It was someone crazy, I guess, and so sad.'

'Billy is dead,' Marquez said, 'and I think it goes back to when you knew him.'

The old editor coughed again and said, 'He died when she died.'

He murmured something else and didn't want to talk anymore. Marquez copied down the name of the church with the cemetery where Rosalina was buried and then he drove north over the Tehachapi Mountains. He dropped into the Central Valley and continued on until he reached the big almond orchards of KZ Nuts.

Now he could smell the land in the dust the wind carried. Dust dulled the late afternoon and reddened the sun. He called Brian Hidalgo at the Field Office and as he waited for Brian to pick up, looked through long rows of almonds to an airstrip with a new concrete extension white in the sun. He studied the KZ buildings, a big ranch house and processing and storage buildings. He saw delivery trucks and an airstrip where a rainbow-colored windsock swelled with wind.

'I've been making calls on this,' Brian said. 'I talked to a friend of mine whose father used to crop dust all over the Central Valley. Sixty years ago that airstrip on the almond ranch was called Dolan's Field. Military planes coming out of March Field, Air Corps planes would use it in an emergency.'

'What about now?'

Papers shuffled, Brian looking at his notes. 'KZ has changed hands in the last few years and is owned by a larger corporation that I'm trying to learn something about. What I've learned so far is that they own eleven other orchards, six in California, two in Oregon, three in Washington. I've got a couple of pages on them. They bought all of them over the last five years. Each has an airstrip.'

'This one has just been enlarged. If they had a plane like the Sherpa they could move shipments of drugs from one orchard operation to another, and then use delivery trucks to distribute.' Marquez counted trucks. 'I'm looking at nine trucks right now with KZ painted on the side.'

'I've got more on the Sherpa too. That plane is a helluva workhorse. It can land in some tough places. I've never told you this, but in Vietnam I had the job of calling in air strikes. In the end there Charlie was all over us and I had to bring the bombs right up to our guys. I knew sometimes we were killing some of our own. You tell yourself you're not because it's the only way you can deal with it, but afterwards you can never really get away from it. I think that's why I'm ready to rock and roll all the time with these cartel freaks.' Hidalgo paused and abruptly switched subjects. 'It's getting weird around here. Holsten came through this morning looking for you. There's some news out of Tijuana.'

That night Marquez slept in a Best Western motel and dreamed of a Mex Fed captain named Viguerra. Captain Vengeance they called him for the way he went after *narco trafficantes*. In his dream Viguerra was smaller, his black mustache neatly trimmed, his uniform crisp and neat in a way it never was in life. He stood near the wreck of a burning plane.

'For every one I arrest, I kill two. I have chosen to fight them. A man can rule a certain amount of territory as a lion rules. As long as he is strong and shows no weakness he can dominate. For now, I am the lion. I have the helicopters and soldiers and the will to kill them, but this is a war with no ending. This is what the Americans don't understand. In this war are beings among us who are not human. They have aspects of us, but they are not of us, and they bring cruelty that is inhuman. Even now, I can feel the presence of one. His men I can kill. Him, I don't know. If you can find for me where he was born, I will give you all the wealth of Mexico. But you will never find that. There is no birthplace or child-hood for any of them. They are not of God.'

'Come on, a man is a man. He's the same as any of us.'

'No, my friend, he isn't.'

But that was just a dream. He woke in the motel room and lay on his back thinking about the leak at DEA. He once had a mission and a purpose and a way of fighting the war on drugs without getting overwhelmed by the scale of it. But he was losing his hold on that. He closed his eyes, saw Captain Viguerra again and asked, 'How do I find Stoval?'

Viguerra laughed.

'You don't have to worry about finding him. That is one thing you do not need to worry about. I promise, when he learns you are looking for him he will find you.'

FOURTEEN

At the Calexico International Airport the air controller was happy to talk shop about the Sherpa. He liked talking planes and was very familiar with the gray fifty-eight footer and its pilot. Calexico International had only one east/west runway. A fully loaded Sherpa needed up to five thousand feet of runway to land, but not if it was coming in empty from San Diego. The Calexico runway was four thousand six hundred and seventy feet, but that was okay, the controller explained. Weaver's routine was to land with an empty plane that then got loaded.

'He ferries cargo for a business in town that distributes products for a group of Mexican manufacturers. They're losing traffic to these new big box stores, so I don't know how much longer it's going to last. Why are you asking?'

Marquez took a chance and handed him a card. The DEA insignia was on it and the controller's reaction was a look of sad regret, though not of surprise. He studied the card as if wanting to collect his thoughts before speaking.

'I know he learned to fly that plane in the Coast Guard and the one he owns he bought as a wreck at an auction. He spent way too much rebuilding it. He'll have to fly cargo to the moon and back to pay it off, but I sure hope he's not doing anything illegal. He's too nice a guy.'

'I don't know that he is doing anything illegal.'

'But you're investigating him.'

'I'm following up on a tip. It doesn't mean anything yet so I'd appreciate you keeping it to yourself.'

'No problem.'

Now Marquez waited for a DEA pilot to fly in. When he did, Marquez walked out to meet him. Then they waited together until the Sherpa landed and loaded. It all went down in under an hour. As the Sherpa lumbered into the air again, a gray beast with its trusslike build, they took off right behind it.

Marquez had counted three men, the pilot and two others who were much younger and more than likely there to handle cargo. They trailed the Sherpa northeast at eight thousand feet. Below the rugged country was colored with shades of brown, the sky ahead a dark blue. He listened as the DEA pilot went back and forth on the radio, and watched as he slid his headset off and turned.

'Your friend here is gradually changing his heading. This isn't the flight plan he filed, so he may know we're here.'

'Can he dump the load?'

'Oh, yeah, that plane is built for it. I've never ridden one of those flying boxes, but they say you have to beat them out of the air. Those two guys with him can slide the cargo doors open and shove stuff out.'

The Sherpa pilot got cleared to land at Mammoth Lakes Airport on the eastern side of the Sierras. His bearing became northeast and at this speed he'd land in Mammoth in forty-five minutes. On this heading he'd cross over Death Valley.

And that's what he did. He took it right up the spine of the Panamint Mountains. Above the deep canyons there the cargo doors slid open and Marquez and the DEA pilot watched slit bags tumble from the plane, spinning, trailing a thin plume of cocaine, some bursting open in a tiny cloud in the air, others lost in the dark jagged rocks below. Marquez videotaped but looking down at the unpaved roads that ran across the big wash and vanished early in the steep canyons, he knew they wouldn't recover anything. Each bag probably held fifty kilos, and still the pilot had to circle the Panamints twice before they were done.

The Sherpa tracked alongside the bone dry land east of the White Mountains, came around Montgomery Peak and descended alongside Highway 395 to the airport at Mammoth Lakes. Two county cruisers were waiting. Drug-sniffing dogs were on the way from Reno. Weaver surrendered without incident and now was in a holding cell in Mammoth. The pair of San Diego gangbangers traveling with him were in separate cells. Marquez tried the gangbangers first. Despite clothes caked in cocaine dust, they gave him nothing but attitude. He called home to the Field Office and talked to Sheryl.

'I need everything we can get on Weaver, the pilot.'

With Weaver they might get somewhere because Weaver looked like a broken man. He slumped in his cell. He wept as Marquez talked with Sheryl about recovering cocaine.

'It's in canyons and on ridges in the Panamint Mountains in Death Valley. It's probably a hundred and ten degrees in those canyons this time of year. We might find a bag or two but then we'd have the problem of proving it was theirs, and even if we did, no DA is going to touch it. Our best chance is to get the pilot to talk.'

He drove three miles back to 395 and then south to the metal buildings and the runway alongside the highway where the dull gray Sherpa sat. The dogs had arrived from Reno and the handler was waiting. The dogs picked up on cocaine as soon as they got in the cargo bay and Marquez wiped his hand across the cargo floor and came up with white powder. He looked at flattened KZ Nut cardboard boxes from the warehouse in Calexico and figured they shipped the cocaine double-bagged and in KZ boxes. He counted boxes as he talked to the dog handler, and then thanked her for coming down and walked back through the afternoon wind to his car.

To the west the high rock on the peaks was white in the sun and he was looking at country he hadn't seen in years.

He felt a wistful familiarity and love of the high clean granite that somehow he'd lost touch with. When he got back into Mammoth he washed the coke off his hands and sat down in a holding cell with the pilot, Del Weaver.

He waited for Weaver to look at him and then asked, 'Do you want to talk and see what we can work out?'

Turned out it was debt, an overdue balloon payment on the plane, insurance, operating costs that he hadn't anticipated, and alimony payments to a schizophrenic wife who would never work again. He put his living expenses on credit cards as he staved off his creditors. The Salazars paid cash and he was only going to do it until his debts were paid off.

Marquez took him through the drill, cited a couple of recent prison sentences of two guys who didn't cooperate, and Weaver rolled over so fast Marquez had trouble keeping up.

'I was supposed to take the load to an almond ranch in the valley, KZ Nuts. I haven't told them I dumped it yet.'

'But they know something has happened. You're way overdue, so what are they thinking right this second?'

'Those guys, they'll think I stole the load.'

'Who's in charge? Give me a name.'

'Mendoza. Raymond Mendoza, but he goes by Rayman.'

'This Rayman works for the Salazars?'

'He's their main guy in California and he's really only a kid.' Weaver shook his head and then put a hand to his forehead, covered his eyes and spoke to the table. 'I can't go to prison. Everything will fall apart.' He looked at Marquez. 'I've got my mother in a nursing home. I'm paying them month to month.'

'That's going to be beyond me, Del. I can write it down and testify to what happened, to how you cooperated after we arrested you, but the decisions you're talking about aren't the ones I get to make. What if you called Rayman now and told him you had to land at Mammoth with mechanical problems but you're almost back in the air? Then I fly with you to the almond farm.'

As he said this, he knew what a leap it was going to be to sell the idea in LA. He could see Holsten frowning, his expression saying, what are you doing in my office asking something so stupid?

'What kind of deal would I get?' Weaver asked.

'That would be up to the US Attorney. But this could go a long way toward helping you.'

'What happens after we land?'

'You taxi away from them and I'll have a lot of backup there. SWAT teams.'

In a perfect world they'd land somewhere first and pick up the SWAT team, come in like a Trojan horse. But there was zero chance of that getting approved. Marquez waited, knowing Weaver was scared and that he couldn't coerce Weaver into doing this, and that it wasn't likely to get far as an idea anyway. He gave Weaver another minute and then pushed his chair back and stood.

'I've got to make a call.'

He called Sheryl and ran it by her with the idea she try to talk Holsten into it. 'It's his bold idea,' Marquez said. 'He keeps talking about us making a bold stroke. Talk up what the press will do with it.' She laughed. 'No, I'm serious, Holsten will hear that.'

Twenty minutes later she called back.

'We're on,' she said. 'Holsten is game.'

'OK, I've got to talk to Weaver again.'

'Talk him into it fast, and then call me before Holsten changes his mind.'

FIFTEEN

They flew south with their shadow flickering over the highway and the dry desert plain. The highest peaks of the Sierra Nevada sat off their right wing. From the co-pilot's seat Marquez looked across at Mount Whitney and remembered the summer he was eighteen and drove his car through the scrub and sage past the outcroppings of volcanic rock in the Alabama Hills and on up toward the granite and pine of Whitney Portal. He hiked the first sandy switchbacks in the last moonlight, strong, young, and alone. Higher up, he watched the sun rise through the V-notch and the sky burn crimson above the White Mountains. He still remembered the cool of the morning and the way the high white rock reflected on Mirror Lake. He remembered how it felt drawing deep breaths and rising along the trail with an electric feeling of elation at the clear light and the high peaks ahead.

None of where he was now could he have foreseen then, though maybe he should have. He felt a strong longing as he looked out across at the mountains, then turned back to Weaver and the acrid sweat smell of Weaver's fear.

'How are you doing?' he asked him.

'Can you get me in a witness protection program?'

Marquez had lied to suspects to provoke a confession, but he never bullshitted a guy on his way down.

'Not with what you'll be charged with.'

'It's not the Salazars I'm afraid of. There's another guy and he's not Mexican. He came to see the plane once and told me he had a lot of money in making this work. I'm pretty sure he was telling me I'd die if it didn't. I was working on the plane one Saturday.'

Weaver pointed toward the back.

'I was back there attaching some strapping and never heard him get in the plane. He came in so quietly I thought he was there to kill me. He stayed maybe five minutes. I never saw him again, but I'll never forget him.'

'What did he look like?'

Marquez listened to the description. He carried a sketch with him now. That came out of his new friendship with Kerry Anderson. He got it out, unfolded it, and showed Weaver.

'That's him,' Weaver said. 'Who is he?'

'When did he come see you?'

'About a year ago.'

'You been flying for them that long?'

Weaver never answered that. They followed the highway out and when they came around the mountains banked right and flew northwest, crossing the Tehachapis as Marquez went back and forth by radio with the SWAT team leader and Sheryl as they got closer. As they started their descent and a white concrete runway rose toward them, two SWAT teams were fired on as they approached the main house and outbuildings. Row after row of almond trees flashed by. The plane bounced hard and Marquez had Weaver run out to the end of the runway and shut the engines down. SWAT vehicles rolled toward them and a helicopter passed overhead as he got Weaver off the plane.

Four cartel guards died in a firefight that ranged between the main house and a storage building where a large stash of cocaine, dope, and pills were found. Rayman surrendered, temporarily blinded by tear gas but able to recognize Marquez's voice. He was clean cut and looked like he could be working at a bank. Marquez watched him guided into the backseat of a county cruiser to get run to a hospital to get his eyes flushed. With Sheryl Marquez walked the storage building, past plastic bags of cocaine stacked on pallets and stamped with images of furniture, a chair, desk, bed, or table, and coded that way so phone conversations were easy. They took inventory.

When Brian Hidalgo and Ramon Green arrived, they were still counting thousands of pills and weighing dope on the almond scales. Hours later he took a break with Sheryl, moving out into the trees in the night. In the darkness he could still feel the heat radiating off the ground. Sheryl talked about the almond farm the DEA would now impound and the TV coverage the bust had already gotten. Sheryl was always thinking about the house she wanted to buy and she made him smile as she looked around the farm and speculated on a DEA auction of the property. She walked close to him, her hand brushing his as they moved out into the trees.

SIXTEEN

Sheryl rode with Marquez. They drove south ahead of the rest of the squad that night and stopped by the house of the on-call judge to get the search warrant for the Calexico warehouse signed, then bought burgers at a Jack in the Box and a six-pack of Corona at an all-night store. They were still an hour's drive from Calexico when they checked into the only motel they could find.

Sheryl unlocked her room, dumped her bag on the bed and showered. She pulled on jeans and a T-shirt, and with her hair still dripping, walked down and knocked on Marquez's door.

He was barefoot, an open beer in his hand, the TV on low. He looked beat, but the energy of the bust was still running hard in her.

'OK if I come in?'

'Of course.'

He opened a beer for her and then showered with the door mostly closed, but not closed, and she wanted to walk in there, but didn't. She watched steam drift out. She flipped through the crap on TV looking for something funny, looking for something to wind down with.

'Find anything?' he asked as he came out.

'Not yet.'

'Keep trying.'

She took a pull of the beer and watched him sit down on the only chair in the room and smile at her. Sheryl loved that smile. It carried the whole day in it. He lifted his beer to her, leaned forward and clicked his bottle against hers.

'We did it,' he said.

'Yeah, we did.'

She took another pull of the beer and felt her heart beating. She didn't know which way it was going to go tonight, but she turned the TV off.

'Weaver said something to me when we were in the air.'

'What did he say?'

'He wanted to know if he was going to be protected.'

'We can get him a prison out of state, if that's what he wants.'

'It's not the Salazars he's afraid of. He said he was working on his plane when this all got started and he got an unexpected and what he described as a spooky visit. I showed him a sketch I carry.'

Marquez took a long pull of beer and debated coming clean with her about what he'd done in Tijuana to Miguel Salazar. But that would make a problem for her. It wasn't fair, though it was strange to carry around something you knew was going to end your career. He put the beer down, got up and fished out a folded piece of paper from his jacket, then sat down next to Sheryl.

'What's that?' she asked.

'A sketch.' He unfolded it and showed her Stoval's face. 'That's who Weaver ID'ed.'

'Where did you get that?'

'Kerry Anderson.'

'And you're carrying it around. What's happening to you?'

'Something inside snapped,' he said and smiled and she couldn't tell if he was joking or not.

They talked about the bust now, ran the highlights over a second beer and turned the TV back on. A late night newscast covered the bust and showed the almond orchards, the Sherpa, delivery trucks, the storage buildings and house as the announcer quoted Holsten calling it a major blow to the Salazar Cartel.

'I'll be there when Rayman gets sentenced,' Sheryl said. She began to wind down. She turned the TV off and looked at Marquez. She could read his face. She could read the quiet. She knew he was thinking about Osiers but she wanted him to put his arms around her in this motel in the middle of nowhere.

They finished the beer. They needed to be out of here before dawn. They needed to be at E.J. Jones & Sons before the owner got there and unlocked the doors tomorrow morning, and she saw John was fading. The moment was fading. She knew he'd spent a lot of adrenaline today. Only John could have come up with the plane idea. She saw he needed to sleep but said, 'I'm going down to my room to grab the warrant. I want to check it again. I'll be right back.'

'Take my room key. It's on top of the TV.'

She scooped it up. She went down to her room and stared at herself in the mirror, looked for the answer there before retrieving the warrant. She didn't really need to look at it. It was all there. They were set for tomorrow. When she went back to John's room and let herself in, he was lying on his back on the bed with his eyes closed.

'Hey, you didn't go to sleep on me, did you?'

'No, I'm here.'

But he was groggy. He'd be asleep in minutes. She shut the door softly and leaned over him, search warrant still in her hand, her heart fluttering. She watched his chest rise and fall, watched him fall asleep and knew she should leave and go to her room. She knew that absolutely. She knew that was the right thing to do, but threw the second lock on the door instead, took her jeans off, got on the bed, and sat cross-legged, looking at his face, her thighs cool in the night air, John's face still and statue like. He made her think of her mother telling her in her cryptic way that if she made a career in law enforcement there wouldn't be opportunity for her. She might never have a family was what her mother was saying, and Sheryl had shaken that off. She lived in a different world than her mother. She'd been sure of that, and now she was thirty-four and single and her mother was dead.

She could wake him. She could touch him, arouse him, and get on top of him. Instead, she watched him sleep. She knew what the rules for agents were. She didn't even have her pager with her. Her gun was back in the room. She knew all the rules for agents and yet she wrapped the bedspread over them and laid down alongside him and smiled as he stirred, rolled on his side and wrapped an arm around her. She undid his shirt, her fingers working quietly, slowly. She put her face against his warm skin and smelled him and closed her eyes.

She didn't want to be anywhere else. A couple of tears leaked out from under her eyelids and she moved her hand up very slowly and touched the skin wet with tears. She didn't want them to wake him. She pressed her hand on his chest. She felt his heart beating. She felt more tears wet the back of her hand and was afraid it was all coming apart now and what should happen with her and John never would. There had been a moment and the moment was sliding by. John was going somewhere else. He blamed himself for Billy Takado getting killed. It was the sketch of Stoval he was carrying. John was on a different road now. She could feel it and pressed her face softly against his chest. She closed her eyes again and tried to make it different, feeling the warmth of his skin and listening to his heart.

SEVENTEEN

The next morning at the warehouse of the distributor, E.J. Jones & Sons, they found employees milling around out front waiting for the owner to arrive and unlock as he did every day. His name was Jim Jones, like the Kool-Aid preacher, and he pulled up in a black Porsche Roadster and sat a long time in the car looking at their DEA jackets. Marquez left him alone and let him adjust to their presence in his own way. Jones was white-haired, well-groomed and acted stunned that the DEA was here. As his employees watched, he made a good run at being indignant.

'Big mistake,' he told Marquez and pointed a finger. 'My father started this business thirty-five years ago and everyone here knows that what we do is distribute for Mexican manufacturers. They bring it to the border and we contract with US trucking firms to get their products where they need to go. You're wasting more taxpayer money this morning. It's no surprise we're losing the war on drugs.'

'We're going to search your building, sir.'

Jones unlocked and said, 'I'll be in my office.'

'I'd rather you wait here for the moment.'

'I've got calls to make, but I guess you wouldn't know anything about running a business.'

'No, but I've wrecked a few. Just stick out here with us for an hour or so.'

Marquez left him with Sheryl and walked row after row of the shelving with shrink-wrapped product on pallets. The air was cool and smelled of concrete and the diesel the forklifts used. Above them, the metal roof creaked and groaned as the day heated. They searched and found nothing. At mid morning, after they knew it wasn't going to come easy, if at all, Hidalgo drove into Calexico and picked up coffee and a box of donuts. Then they all met in the middle of the building.

'Maybe I got it all wrong,' Marquez said, 'but I really don't feel like apologizing to this guy yet.' He picked up one of the extra coffees and looked around at the squad. 'Let's go take another look at that room in back where they box product.'

The room held packing machinery and they'd looked it all over earlier, but not opened anything. Marquez put his coffee down and used a knife to cut into a pallet of folded cardboard boxes. He folded back the heavy protective paper, cut the bands, and pried one loose so he could read the label.

'Here we go,' he said, and worked one of the folded boxes fully loose. He held it up and showed the KZ Nuts emblem. 'They package and load here.'

No one responded because the owner had already told them KZ grew and shipped more than almonds. Some of the nuts were grown in Mexico, so no big deal. They were bound to have boxes. Still, the squad came over for a look and Green knocked over Marquez's coffee.

'Sorry.'

Marquez watched the coffee drain slowly under the pallet, thinking he really wanted that coffee. Then he heard dripping. The coffee had spilled on a concrete slab, so what was dripping? He got down and looked under the pallet. Couldn't see that well, got up, walked over to a forklift, drove it back and lifted the pallet away, exposing a hinged steel lid, roughly three feet by three feet. He parked the forklift, walked back and then heard a sound below, a man coughing and voices. Marquez motioned everyone back, grabbed the handle and lifted the trap door.

A man wearing a backpack stood on a metal rung blinking at the light and smiling. Beneath him was another man and Marquez said, '*Hola*,' and waved them up. One after another, ten came out with their loads of cocaine. They separated them, busted them, got statements and arrested the owner pending charges.

Marquez made a run at getting him to talk, but he lawyered up and when they finished with evidence collection they returned to LA. He got called into Holsten's office the next day. On Holsten's desk was a *San Diego Union-Tribune* article about the bust and the drug distribution system that made use of a restored Coast Guard plane. The Sherpa got a photo and caption, *Military workhorse goes bad*.

Holsten said, 'You're quoted in there. If I didn't know better, I'd think you were running Group Five.'

'Well, we both know better.'

'Congratulations on the bust.' Holsten smiled in a cold hard way. 'I have several things to talk to you about today. First, we have a strange request from the Mex Feds. A Captain Viguerra is planning a large raid and he specifically wants you and two agents you choose as observers. Do you know him?'

'I've met him a few times. He's former military but working for the judicial police now. He's a charismatic guy. His men are very loyal to him. Where is this bust going down and why does he want us around?'

'I don't know why he wants you. All of this is coming through the El Paso Field Office and they don't know either. We're all hoping you can tell us.'

Sarcasm, the cold smile again, and Marquez knew today was the today. He stared back at Holsten and said, 'They must have a theory in El Paso.'

'They think he's afraid of getting betrayed by someone on his side and that three DEA agents as ridealongs are a form of insurance. It's not a request I would ever normally consider, but he's managed through his contacts to get headquarters engaged. There are people in Washington that want us to show we can work with the Mex Feds. So if you want to go I'm going to let you go conditionally.'

Holsten let him digest that. The DEA didn't send ridealongs into a bust and he was being very careful to make sure Marquez understood if he went it would be voluntary.

'In El Paso they're not sure Viguerra is legit,' Holsten said. 'How did you and Viguerra become such good friends?'

'What is it you want me to do?'

Marquez could have added *sir* to the end of the question, but there didn't seem to be any point anymore.

'I want you to answer my question. How did you become such good friends that he asked for you?'

'I don't know him very well, but I heard he wasn't corruptible and went to meet him when we were trying to get a handle on the Salazars. We heard the Salazars put a contract out on him and I wanted to offer an alliance.'

'Is this in your reports?' Marquez nodded and Holsten was quiet and then asked, 'What do you think of his request?'

'I'll do it, but I'm not sure I'd ask anyone else to.'

'Hidalgo and Green have already volunteered to go.'

'When does this bust of Viguerra's go down?'

'You'd have to leave today, but that depends on what happens with a conversation I want to have with you away from here. Let's go get coffee.'

So it was going to be the famous ride in Holsten's car to Starbucks. Marquez waited on the curb for Holsten to pull out of the parking garage. When he got in the car Holsten didn't waste any time.

'In my opinion your DEA career is over. Even if you survive the disciplinary hearings, you'll never go up.'

Holsten drew a horizontal line in the air and Marquez could almost see the line as he lowered his hand. He felt a tightening in his chest and realized he wasn't as ready as he thought.

'You'll go sideways. You'll end up transferred to a back-water office and it'll break your spirit. You're young so you'll go sideways for a long time. After that, you'll quit or sink away.' Holsten shook his head. 'What in the hell was going through your head?'

'A copy of the autopsy report on Jim Osiers got left wrapped in my morning newspaper. When I read it, I had to do something. I drove to Tijuana to a restaurant Billy told me Miguel frequents. I got into it with a couple of wannabes inside, and outside when I was leaving Miguel showed and drew a gun when I started toward him.' Marquez shook his head. 'Everybody in the Judicial Police knows Miguel Salazar murdered Jim, and I was there when he shot Billy Takado. He's walking away from both killings, and I couldn't handle that. No one cares about a dead informant and Jim Osiers is being painted as dirty. Once he's dirty the investigation into his murder will end. I couldn't handle that.'

'I take that last comment very personally.'

'You should.'

Holsten's face reddened.

'But I'm sorry I let the department down. I let myself down.'

'I could fire you without any disciplinary hearings, without Internal Affairs or Office of Professional Responsibility investigations.'

'Then fire me.'

'I don't want to fire you. I want you to quit after the Viguerra ridealong.'

'Why do you give a damn about this ridealong?'

'I don't, but my superiors do. After Osiers we have to show the Mexicans we still want to be their partners. It's connected to the trade negotiations. It's way over your head, Marquez.'

'Viguerra is crazy. Don't send Green and Hidalgo.'

'I'm not. They volunteered.' Like fuck they did, Marquez thought, and Holsten changed the subject. 'What's happened with you is something I've seen happen several times before, in particular with undercover agents right around your level. I've seen it happen to the best. They have some success and then the boots get a little too big, the stride a little long. Overconfidence clouds thinking and out in the field they start acting like they run the DEA.'

Holsten, tall spare SAC with his sterile view of the world,

laid it out and Marquez riding shotgun, lean and young still, but with far more experience in the field than Holsten, listened knowing that something else had happened to him. He knew as he crossed the border into Tijuana that morning that he was severing his connection with the DEA.

Holsten nosed over to the curb a half block from Starbucks, still wanting his coffee. On the sidewalk before they went in Holsten turned with his lips pursed and shook his head, lamenting, 'KZ Nuts, the warehouse in Calexico, these are significant busts. You made them happen and it was a very big deal. You saw the Salazar organization developing before anyone else. If you hadn't gotten scared after Takado was shot and lost your sense of purpose and gone after Miguel Salazar you'd be in a different place. But in our organization there's no room for those kinds of flaws. I'm guessing you'd rather quit than go through the Internal Affairs investigation, the hearings, the whole show.'

'I'll resign, but between you and me you made a poor decision telling me to wait at that pass with Takado's body. It showed a critical lack of experience, but fortunately for you experience in what we really do isn't required in the upper levels of management. So I think you'll be fine.'

He could see how angry that made Holsten and Marquez found it didn't make him feel any better. He waited outside in the sunlight as Holsten went into Starbucks and ordered. When Holsten came out and they were back in the car Holsten said, 'I took a cheap shot at you and you took one back. That's fair, and right now you may not believe it, you may never believe it, but I'm very sorry to lose you. That's probably why I'm so angry with you. No one I've ever known has shown as much promise. No one else in the LA Field Office could have made that KZ bust happen. Between us we'll work up a good reason about why you're moving on and I'll write a strong recommendation letter. I'll write it this afternoon and we'll bury what happened in Tijuana and I'm sorry about the call I made after Takado's murder. Leave your gun in El Paso before you cross the border with Green and Hidalgo and leave your badge there when you get back. I'll mail you a letter of recommendation.' Holsten turned, offered his hand and said, 'You are the best talent I have ever seen. I wish you all the luck in the world with your next career.'

EIGHTEEN

*I*n an El Paso motel Marquez dreamed a memory of child-
*hood. The day was bright and blue and cold. He sat in a
chair in an elementary school office that smelled of warm
spoiled milk and carbon paper. Through a window he watched
an American flag snap back and forth on a pole, and beyond
the flag in the far distance he saw snow on the mountains.
Behind the counter a typewriter clacked and stopped and a
large woman in a blue suit led him into the principal's office
and pointed to a chair. Marquez sat down. His ear stung from
where he'd been hit. His right cheek was raw and he had a
lump in his throat because he didn't start the fight. They
ganged up on him but the school principal squatted down in
front of him now to tell him that wasn't true.*

*'You don't belong here. You don't fit and your parents aren't
fit for our community. We were forced to let you go to school,
but your family won't last here and we don't want you to stay.
Do you understand?'*

'Yes.'

'You're in my office today because you started a fight.'

'I didn't—'

*'I want you to get in another fight. Today I'm going to
suspend you, but next time I'll expel you. Do you know what
expel means, son? It means I'll get rid of you.'*

Marquez kept the subsequent fights after school and off the
school yard, but it didn't matter. The family moved anyway.
They were always moving. 'We're nomads following the Great
Dope Route,' his father had said. 'Like Marco Polo,' and his
mother would giggle, though they had nowhere and no one,
and now he was leaving again, leaving the DEA and all of
his friends, everything he was connected to. He tossed in the
bed and sweated. He pushed the covers back, dozed, dismissed
the childhood dream, and much later that morning crossed
from El Paso into Juarez with Hidalgo and Green.

They drove over the concrete trench that had once been a
river and now was lined with fences. In Juarez dust and litter

swirled in wind as they followed Viguerra's lieutenants to a warehouse on the outskirts of the city. Inside the warehouse, Viguerra broke from his lieutenants and greeted them.

'You'll ride with me,' he told Marquez. 'We're inviting ourselves to a meeting at a big hacienda.' His eyes lit with sudden humor. 'A cartel meeting where one of the things they're voting on is raising the price on my head.' He tapped his sidearm. 'I'll be voting.' He winked at Hidalgo and Green. 'If anyone asks, you must say you are American water inspectors making sure that none of the river that used to flow to Mexico still does. You are here to check for leaks. All of the local people will understand.'

Last time they met Viguerra told Marquez, that yes, it was true, that officially he was of the Mexican Federal Judicial Police, but that he thought of himself as a soldier, not a policeman. 'I think like a soldier and we are in a war, a guerilla war where we are not the ones in power. The drug cartels are the powerful ones. They have control but with the people's help I fight them as if from the jungle.'

An hour after reaching the warehouse Hidalgo, Marquez, and Green climbed into the Vietnam-era Huey copter that Viguerra intended to use in the assault. In the seats around them were Viguerra's 'troops.' They flew south staying low and flanking dry hills. Outside a military encampment the helicopters landed and unloaded most of the men and equipment, then sat with rotors still running as Viguerra walked among his men before they loaded into jeeps and two troop carriers. Marquez rode with Viguerra and Hidalgo and Green rode in a troop carrier.

'It's an hour from here,' Viguerra said.

The assault began at dusk with the cutting of phone and electrical lines and the sniper shooting of two cartel guards in the gatehouse. Two helicopters rose from hills behind the hacienda and with heavy machine gun fire pinned down the guards inside the courtyard gates, then fired rockets into the cars parked there. When the thick wooden courtyard gates blew off their hinges, return fire flashed from the house. Windows shattered. Roofing tiles slaked off and fell three stories on to men fighting below as the helicopters poured fire into the house.

Viguerra's men fought their way into the lower floors and the return fire died down to sporadic shooting from the upper floors, clearing fire likely as Viguerra's men moved in and up. Then in seconds everything changed as a missile struck the lead helicopter. It spun, rolled to the right, then dove into the vineyard below the house. A second helicopter went down and the third was burning as it raked through the air above Marquez. Its tail snapped on landing and Marquez left Viguerra and ran down to try to help the men inside get out.

They burned before he got there but he was near the helicopter, sheltered by it when the blast came. The concussive roar enveloped and deafened him. He felt it from the inside out. Splintered rafters, shards of roof tile, and chunks of adobe rained down into the fields around him. A widening billow of gray-black smoke rose from where the house had been and it took him a moment before he could accept what he saw, that the house was gone. He watched a length of the adobe wall surrounding the outer courtyard slide down the slope and topple over.

Then men emerged from the ground like ants into the orchard. Armed men, cartel men, and that meant a tunnel, an escape route and he realized the house had been booby-trapped for a raid. It was why Viguerra and his men met so little resistance.

Shooting started in the fields, but the cartel gunmen outnumbered Viguerra's men and the shooting quickly died. There were shouts, vehicle engines starting. Marquez climbed back to where he'd last seen Viguerra and the jeep with the keys in it, but not Viguerra. For ten minutes he searched and when he didn't find him he drove the jeep back out to the road. Someone shot at him as he drove the perimeter of the orchard trying to find Hidalgo and Green.

NINETEEN

Seven or eight cars and pickups were pulled over and a small crowd had gathered near a concrete power pole. He slowed to a stop and as he got out of the jeep he watched a man turn a young boy's head away so he couldn't see what the crowd was looking at. He worked his way in, asking as he did what vehicles anyone had seen coming out the hacienda road. Then he got a view.

Ramon Green and a young judicial police officer were chained back to back against the pole, heads bowed in death, intestines pulled out, flung like rope in the dirt. He knew what he was seeing, but still had to touch Green to be sure. He took Green's wedding ring off and knelt there. Brian Hidalgo wasn't found until the next morning. Many regular *federales* were part of the search and it was *federales* who told Marquez Viguerra was decapitated, his head left on a stake along the highway shoulder, and *federales* who drove Marquez miles out a road following a dry creek to an abandoned adobe house. Inside the house they showed him Hidalgo's body, and then he sat for a long time outside on a rock near the dry creek.

Later in the afternoon, a Mex Fed contemporary of Viguerra told Marquez, 'I've seen these kinds of wounds before. This is a man who works for the one you asked about. They brought your agent here to question him. This man who does this is not a Mexican. This is not something that a Mexican would do. You need to understand that.'

Marquez spent days getting debriefed by agents in the El Paso Field Office. Holsten and Boyer flew out. He spent hours with Holsten reconstructing the events, then handed over his badge and flew home to LA.

Three days later, Marquez broke the lease on his apartment and crossed back into Mexico and began to hunt Stoval and the man who worked for him whose name he'd learned was Kline. He communicated half a dozen times with Kerry Anderson, who helped him and passed on information. He didn't talk with anyone else other than Sheryl. In August he picked up a message from her telling him she had applied for a transfer to headquarters in Virginia and it looked like she was going. He didn't call her back but he wished her luck.

Near Guadalajara he picked up a lead on Stoval's man and followed that south to Mexico City, and when that went nowhere he went much farther south into jungle villages where he heard this Kline was often seen. He searched for six weeks before backing away from the jungle. Late one afternoon, sitting with a beer outside a bar along a dirt road, he was approached by an American who did not identify himself but told Marquez he needed to hide or fly home.

'Why is that?'

'Because the men you're looking for are looking for you. Come here, let me show you something.' He led Marquez to the cracked side mirror of a pickup truck and turned the mirror so Marquez could see himself. 'Look at yourself.'

Marquez turned away instead and from behind him the man said, 'I'm your only friend here and I'm warning you, don't stay here tonight. They know you're in the area. Questions are getting asked about you, not just here but in the States. Information is being traded. You're being branded a rogue so your government can disown you. Stoval has a contact within the CIA that he provides information about the Salinas government in return for information he needs. He knows you're no longer with the DEA and one of his men extracted personal information about you from one of the DEA agents killed here. Are you hearing me?'

'Yeah, I'm listening.'

'They're hunting you. They're asking more questions.' The man tapped his chest. 'If I found you, believe they can.'

'Who asked you to find me?'

'I'll give you his initials. KA. Does that make sense?' Marquez nodded and the man offered his hand. 'Fly home, Marquez.'

TWENTY

Emrahain Stoval walked out along the General-Guisan-Quai. He did not mind the tourists as many did and liked the reflection of light off the water at this hour. He liked the smell of the air. He liked Zurich. It was a walking city and walking helped him think. He pondered this John Marquez, former DEA agent. Marquez had eluded them for months. He should be dead by now. According to one source Marquez was an embarrassment to the DEA and incompetent, but Stoval, who judged the DEA incompetent, had concluded that Marquez was just the opposite.

Mexican police officers who had taken his bribe money had promised that it would not take long to find him, but after months of nothing they talked as if they were pursuing a ghost.

But now there was new information that Marquez was back in the north, not far from El Paso or possibly in El Paso. Taking him in Mexico was better, but he couldn't count on that any longer, and he didn't see sending the same people in the same way again. It just wasn't getting done.

Stoval guessed that he probably knew more about this John Marquez than his former employer, the DEA, ever had. He'd read the account of the Kenyan police of the young man who without any real help tracked down the elephant poachers who'd raped and murdered his wife. Marquez had done that with next to no resources. The relentlessness impressed him.

He read a *San Francisco Examiner* article printed from microfiche.

Daring Rescue Off Alcatraz

Seventeen year old John Marquez jumped from the stern of a Blue & Gold ferry yesterday afternoon to rescue a father and daughter whose small sailboat had capsized near Alcatraz. Captain Tom Marks said he left the dock in Tiburon at 3:00 bound for Pier 35 in San Francisco with a full load of passengers and that neither he nor his crew saw the capsized boat and struggling pair in the water. 'It was very choppy,' Marks reported, 'and we had fog coming in. I don't know how he spotted them and not many people would jump in the water in those conditions. He must be a helluva swimmer. He's lucky to be alive.'

But not as lucky as Warren Dorland, 45, of Novato, and his eleven year old daughter, Bailey Dorland, who according to the Coast Guard was saved by Marquez's prompt response. 'The tide was running out through the Gate and the girl had lost grip of the overturned boat hull. With the fog coming in we would have had a very difficult time finding her.' Marquez, who will be recommended for a heroism award, was unavailable for comment. His older sister, Darcey Marquez, told reporters that despite being treated for mild hypothermia and released last night, her brother had left on a trip with friends this morning. She said the rescue didn't surprise her. 'That's just John,' she told reporters. For a grateful family last night it was much more.

He researched family. Marquez had none other than a sister. She'd been located in Alaska and Marquez lived in a cabinlike house on the side of a mountain in the San Francisco area. He'd inherited that and had some minor savings but no real wealth or prospects. Sooner or later, he would abandon his search and go home, but would he ever really give up? That, and if he didn't take Marquez out cleanly, Miguel Salazar would do it crudely and the DEA would react.

Marquez had no fear in his eyes in the bull ring and without turning around he'd intuitively understood what to do to try to get Takado away from Miguel Salazar. Diving into San Francisco Bay when the fog was coming in and the water rough said he was capable of focusing everything on a moment. The elephant poachers, that was unusual. He knows we're hunting him, Stoval thought. He knows and he's not running. I'll bring Kline north and we'll focus on El Paso. I don't want him moving again. It needs to be now.

TWENTY-ONE

Sheryl was in Virginia, four floors up at DEA headquarters. Marquez was in a pay phone in El Paso, Texas. She sounded engaged in the new job and happy, though worried about him.

'You wigged out, John, that's all there is to it, but I'm glad you're back in the States. Where were you all winter?'

'Guadalajara and farther south, then in Thailand and Indonesia.'

'How are you paying for all this?'

'I'm eating through my 401K.'

'That's insane.' She exhaled into the phone. 'Look. I'll be in LA next week. Why don't you meet me there?'

'I need a favor, Sheryl. I need you to check something for me. I heard something from a judge in Mexico named Carlotta. He's very well connected. He told me the CIA got the Kiki Camarena tape from someone who was in the room during the torture. Anderson told me Stoval was a source for the CIA. Tell Anderson I've learned something more

about the black letter and ask him if he knows anything about
Carlotta.'

'What black letter? What are you talking about? You sound
like a nutcase babbling about secret UN helicopters. Next thing
you're going to tell me is that Stoval was behind the Kennedy
assassination. And what's Kerry Anderson doing talking to you?
You're not a Fed anymore. He shouldn't be talking to you. Is
he passing you information?'

'Do that for me. I'll call you back.'

Marquez left the phone booth. Some of what Sheryl said
stung him and he tried to shake it off. He hadn't known
Kiki Camarena personally, but everyone in the DEA knew of
him. Camarena was the first DEA agent kidnapped, tortured,
and murdered in Mexico. His killers were never caught and
Marquez hoped Carlotta was a new lead.

Marquez was leaner and in better shape than he'd been in
at the DEA, though sick lately with something he picked up
in the jungle. At night he'd get a fever. He'd lost weight. His
hair was longer, face tanned. He looked civilian and he didn't
carry a gun anymore, though in his car was a Kimber pistol
and he had another hidden in the rundown house he rented.

After hanging up with Sheryl he crossed back into Juarez
and took up the same position in the same room in the same
apartment across the street from the offices he'd watched for
the last ten days. But again, no one showed up, and when he
crossed back to Texas it was 3:30 in the morning and with a
fever the trapped heat in the dusty rental house was stifling.
He opened windows and splashed water on his face. He
stripped off his clothes and lay down.

When he woke the sheets were drenched in sweat and he
heard a vehicle slow on the street. When he didn't hear it pull
away he slid over to the side of the bed and sat up. Seconds
later, he heard a door downstairs kicked open. It slapped
against the wall and hob-nailed boots clicked like hooves across
the floor as above Marquez scrambled for his gun. He heard
splashing, a sloshing of liquid, and then the smell came in a
wave up the stairwell, stronger than gasoline, sharp as acetone,
vapors that stung his eyes as he dragged the dresser over,
climbed up and broke the skylight loose. He pulled himself
up and on to the roof just ahead of the roar of heat and light.

Later he had little memory of sliding, of the brittle old

asphalt shingles slaking away underfoot. The rotted gutter held just long enough to slow him. He remembered a doctor leaning over him, skepticism in his eyes about Marquez's ability to comprehend his words but saying it anyway, 'You're a lucky man.'

His search for Stoval ended there. He knew he couldn't even risk staying in the hospital. He limped across the lobby and out into the heat. An hour later he was on a bus headed out of Texas. He zigzagged north and got his health back in small mountain towns in the Rockies before returning to California and then lived out of a motel for five months using a false name.

But he also made contact with friends in law enforcement. He had his letter of recommendation from Holsten and he got his resume together. He tried the Department of Justice, hoping his resume would get him an interview at DOJ and maybe a job. It didn't get him either.

When his tenants blew out of the lease on the Mount Tamalpais house his grandparents left him, he moved in there and applied to the San Francisco Police. SFPD was interested in his experience dealing with gangs, but they sensed what DOJ had, that something was missing, so he went to work for a private eye friend. But he still couldn't move forward. On a Friday afternoon when a case was resolved and it didn't look like his private investigator friend needed him in the near term, he got out his backpack.

He called his sister first, and then a woman named Katherine that he'd met recently and found himself thinking about every day. He told both and the next morning turned the water heater off and shut the house up.

Two days later he was along the Mexican border again, only this time he turned north. He took his first steps along the two thousand six hundred fifty miles of the Pacific Crest Trail. He figured this was where he'd get his life sorted out. It was a safe place to think and plan, and he wouldn't spend any money or at least not much. He'd made mistakes and Sheryl was right, he'd lost his way. He hiked into the highest mountains and it was okay being alone. It was fine to be alone and think about what had happened and where to go from here.

Marquez was north of Whitney at Rae Lakes when they came

for him again. His tent was pitched so that an outcrop of rocks sheltered him from the night downwind off the peaks. A warning had been passed along about a black bear in the area and though he had his food in a bear canister, it was the bear snuffling around the tent that woke him and it was the bear that scared one of the two men into talking.

A few words called out, a hushed whisper, and Marquez had time to get out of the tent. They fired twenty or more silenced rounds through his tent before checking inside. When they did he hammered a rock down on to the skull of one and drove the same hard granite through the lenses of the night vision goggles the other wore. He struck the eyes again and again as the man clawed at the goggles straps. Marquez stripped his gun from him and left him kneeling, nearly blinded.

At gunpoint he forced both to walk into the cold lake. He questioned them, flashlight in one hand, gun in the other, the one man unable to see and supported by the other.

'You'll die here if you don't tell me who sent you.'

They gave him a name and when the name didn't mean anything he got angrier. They gave the same name again, where they were contacted, how it worked, how they got paid, the photos they were supposed to take of his body. But their contact name still didn't mean anything and he used the silenced gun of one and shot into the water near them. He forced them back. He listened to their ragged breathing and kept the flashlight on them as he packed his gear. He took their clothes, shoes, and guns, and then walked away when they were still in the water. The one with the eye wound wouldn't last another four hours. Hypothermia would get the other.

'You guys have a nice night.'

But half a mile away from them he did a thing he'd think about for years after. Slipping the pack off, he removed their shoes, clothes, coats, and walked back. He found them stumbling along the trail around the lake, the one he'd blinded crying out and shivering uncontrollably. He dropped their gear with them and left them a flashlight, and in a strange way letting them live freed his heart from an anger he'd carried since Takado's murder.

He hiked out. He called. He made sure Darcey and Katherine

were fine, and then returned to the trail. Three weeks later, on a ridge along a canyon on the west shore of Tahoe, he stopped to eat, and sitting on a granite shelf looking down at that graceful improbable lake moved him in a way he couldn't put in words. The moment marked him and months later in the fall, as he ate a lunch of hard flat biscuits, tuna fish, and half a chocolate bar and black coffee with a game warden in Oregon, it began to gel. The warden was working a bear poaching case. Marquez stayed at a campsite three nights to help him. He taught the warden some undercover tricks and was there when the warden took two poachers down.

On the first of November after completing the Pacific Crest Trail he shaved his beard and called Katherine. He'd sent several postcards and a couple of letters and it was great to hear her voice. He smiled as he talked to her. He flew to San Francisco the next morning. The next day he drove to Sacramento and dropped his resume with the California Department of Fish and Game. Two days later he got a call from the chief of Fish and Game who said, 'This job is only for someone with the passion for it. It doesn't pay well. We can't even pay you what you were making before.'

'It's where I belong.'

'You need to be very sure about that.'

'I've had time to think about it.'

'Then come back this afternoon and let's talk. You might be just what we need.'

II
Green Book
(June 2009)

TWENTY-TWO

Moat Creek, California

Every warden in California's Department of Fish and Game keeps a logbook, but only the SOU, the Special Operations Unit, carries the green, hardbound Boorum & Pease. In fourteen years as patrol lieutenant of Fish and Game's undercover team Marquez had filled six logbooks. They rode with him, were water and coffee stained, and held countless notes about interviews, suspects, tips, vehicles, busts, court appearances, and anything that might help solve or make a case now or later. The books were the record of his time. They told of the war against poachers fought in California at the end of the twentieth century and into the first decade of the new one.

This morning half of the SOU team was along the north coast with Marquez sweeping down from Fort Bragg, checking beaches and coves for abalone poachers. In California you couldn't legally dive for abalone with air. You had to free-dive and today there was a very low, minus two-foot tide, so the dive was shallower and easier. Before dawn the beach lots and access roads filled with cars. South of Bragg and not far from Moat Creek the team picked up on four divers in an old gray Chevy. The divers visited three coves, each time staying long enough to dive, yet returning to their car empty-handed. Which can happen, but this didn't feel right.

Lieutenant Carol Shauf ran point as the team tracked the foursome. Shauf called out their changing locations over the radio and as Marquez heard her description of one of them he eased over to the road shoulder north of Moat Creek.

To his left beyond the road and the cliffs was the dark blue of the Pacific, to his right a barbed-wire fence and pasture. In the distance, dark trees on the coastal mountains. Fog blew overhead, but it was burning off and the green field to his right alternately darkened and brightened. Sunlight and shadow touched the pages of one of his old logbooks as he flipped through the pages. He listened to the back and forth over the radio as he worked his way back in the logbook. He found what he was looking for just as his cell phone rang.

'John Marquez?' a voice asked, and Marquez recognized him right away. He remembered the distrust in Desault's stare the day of the lie detector test. 'It's Ted Desault. Remember me?'

'Sure, I remember you, Ted. You must be calling to apologize? It's taken you long enough.'

Desault chuckled and Marquez could ask how he got this phone number, or what it was he needed so badly that after twenty years he was calling, but he decided to wait for the explanation.

'I head an FBI task force to take down Emrahain Stoval.'

'Stoval.'

'Yes, and I know you keep tabs through Kerry Anderson.'

'I try not to think about him much anymore. I've got my hands full here.'

Marquez listened to a quick back and forth between Shauf and another of his team. He knew Desault could hear it too and he wanted him to.

'I need your help, Marquez.' If you didn't need something, you wouldn't be calling, Marquez thought. 'Stoval traffics in animal parts. We think he's vulnerable there.'

Marquez knew about the trafficking. Desault was right, he still kept track through Anderson. But he was also two decades away from what had happened then. According to Anderson, Stoval had made himself untouchable after 9/11 by providing continual intelligence about terror related smuggling through Mexico. But then that was the kind of thing Anderson would say. Anderson and Sheryl Javits were about all the connection he had left from those days. Sheryl was at the wedding when he married Katherine. Sheryl came to dinner occasionally at their house. She was well up in the DEA brass now. It was Sheryl who had confirmed years ago that after Miguel Salazar was killed the contract on Marquez had gone away.

'I want to talk face-to-face,' Desault said. 'I've got an offer I'd like to make you. I think you'll like what we're doing.'

Marquez looked out at the ocean and said, 'Give me a number where I can reach you.'

'When can we meet?'

'I'll call you. We're in the middle of something, right now.'

But Desault knew that. He'd heard Shauf. As he hung up, Marquez thought of the passive distrust in Desault's eyes the day of the lie detector test. He got only a few seconds to think about it before Shauf's voice crackled over the radio.

'Hey, they're back at the first harbor. I'm betting they left a dive ring down there full of ab and will bring it up now.'

'Can you see the driver?'

'I'm looking at him.'

'Has he got a tatt on the right side of his neck?'

'If he does the wetsuit collar is hiding it. He's got a buzz cut. He's big. No, he's fat. Black wetsuit, bright blue stripes on the arms. Why are you asking?'

'I recognize him.' Marquez had found the page with the notes from 2003 on a poacher named Greg Lahzouras. Images from long ago, Billy Takado's face, buzzed in his head, but he made himself focus. 'If it's who I think it is he's got a tatt that's supposed to be a dragon, but looks like a red lizard on his neck.'

'You might be right. This looks like a guy we busted in Shelter Cove in '03 or 4. Remember, he got off with almost no fine? What was his name?'

'Lahzouras.'

'Yeah, yeah, you're right, it is him.' Her voice speeded up. 'OK we've got some more action, the backpacker we saw out on the road earlier is walking back up like he's carrying a dead body on his back. I think they filled his pack with ab. If I'm right they'll pick him up when he reaches the road, unload what he's carrying, and do it again at the other places they dove.'

And that's what happened. The backpacker let other cars go by and then stuck his thumb out as the Chevy with the divers approached. They put his pack in the trunk alongside a big cooler and he got in. At the next beach lot the divers went down to the water, leaving the backpacker to transfer the abalone from the backpack to a big cooler in the trunk. When he finished he strolled down to the beach with the empty pack. Not the most sophisticated method, but it was getting the job done.

They watched this routine three times before the divers left the coast, drove east through coastal mountains, and north on 101 forty miles to a convenience store lot, where in about sixty seconds they moved two big coolers from the Chevy into a white minivan. The Chevy with the divers headed south back down 101 and Marquez sent three of the SOU with it. Shauf and the others stayed with him and trailed the minivan to a small airport way up in Yreka.

As he drove he thought about Desault's call and the time that had passed. His face showed the years of wind and sun. He was gray at the temples now. Gray was the color when he shaved and washed the razor, but he still had the rangy broad-shouldered strength and lankiness. Wildlife enforcement had been the right decision long ago, but he knew also that his role as patrol lieutenant of the SOU was going to end in the next few years. Chief Blakely, who headed the law enforcement end of the California Department of Fish and Game, wanted him to accept a promotion, move up the ladder, and bring his experience into one of the regional offices.

He'd floated a different idea with Blakely, that she create a new job in the field for him as he left the SOU. Her bemused smile told him how ridiculous that was. Thirty-eight warden positions were currently unfilled because the salary was so low. There was absolutely no way she could create a new position. How much of that did Desault know, and where did Desault get his cell number if not from Blakely? It would be easy to ask her.

Marquez had married Katherine and helped raise his step-daughter, Maria, from age five and a half to adulthood. He was a legend among the commercial market poachers, but he took fewer risks nowadays. Poachers who had tried to track the team told stories and speculated that the SOU had secret airplanes and helicopters because they seemed to disappear and then arrive impossibly fast on the other end of the state. But that was the art of casting a long shadow, and that's what they were up to again tonight. Half the team was with him and the rest working a sturgeon operation in the delta.

They could have busted the abalone poachers at the little airport in Yreka, but instead videotaped the coolers getting loaded into a Cessna. An hour and a half later, Oregon game wardens arrested three men, including a well-known Portland restaurateur as he came out to meet the plane when it landed. Meanwhile, Marquez and the team followed the minivan driver back out to the coast and arrested him and his companion outside a Crescent City bar.

Crescent City is way up on the north coast of California and Marquez didn't get out of there until late. He never found the time to call Desault back and he didn't get as far south that night as he'd hoped to. He slept four hours in a motel in Ukiah and at first light was on the road south again. He was late and as a consequence didn't meet up with one of the ten wardens on his SOU team in time. An investigation would later determine fault, but for Marquez the results of the investigation would never matter. He believed that if he hadn't slept in Ukiah, if he'd just pushed on, it would have gone down differently. He would always blame himself.

TWENTY-THREE

The sturgeon poacher, Jeff Holsing, parked in the lot outside the Cache Creek Casino and went inside. As he did, SOU warden Brad Alvarez eased his truck into a parking slot where he had a good view of both the casino and Holsing's van. He flipped open his cell phone and called the warden he was working the operation with, Melinda Roberts.

'Holsing just went into the Cache Creek Casino. How far away are you?'

'An hour and a half, unless there's traffic.'

'I'm going in.'

'Keep your distance.'

That went without saying and Alvarez passed over it. He glanced at the glass doors leading into the casino. He's got to be meeting somebody in there.

'Look for me at a blackjack table,' Alvarez said. 'Or maybe slots. Text me when you get close and I'll order you a drink. What do you want?'

'Margarita, no salt.'

'You got it.'

She laughed and Alvarez, sitting in his truck, smiled. Truth was they'd both been up most of the night, and what he would do in the casino if he got the chance was get coffee and food.

'I talked to the lieutenant,' she said. 'He said to tell you he's on his way but still two hours out.'

'I got a message.'

The real message was Marquez wanted them to be very careful. Marquez thought Holsing was already looking over his shoulder before they started tracking him. He thought Holsing was too jumpy and likely to be carrying a gun. But Alvarez wasn't worried about whether Marquez got here in two hours or three. What mattered was that they didn't lose Holsing as he delivered the sturgeon. They left it that Roberts would text when she was ten minutes away, and if Holsing moved before that he'd be back on the phone with her.

He saw rows of slot machines as he walked in. Even at this early hour Cache Creek was crowded with players. But Holsing wasn't here for slots. He was at a café table eating breakfast with Carl Talbot, a twenty-four year old carpenter that Holsing had met with last week. The SOU didn't know Talbot's role yet, though it was Alvarez's guess that they'd find out today.

When he was confident they weren't moving soon, Alvarez checked out the food court and bought a mocha and a bagel. He sat where he could still see their table and ate the bagel, but left the mocha alone. He wanted the mocha to last, because who knows where it was going from here. Following Holsing was like watching a bad reality show. This one had started at 4:30 this morning when Holsing loaded five sturgeon into his van and then drove around in circles until meeting up with a middle-aged white male in a black Hummer at a Chevron station in Fairfield. He figured Hummer man was their buyer, but the sturgeon stayed in Holsing's van.

When a waitress arrived with their check, Alvarez moved back outside and then to his truck, thinking, come on, Holsing, you can't drive around with the fish on ice forever. He watched both come out of the casino. Holsing crossed the parking lot to his van, a tall skinny nervous guy with enough opportunistic charm to get by. He was also cruel. They'd watched how he beat his dog. He was in his van and backing up when Alvarez updated Roberts.

'Holsing is rolling and it looks like Talbot is leading him into the Capay Valley. Where are you at?'

'Stuck in traffic.'

'How long?'

'Forty minutes.'

'OK, I'm going with them.'

Ahead, Talbot's pickup turned left off the one two-lane road running through the Capay. Holsing followed closely on to a gravel road running across the valley floor toward the base of the mountains. When Talbot turned off that road it was on to a dirt and grass road leading up to a property that backed up to the base of the mountains. Pasture land and a ranch house. A big piece of land and he got the address as he rolled slowly past.

He gave Roberts the address and said, 'I'll go up that Forest Service road. I should have a view from there. Do you know where I mean?'

She did, and now Alvarez unlocked the Forest Service gate. He drove up to a bend where he could look down over the trees and see the house, Holsing's van, and Talbot's blue Ford pickup. He got out of the truck with his binoculars and phone and what was left of the mocha.

Below, and across the valley, the land was green with spring, though on the south and west slopes the grass had already gone brown. Ground fog lay in thin strands in pockets in the fields, but it would disappear soon. The light rain that fell in the late night had left the land damp, but the sky was clear now and the morning warming. After the night and the cold in the delta, the sun on his face felt great. He finished the mocha and checked out the house again with the binoculars before deciding to move up the road to the next bend.

When he did, the cell reception sucked. The conversation with Roberts broke up, but that could be where she was driving through so he didn't move again. They weren't doing too well with the radio today either, some problem with a repeater this morning. Still, with the radio he was able to communicate to her where he was.

Now Holsing and Talbot came out of the house. Talbot shouldered a pack he didn't look happy to be carrying. He tossed his cigarette in the grass and they started across the pasture toward brush at the base of the mountains and Alvarez tracked them with binoculars until they disappeared into the brush.

Then he walked around the truck, reached in for the radio, and felt a rush of excitement as he got Roberts.

'They've hiked into the hills with Talbot carrying a back-pack.'

'What's that about? A backpack? Meth lab,' she guessed.

'I'm going to walk out and across the slope and try to get a look at where they're headed.'

'Brad, I think you should wait.'

'I'll be well above them and I'll call you. I'm not going far, I just don't want to lose them.'

He locked the truck and followed a deer trail into the trees and then across the slope a quarter mile through brush, scrub oak, and dry grass. Farther than he'd planned to go, but he could still get back to the truck pretty easily if Holsing popped back out. Up ahead, the slope dipped into a ravine and then the terrain looked rougher, but it was worth it. Holsing and Talbot weren't up here on a nature walk.

He climbed down into another ravine, then up steeply through brush on the other side. He started to sweat. He should have left the extra shirt in the truck. The slope was humid as last night's rain evaporated and it was tougher than he'd expected. It was slow going until he spotted a deer trail. Once on it, he found footprints and followed those down and across to a small stream, moving quietly now, watching everything. A stream would fit with a meth lab. They'd need water.

He worked his way down and kept an eye on the pasture because he was a ways from his truck and if Holsing headed for his van, he'd have to really move to avoid losing him. Then suddenly it was worst case. He caught sight of them coming out of the brush back into the pasture. Talbot still had the pack on. Holsing led and Alvarez watched him stop near his truck. If he got in it, there was no way to get back across the slope, down there and follow him. They'd been up here twenty, maybe twenty-five minutes, and he saw Holsing was going to leave. He stood near his truck talking to Talbot and Alvarez tried reaching Roberts.

'Come on, Melinda, answer,' but the call kept dropping after one ring. Marquez would be all over him for going out here alone, especially with drugs possibly in the picture. Marquez was getting more conservative and as he thought it over it made sense to search for whatever they had visited up here.

If it was a meth lab, Holsing could do serious time, much more than he'd get for poaching sturgeon. I'm going for it, he thought.

He followed the stream down and when it happened, it was like, bang. He came around a tree and there it was, a little dam, a grow field, and a bunch of trash. He was looking at maybe two hundred marijuana plants. He got his phone out, took pictures, and wouldn't need to hang out here long. He could easily find his way back. He'd bring Marquez, Roberts, and whoever the DEA or county sheriff sent.

He got photos of the dam and where they'd channeled the overflow down into the plants. Black plastic irrigation hose ran down between the rows. Bags of fertilizer were stacked along one side. He took a picture of a pump and a generator and a five gallon gas can resting on a dirt bench cut into the slope, then started back up, hurrying, because who knows, maybe he'd still make it back in time to follow Holsing or give Roberts a heads-up as Holsing drove out.

Several years ago a warden had been shot and wounded at a grow field in Palo Alto, but he figured the footprints on the deer trail were Talbot's, though the pack Talbot carried could be supplies for someone taking care of the plants. He watched ahead, didn't expect anybody, but watched anyway and still hurried. He made more noise than when he came down. He took another careful look upslope before climbing on to an open grassy patch, and there he stopped long enough to text Roberts. Sometimes a text message went through when you couldn't make a phone call work.

we've got Holsing nailed. he got

Alvarez never finished the message but he did press Send as he spotted a man up the steep slope thirty yards standing between two trees. He reached for his badge instead of his gun, and he got the badge up and heard a shot as he felt a blow and a burning in his chest. When he tried to breathe he couldn't and the sharp burning spread rapidly under his ribs as he sat down. His badge dropped and he fell back and tried to roll on his side, getting some air, not much, and feeling for the wound, knowing it was bad and scared. His kids were at home. Didn't want to die over a grow field. He pressed against the wound with his left hand and tried to get his gun loose, but couldn't seem to do it, couldn't make his fingers work.

His hand slipped off the holster as a man leaned over him and blocked the sun. Alvarez saw the man's face and then the barrel of a rifle. He tried to speak, tried to reach his badge. He moved bloody fingers across the grass trying to find his badge, and then saw the barrel adjusting and cried out and moved his hand through sunlight toward the rifle barrel as the finger on the trigger gently squeezed.

TWENTY-FOUR

'Lieutenant, I've lost contact with Brad.'

Marquez knew that Roberts would have tried everything before calling him to report that. Yet Brad was likely fine. Good chance the problem was cell or radio reception in the Capay Valley.

'You at his truck, right now?'

'I just came down from there. It's up on a Forest Service road above me. He walked from his truck across the slope above Talbot's house when they hiked up into the brush.'

She explained that and Marquez got a clearer picture. He hadn't known about Holsing, Talbot, and the backpack.

'Is Holsing still at the house with Talbot?'

'Doesn't look like it, but I can't say for sure. His van is gone, so he's probably gone. Talbot's truck is there.'

'And you're sure Brad didn't have any contact with Holsing at the house or on the slope?'

'He drove past the house and then took a position on the Forest Service road above them. When they started up he hiked out across the slope above them.'

'Rough terrain.'

'It is.'

'So maybe he's up working his way back.'

'Sure.'

Marquez heard it in her answer. She didn't believe Alvarez was up there working his way back. She was scared. He went over the timeline with Roberts again, and then asked, 'Was the Forest Service gate locked when you got there?'

'Yes.'

'OK, read the text message again.'

Marquez pressed the cell closer to his ear and accelerated away from the truck alongside him. Roberts spoke slowly.

'"*we've got holsing nailed. he got*", and that's where it stops.'

'How long ago was the text sent?'

'Forty-eight minutes.'

And she'd walked out and looked for him, and didn't find him and couldn't get him on his cell. Forty-eight minutes and Holsing's van gone. No way would Brad let that happen without communicating, so he was up on that slope. But maybe it was a badly sprained ankle and he was sitting in a ravine or working his way slowly back. But if Brad was anything, he was tough and this long out of communication he'd be worried about the operation. He would have found his way back to his truck.

'Let's get everybody there we can.'

'That'll blow the operation, Lieutenant.'

'It will. Get everybody and let's get help from the county.'

TWENTY-FIVE

County officers and wardens worked a grid across the slope and a helicopter sat over an area just north of Brad's truck. A K-9 unit was on its way. Inside the house, Carl Talbot repeated his story to Marquez, complaining that he had already told it to both the county and the girl wardens. He'd eaten breakfast at the casino – where he always ate – then came home and started work. A two foot deep trench lined with black filter cloth ran along one side of the house foundation. A plastic perforated pipe ran down the center of the trench. Marquez looked at it before going in to talk to Talbot. Talbot claimed his whole day was breakfast and working on the drainage trench.

Marquez looked through the window at the helicopter

hovering over the slope, and then at Talbot. Streaks of dried
sweat ran along the sides of his face. An angry looking boil
sat low on the left side of his neck and he kept touching it.
His hair was greasy, clothes dirty, one sideburn lower than
the other. He was young and underneath the attitude, nervous
and scared. He had to be worried that the search would find
whatever he and Holsing had up on the slope. But he was
sticking to his story that he didn't know anybody named Jeff
Holsing, never heard of anybody named Holsing.

Talbot answered questions in a monotone as though he
was a prisoner of war reciting name, rank, and serial number.
He slouched on a couch, a TV remote in his right hand.
When Marquez walked in he'd turned on a NASCAR race
and then muted it but wanted to leave it on as he answered
questions because he'd waited for the race all week. He turned
it back on now and Marquez walked over and unplugged the
TV.

'You can't do that, man, this is my house.'

Marquez sat down next to him. He held his cell phone so
Talbot could read the screen. 'I'm going to show you a text
a warden on our undercover team sent this morning.'

He smelled the mud on Talbot's boots and the sweat that
had dried in his shirt. At the shoulders his shirt was wrinkled
and sweat-stained where the backpack straps had rubbed. He
hadn't thought to change his shirt, or maybe he had no idea
that Brad was on the slope and that the police would show
up. Could be he had no clue about the sturgeon.

Roberts had forwarded the text to him. Talbot glanced over
long enough to read it. Then his gaze returned to the blank
TV screen.

'I told the warden chick everything I know.'

'Before Brad Alvarez sent that message he described
Holsing and you hiking up there. We've had surveillance on
Holsing for weeks.' He let a beat pass and added, 'There's no
way around that for you.'

Marquez pointed at the dark blue backpack in the corner
of the room.

'You were carrying that, so before this goes to the next
level, I want to make sure you understand that everyone here
knows you're lying. If you stick with that lie, it could make
things much worse for you later.'

'I'm going to watch the race.'

A Yolo County deputy poked his head in the front door now and said, 'They've spotted two guys up there moving across the slope away from the dogs.'

That hit Marquez hard. It touched his worst fear and he stood. He asked Talbot, 'Who's trying to get away?'

'Probably some fucking illegals working on a farm around here and living in the hills.'

Marquez pointed through the window.

'Those are SWAT team officers they're lowering out of the helicopter. The pair trying to get away won't get much farther.'

'Whatever, man, if they shoot them that's OK with me. They ought to kill those guys at the border or build that fence they keep dicking with.'

Marquez looked through the window as he talked now. He looked for movement on the slope below the helicopter.

'I was in the DEA for a decade before I came to Fish and Game and if it's a grow field up there and the two men trying to get away were tending it, you're completely fucked, because when the Feds put you and Holsing in separate rooms Holsing will have something to trade and you won't. You're just another guy hired to watch the farm. Holsing will trade names. He'll trade his way to a minor sentence and they'll hang the grow field around your neck. You'll do the real time. I've been there; I know how it works.'

'Whatever.'

Talbot got up and plugged in the TV. Marquez watched him sit back down, pick up the remote, and click the NASCAR race on. He left Talbot as Chief Blakely called. He took her call outside. Everyone at Fish and Game headquarters was focused on what was happening here.

'The CHP just found Holsing's van on the side of an eastbound freeway onramp in Auburn Ravine,' she said. 'Sturgeon are inside and the California Highway Patrol is asking what we want to do. I can get a warden there to watch the truck or they can impound it.'

'Let's get a warden there.' As he said that it hit him and he reversed himself. 'No, check that, let's impound it. He abandoned the van. Somebody met him, picked him up, and he's on the run. He's scared.' Fear for Brad ran hard in him again. 'Chief, can you text me a message that reads, Holsing stopped on 80 and arrested. He's in Sacramento and has told investigators about the grow field and that it's Talbot's deal.'

She repeated the message he wanted sent and then hung up. When the text came through Marquez was back in the room with Talbot. Talbot turned slightly as Marquez's phone chimed. He flinched when Marquez put the Blackberry screen where he couldn't avoid it.

'This is about you. They got Holsing.'

Talbot muted the sound and Marquez shook his head no and pulled the phone back.

'Turn it off.'

Talbot clicked the TV off. He read the text and without saying a word turned the TV back on and the sound way up.

'No sweat, Talbot, we don't need you anymore. Let me know who wins the race.'

Marquez walked out but it didn't surprise him that Talbot caught up to him as he crossed the pasture.

'I didn't even know it was up there. They didn't tell me until I got here. I don't even smoke the shit.'

'What do you get out of it?'

'Ten grand for keeping the Mexicans supplied with their fart food.'

'Did you see our warden this morning?'

'No, I didn't even see the Mexicans this morning. I left their stuff for them while Jeff checked the plants.'

'Show me. Let's go.'

TWENTY-SIX

A county deputy walked with them. Behind Marquez, the deputy's equipment jangled with each step. The trail twisted as the slope steepened and brush went from waist to chest high. He didn't question Talbot as they climbed over fallen trees and pushed through the brush. He waited until they were well up the slope and following footprints, but all he could think about was Holsing abandoning his van, the sturgeon, everything, and fleeing. Higher up, the ground became muddy from seepage. Marquez smelled marijuana.

He saw the edge of a grow field and stopped at a deep set of boot prints.

'Lift yours,' he said to Talbot. When Talbot lifted his boot and showed the sole, Marquez said, 'OK, so this is your print here, but who is this walking next to yours?'

'I don't know. I'm not like a tracker.'

'Was Holsing wearing boots?'

'I don't know.'

'When did you talk to him last?'

'He took off after we were up here.'

'Where was he going?'

'He didn't say.'

'Didn't tell you anything?'

'He doesn't talk to me, dude.'

'Our warden said you were slow opening the door this morning. That's because you needed to call Holsing first, right?'

Talbot wouldn't answer, but Marquez knew that's what had happened. Talbot called Holsing and warned him, and Holsing told Talbot just play it cool, don't admit anything and tell them you don't know me. Then he decided to make a run for it. That's why he left his van on the side of an onramp.

'Where do the Mexicans camp?'

'Higher up somewhere. They drink the creek water and crap in the weeds. They aren't allowed to come down. I just leave their food by a tree and let them beat the animals to it. When they brought me in to work on the house, I didn't know about any of this. My old man was a contractor. I'm a carpenter.'

He kept talking about himself and Marquez heard dogs baying. The K-9 team had arrived and gone straight to Brad's truck. They ran the dogs from there and the dogs were on the slope above and to their left. He couldn't see them but knew from the baying the dogs were coming this way. Marquez looked at the deputy's solemn face. The deputy knew something bad happened up here.

Marquez led now. He took in the grow field, the stacked bags of fertilizer, irrigation lines, the dam, and the damage to the land the growers always walked away from.

'What kind of weapons do the guys tending the field have?'

'I didn't have anything to do with that. Jeff gave them those.'

'What do they have?'

'AK-47s.'

'Did you hear any gunfire today?'

This time Talbot's answer came very fast.

'Nope.'

'Did you climb any higher than this today?'

Talbot shook his head. He pointed at where he'd left the food. It looked as if he'd just turned the pack upside down and dumped the supplies out. He licked his lips and Marquez left him with the deputy and called Brad's name as he climbed higher.

Above the small dam he picked up a trail and found a fresh mark that could be Brad's. He recognized the Vibram pattern and followed the boot prints. They continued up through brush and out on to a grassy open slope, and then he saw blood on the grass. He heard the dogs and their handler. The dogs were closing. The dogs smelled the blood, he guessed.

'Hold up, there,' he called out to the handler, his voice suddenly hoarse.

The handler answered and then Shauf.

'Is that you, Lieutenant?'

'Yeah, Carol, it's me, come on over alone. The dogs shouldn't come any closer.'

When she pushed through the brush, Marquez was kneeling. A droning sound like a cloud of locusts buzzed in his head as he picked up Brad's badge and saw a bloodstained trail of crushed grass. Without speaking they followed it to where a shovel had been discarded. He saw a mound of newly turned earth with rocks heaped on top, and went forward alone. On his knees he lifted away rocks. He brushed away soil. He dug with his fingers until he reached a dark blue collar and then skin. As he cleared dirt from Brad's face a terrible grief flooded him. He stared, brushed more dirt, and then had to turn away. He looked at Shauf but couldn't find words. He knelt again and his knee sank in the soft newly turned soil. Shot him, dragged him up here, and tried to hide his body. Shauf's voice was leaden, dead. Her hand touched his shoulder.

'Lieutenant, we shouldn't touch anything. We shouldn't be this close.'

Marquez understood that and stood and backed away. He lifted his radio, hesitated, lowered the radio to his side, as if he could change the truth. When he raised the radio again, he keyed the mike, drew a deep breath, and called it in.

TWENTY-SEVEN

The two men trying to escape across the slope surrendered less than half an hour later. Turned out they were
Mexican illegals and didn't speak any English. There was
radio chatter as they were taken into custody. Marquez watched
it from way up on the slope and far away in his head.

After the county helicopter flew away it was quiet. He
waited with Shauf. He waited thinking Sheryl Javits had
warned him that the cartels were smuggling in farmers from
rural areas of Mexico, paying them fifty dollars a day to
tend the crops, and arming them with the warning that if
anything happened to the marijuana, their relatives were in
danger. Drug cartels had figured out that some of the remote
areas of California's parks and wildernesses made ideal grow
locations. They were treating the land as their own and like
everything they touched they left it damaged or ruined when
they were through.

Brad was dead. A good friend dead. One of his team
dead, murdered, a family left behind. Brad with his love
of the job killed like this. Marquez couldn't get his head
around it. He looked out at the mountains and hills across
the valley as an FBI Evidence Response Team climbed the
trail toward them. When they arrived he introduced himself
and Shauf and took them in with a numb awareness. He
showed two AK-47Ns to the FBI. He showed them the shovels
thrown down in the grass and tracks the men left, and where
he'd knelt near Brad's body. None of it would change
anything. If he had made the bust earlier and not chased the
ab poachers out to the coast last night, none of this would
have happened.

The ERT leader wanted to hear Marquez's full account and
Marquez went through it with him, and then watched as they
ran tape, set up a perimeter of tape and a second ring beyond
that. They placed markers, collected bloody grass, bagged the
shovel and guns, and found a spot on the slope for what the
ERT leader called his field station, a Nikon NPL-821 that

projected a grid they mapped the evidence on. Marquez recorded all of this in silence, watching as if his presence here helped them get it right.

At dusk as the FBI finished and packed up, Chief Blakely arrived at the ranch house. She radioed Marquez from there.

'I think you should be there with me when I go out to the Alvarezs' house.'

'I'll follow after Brad is off this slope. I won't be far behind you.'

Near sunset Marquez helped strap Brad's body into a basket lowered from a helicopter. After Brad was in a coroner's wagon and the wagon was moving, Marquez left the Capay. He drove toward the Alvarezes' house with Shauf following, though later he wouldn't even remember the drive.

Brad's wife, Cindy, looked both bewildered and in pain. Chief Blakely was there as were other friends of the family, but Cindy couldn't accept what they were telling her. She'd been waiting for Marquez.

Brad's six year old son, Shane, asked Marquez, 'Is Daddy dead?' and Cindy answered, 'No, Daddy will be home soon.' She looked at Marquez and asked, 'Who was it that got killed? I'm so glad you're here.' Her face flushed bright red. Tears sprang from her eyes. 'Chief Blakely thought it was Brad, but who was it really?'

Then, as she studied Marquez's face, hers crumpled.

'John, you know Brad is magic. You know it better than anyone. You know how he is. Nothing can happen to him. He always makes it home. You know that. Please, no, please don't say that it's him.'

She reached and gripped his arm, eyes lit with fear, and then welling again with tears.

'Please, John, if he's been shot and he's hurt, I'll make him well. I'll take care of him. I can make him well again. Where is he?'

Marquez took her hand and racking sobs started from deep inside. He held her. She sank down and he got her over the couch as her son started to cry. He understood what she meant about Brad being magic. He knew exactly what she meant.

After her family arrived, he moved outside with Cindy's father, who trembled as he stood on the porch and smoked, his voice gravelly and sad as he spoke.

'I remember the day she met him and I don't know what she's going to do without him. What's the boy going to do without a father?'

There was no answer for that either.

TWENTY-EIGHT

Late that night word came that the men had confessed to shooting and burying Brad Alvarez. Marquez and Roberts were at Holsing's van pulling the sturgeon when the call came. They laid the sturgeon out and measured and videotaped. Holsing had modified the van, removing the backseat and attaching a metal pan with sides high enough to hold fish this big on ice. The pan was six feet long and stainless steel. It conjured autopsies. The bed of ice had melted and drained through a copper tube that dripped out under the van and Marquez shined a flashlight underneath and looked at where it was dripping still.

Two of the sturgeon were just over five feet long, so juveniles somewhere around twenty years old. The life span of a sturgeon was close to that of a human being. They lived a little longer than us, and they'd been around a lot longer, close to two hundred fifty million years, here with the dinosaurs, but unlikely to survive us. Ten pounds of roe got you twelve hundred black market dollars and the meat three bucks a pound. Marquez weighed, measured, and wrote mechanically. None of this was for tonight. They slid the sturgeon into garbage bags, double-wrapped them, and then put them in Roberts' van. She'd drive them to Sacramento and cold storage. They wouldn't be kept long. He watched her drive away and then searched the van again, finding three joints and some pills they'd missed.

When he'd started at the DEA, the HIDTA, the High Intensity Drug Trafficking Area teams, had just come into being and were focused on the Caribbean and Florida. They had some success, but with a predictable twist: as the balloon got squeezed, it popped out somewhere else. Cartels moved their shipping lanes to Mexico. They dug tunnels, floated dope

on the Rio Grande, modified boats, trucks, and cars, and flew
over the border in small planes that they sometimes abandoned
after unloading.

Marquez had fought trafficking for a decade. He knew how
the stings, the busts, the hype and press conferences worked,
but the only real measure of whether the law enforcement efforts
were working was answered with a question, are drugs cheaper
now or more expensive? They're cheaper. Paradoxically, law
enforcement had gotten better at intercepting shipments, and in
response cartels reduced shipping and bribery costs by moving
operations into the United States. That was what happened today.
The SOU ran into that change today and Brad died, he thought.

The super meth labs were still in Mexico and big ware-
houses sat on the border filled with drugs and protected by the
police, but some of the meth production had migrated north
along with a lot of dope growing. That's what the KZ Nuts
operation had been so long ago, the Salazars establishing a
distribution system in anticipation of growing large amounts
of dope in California. He felt drawn back into that world tonight
as he drove toward home. Its dark presence rode with his grief.

He drove through the delta on the way home. He stopped
at the dock in Potato Slough and looked at Holsing's boat. In
the dope operation he knew Holsing was a low level manager
who probably handled a dozen grow fields. Sheryl would know
much more. He'd talk with her in the morning, but he called
Katherine from here.

She started to cry as he told her Cindy Alvarez's reaction.
Brad had been at their house many times. He drove on now.
They'd board Holsing's boat tomorrow and go through his
house. Moonlight turned the old eucalyptus along the delta
road spectral. Dawn wasn't that far away when he rose along
the curve of the Antioch Bridge. At home he sat outside in
the early light with Katherine. She made coffee. He picked
at food and tried to communicate the depth of the loss and
the responsibility he felt. He showered and held her and fell
in and out of brief shallow sleep.

Later that morning Sheryl Javits drove up to the delta and
was there when the SOU went through Holsing's boat. Like
Marquez, Sheryl had grayed. She'd thickened a little in the
middle, but still had the face you could put on a coin and trust.
Decades of law enforcement blunted the emotions of some,

but not hers. That was her gift. Her sad smile today acknowledged the reach and the depth of the cartels and she told
Marquez what she said she shouldn't.

'We know Holsing. We're working a large operation he's
part of. We're closing in on a very big bust.'

'Did you know about the Capay grow field?'

'Yes.' She added, 'They're using Zetas to keep the farmers
in line. They have more sleepers in California than anywhere,
except maybe Texas.'

Marquez nodded. It made sense. The Zetas were hired assassins who later formed their own cartel Kerry Anderson taught
him about the Zetas years ago.

Nothing came of the search of Holsing's boat and mid
afternoon Marquez was at Fish and Game headquarters as a
grim-faced Janet Blakely told reporters the SOU would stand
down pending the investigation into the death of Lieutenant Brad
Alvarez. She said it was a great loss for the department. She
didn't answer any questions about the killing. That night Marquez
saw a sound bite from the press conference on Fox News. They
showed Brad's photo and those of the two shooters, now identified as illegal aliens working for remnants of the Salazar Cartel.
Below the TV reporter in large white letters was the question,
'Are Mexican Cartels Stealing America?' By itself, the murder
of a game warden wasn't enough to sell TV news.

Brad's body was autopsied and released to Cindy Alvarez
four days later. He was cremated and a service was held in
Folsom on an afternoon when thunderclouds boiled over the
Sierras. Marquez attended the service in uniform. Katherine
and his stepdaughter, Maria, came with him. He spent the
next day with Yolo County detectives jointly investigating
Brad's murder with the FBI. He walked back up to the grow
field with them.

A fugitive warrant was out on Holsing, but there were no
leads, and that night Marquez packed and told Katherine he'd
be back in three days. At first light the next morning he left
for the Sierras. He crossed to the eastern slope and drove
down to Mammoth. There, he caught the shuttle out to Red's
Meadow and hiked into the Minarets and up the trail to Lake
Ediza, arriving after the sun had fallen behind the rim of the
mountains and the small lake rippled with cold late afternoon
wind. There was little snow this year and even now in late

May the stream that fed Ediza was easy to cross. He drew water from the lake and set up a camp.

Brad was always collecting things and the running joke between Marquez and him was that he always later imbued those things with special powers, the smooth quartz pebble that carried good luck, a bear claw pulled out of tree bark that warded off evil, part of an antelope horn, a polished piece of petrified redwood he'd once given Marquez. He wasn't a guy who wore ornaments or believed in much he hadn't seen firsthand, yet he was funny about these natural fetishes. And he was passionate about Fish and Game work.

Marquez understood that. You didn't get into this work for the money. It was a calling and Brad just liked being out there. When he'd started across the slope to see where Holsing and Talbot were going, good chance that a part of him was just glad to be outside on that open slope in the spring morning.

Marquez carried the piece of redwood with him, zipped it into the pocket of the jacket he'd wear tomorrow. He heated water on a gas stove as the Minarets reflected the setting sun and snow on the shoulders of Mount Banner and Ritter turned a rose hue. Before it got dark he slid his sleeping bag into his bivvy sack and got out the things he would carry up the mountain tomorrow.

Then he boiled water and cooked noodles and cut up two tomatoes he'd bought in Mammoth. He emptied sardines out of a tin on to the noodles. He tore up basil leaves, folded everything in, and cracked pepper onto the pasta. He ate out of the pot. It felt good to eat. He used the last piece of bread to wipe the inside of the sardine can clean and left the gas stove out to boil water for coffee in the morning. He washed the pot and packed up everything else he would carry out. Black bear were always around, but he doubted any were up here yet in this part of the late spring, and left his pack cinched tight, leaning against a rock. And maybe it was the grace of the mountains or the exertion of the hike in and finally eating. Whatever it was, he was able to sleep.

At dawn it was quite cold and he made coffee, ate bread, cheese, and dates, and then walked down to the lake and filtered enough water for the hike up. He slid the water bottles into the pack. He slipped the pack on and started up with an ice axe in his right hand.

There was no trail or any real need of a trail. The weather was fine and he could see ahead and knew his route. It was steep and long and jumbled with granite and talus, and then he climbed on snow. It was steep and there were places where you wouldn't want to fall, but nowhere did he need a rope. On the saddle between Banner and Ritter he drank half his water and cleaned his sunglasses before starting up again. Here, the snowfield steepened and he kicked the toe of his boot in harder and used the ice axe.

When he summited Mount Banner just before noon he could hear Brad's voice in his head. On top, it was cold and clear. Over the Minarets the sky was dark blue. He caught his breath sitting on a rock looking down at Lake Ediza, small and beautiful below, and at Thousand Island Lake and east toward the desert, and then down the long reach of the Sierras. This was a place Brad loved and Marquez walked the summit looking for a spot, then climbed down between rocks and found a place to tuck in Brad's good luck talisman.

We do things to say good bye that defy rational explanation. You take what you remember and loved in a human being and you hold it in your heart, but still at times you need a photo or a ring or piece of clothing, something you can touch, a tombstone to visit where you can talk. Marquez knew from time to time he'd come back to this mountain. When he could no longer climb it, the mountain would still be here, and if part of Alvarez's spirit lingered with it, and if the talisman held any good luck, the mountain would be safer for those that climbed. What better spirit to guard climbers than Brad?

TWENTY-NINE

Marquez was in Sacramento in Chief Blakely's office on the thirteenth floor of the Water Resource Building. Blakely moved out from behind her desk and they sat at the table and talked.

'You're not going to be suspended, but the SOU won't do any undercover work until the investigation is over.'

'On some of our ongoing operations it's going to be hard to pick up the pieces later.'

'I know.'

'How long will we be down?'

They looked at each other, Marquez with his big right hand resting on the table, his sun-weathered face in the shade of this room, Blakely not wanting to answer.

'You've got court dates coming up and paperwork to do. You can check out leads, but the SOU can't initiate any new undercover operations.'

Blakely didn't address the real question, so he did it for her before leaving.

'Melinda Roberts could step in for me.'

'No, we're not going there yet. There aren't going to be any snap judgments. Go pick up the loose ends. Finish the reports. Get your team to focus again. If you want to check out the bighorn tip, that's fine, go do that.'

The Fish and Game hotline, CALTIP, had recorded a call last night from a young woman reporting an alleged illegal bighorn hunt in the southern Sierra. That might be trophy hunters or bone merchants. A pair of the horns could net you sixty thousand dollars on the black market. The young woman who left the tip also left her phone number, and Marquez had left her a message.

When he walked out the temperature was close to a hundred degrees and the valley sky a hazy white-blue. He drove through the delta on the way home, past Holsing's boat and then out to Holsing's house in the Green Valley, a three thousand square foot, cedar-sided, two-story house there was no way Holsing could afford, yet had bought for cash. The house had been searched after the boat but the only thing of interest was a notebook and Holsing's private cocaine stash. In the notebook was a page of handwritten codes that looked like this:

N178SW43

SE47N634

SW212NE21

WSW98S65

ESE015WNW87

Marquez had jotted the codes on a page in his logbook and the DEA was trying to unravel their meaning. He doubted Holsing came up with them on his own and Sheryl backed that up, saying the DEA believed they were part of a Salazar Cartel code. They'd seen something similar on another case. He parked in front of Holsing's house, walked up and looked through a window near the door. Nothing looked any different. The DEA would keep an eye on the house and collect Holsing's mail for him while he was away being a fugitive, but no one was doing anything about the newspaper delivery. Marquez stepped over yellowing newspapers as he walked back out the driveway.

In the Bay Area gray fog sucked in by the valley heat darkened the sky as he drove across Marin County. He took a call from his stepdaughter, Maria, after he was on Mount Tamalpais and climbing toward the house.

'Dad, when are you getting home?'

'I'm almost home. What's up?'

'Mom says you might lose your job. How could that happen if you weren't even there?'

'I was Brad's supervisor.'

'But you weren't even there.'

'I'm responsible for my team wherever they are. That's the deal.'

'You can tell me to shut up, but how can that be fair?'

Brad's death was about chain of command and he tried to explain that, but wasn't sure he got through. Then Maria revealed that she called for another reason, as well.

'I broke up with a guy I've been seeing.'

'That can't be easy.'

'It's not.'

'When did it happen?'

'Last week, and I'd like to talk with you, but not on the phone.'

Maria shared a house with three roommates in the Noe Valley in San Francisco. She worked part time for a web designer and part time for a guerilla web marketer. She was bright, quick, and restless, twenty-three and trying to figure out what to do with her life. She was an inch taller than her mother and with dark hair and a body made lean by cycling. She was currently anti-car and very worried about global warming. She'd also had something of a political awakening and asserted her opinions with the confidence of a TV preacher.

That night Katherine asked, 'Did Maria call you?'

'She did.'

'I'm glad she's breaking up with him. I didn't like him at all.'

Later that night Katherine woke him by kissing him. He was never going to be exactly what she hoped for in a marriage. He loved the warden work, the SOU too much. He needed the feeling he was making a difference more than he needed money, and Katherine would never say it but she was more than ready for his undercover career to end. But sometimes you forgive a person for being who they are, as opposed to what you want them to be. He and Katherine had been separated once and close to it a second time, before they found a way through. He woke to her kisses on his face and chest and belly, and drew her close, and she whispered with her face pressed against his, 'They'll never have anyone ever again as good as you.'

THIRTY

'Kerry Anderson is going to call you,' Sheryl said. 'I talked to him this morning.'

Marquez was with Sheryl at a coffee place in Sausalito that he liked. Wardens worked from home and he came down here sometimes in the afternoons with a file, mostly in the winter when they tended to have fewer operations running. Everything lit up again in early March when the stripers and sturgeon started jumping on the Sacramento River and the bear came out of hibernation and deer herds congregated around the new grass. Most of this morning he had been on the phone with his team. Most of that conversation was about Brad, but he also gave them assignments.

'OK, why is he calling?'

'That's the weird part, stranger even than Anderson. He says he has recent information on a phone intercept in Mexico where Stoval was talking about you. Maybe you know this, maybe you don't, but Anderson's role changed after 9/11. He does more analysis and shares more and that goes out to several agencies. He straddles several of the agencies. Anything they think is terrorism related they share and Anderson is pretty good at cooking that up. As you know, he'll talk to anybody about Stoval. He'd talk to you if he was sitting next to you on a bus. I've never met anybody so obsessed with one person. Can you imagine what it would be like to be married to Anderson?'

'He's not married.'

'Talking to him you'd think the only analysis he works on is Stoval.'

'Where are you going with this?'

'You are so patient, John. You've never changed. Where I'm going is Anderson called me yesterday fishing for anything I know about this Stoval task force that Ted Desault is heading. Talk about a blast from the past. Ted Desault – there's a name I hoped I'd never hear again.'

'Desault wants to meet with me. He wants to make me an offer. He called me just before Brad got killed.'

'No kidding?'

Marquez nodded. They were sitting outside in wicker chairs in the coffeehouse garden less than a hundred yards from the bay. There were gulls, boats, tourists, and a chill wind this afternoon. He thought about Desault's call and why he still hadn't called Desault back. Now it hit them both at the same time and Sheryl said it aloud.

'Stoval knows an offer is going to be made to you. That's it, isn't it? Is that scary, or what? He's hooked into Desault's task force. What kind of offer did Desault make you?'

'I haven't heard it yet.'

Marquez looked at a gull wheeling out over the water and Sheryl talked quietly about Stoval and the regeneration of the Salazar Cartel.

'He's still there. He still bankrolls short term loans for drug smugglers and we think he's more involved in the new Salazar operation. And he doesn't use the same contract killers to make sure he gets paid back. He does what the cartels do, he uses the Zetas.'

'What's anybody's guess about his net worth now?'

'Anderson says one point seven billion.'

'He's done well.'

'Yeah, a lot better than you and me.'

'What are you talking about? You've had a great career.'

'You know what, John, the Group Five days were the best. When it was just our squad and we were working the Salazars and nobody else, that was great. Remember how close we all were? I hit a real low point after you left and after I moved back to California.'

'When you married Phelps.'

'Yeah, that two and a half years of marriage was the absolute rock bottom of the ocean.'

Marquez rarely thought about Pete Phelps, the ATF officer who'd been in Baja when they were there. He no longer felt any animosity toward Phelps, which was saying something.

'I never told you I caught him in bed with my neighbor,' Sheryl said. 'I almost shot him, and I still think the only reason I didn't is that it would have been one more mess of his to clean up.' She sighed. 'I have something else to confess. It's why I drove over here. It's why I didn't want to talk on the phone. Stoval mentioning your name isn't a surprise to the Feds, or at least this is what Anderson told me and should tell you. They know there's a leak and they're playing a cat and mouse game with it.'

'I'm not following.'

'OK, well, it's possible Desault doesn't know that Stoval mentioned your name in a phone intercept. Anderson knows because he's lead analyst. He told me because he knows I'll tell you, but it's possible no one on the Stoval task force knows because the Bureau is frantic to find the leak. They have the same problem we had back in the Group Five days and I don't know exactly what Anderson is going to tell you, but you shouldn't go anywhere near the FBI task force. Stoval hasn't forgotten that you went after him all those years ago. There's probably nothing he'd like more than you coming after him again. These many years later and he's keying off on your name. Maybe I'm getting older and less brave, but of all of them over all the years, Stoval scares me the most.'

'I owe Desault a call.'

'Don't do it, John. I really mean it, don't do it.'

THIRTY-ONE

Marquez googled Zetas and came up with a *Dallas News* story.

American youths did Mexican drug cartel's dirty work
Court records describe how Zetas gave money, instructions to hit men

09:32 A.M. CST on Saturday, November 10, 2007
By DAVID McLEMORE / The Dallas Morning News
dmclemore@dallasnews.com

LAREDO – Rosalio Reta killed his first man at age 13. He didn't like it much, he told police. The guy was tied up and kneeling. Mr Reta just had to pick up a pistol and shoot him in the head.

Rosalio Reta
'He told us that wasn't his style. There was no challenge,' said Webb County Assistant District Attorney Jesus Guillen, who successfully prosecuted Mr Reta for murder. 'He preferred to run surveillance on a victim, pick the right moment and surprise him. Like he was playing Grand Theft Auto.'

By July 28, 2006 – one day after his 17th birthday – when Laredo police charged him with the contract killing of Noe Flores in Laredo, Mr Reta had been involved with 30 murders, Mexican and Texas investigators believed. All were on behalf of the Zetas, the ruthless enforcement arm of Mexico's Gulf Cartel drug smuggling operation.

His trial last summer for the Flores killing offered tantalizing glimpses into the shadowy workings of the Zetas and the inroads of cartel violence into this border city.

Court records revealed a portrait of a group of young American killers who were well-paid to do one thing: kill people the Zeta leadership in Nuevo Laredo wanted dead. And they highlighted a group of young killers who followed orders from Mexican drug lords with ruthless efficiency while often behaving like teens with poor impulse control.

Mr Reta sought his own extradition for the murder. He called a DEA agent and Laredo homicide Detective Roberto Garcia from a prison in Mexico, saying he wanted to stand trial in Texas for two homicides.

He told US investigators he feared reprisals from the Zetas over a botched hit in Monterrey – a grenade attack on one of the city's nightclubs that killed four and injured 25. He was supposed to kill only one person, police said, but had missed the target.

Laredo police had already identified Mr Reta as one of three people responsible for the Flores killing. Their investigation had linked him to one of three three-member scicarias, or hit man cells, the Zetas had set up in Laredo. They believed Mr Reta was responsible for at least five killings in the city – either as a shooter or organizer.

After he was charged in Laredo, Mr Reta gave a state-ment to Detective Garcia, detailing the Flores killing and his role in it.

Mr Reta told police he drove on the night of Jan. 8, 2006, when his three-man cell hit Mr Flores in a Laredo residential neighborhood. He described how one of his cell members, Gabriel Cordona, walked up to Mr Flores and calmly fired eight bullets into his body – three of them into his head. And he told how the third member, Jessie Hernandez, panicked and began firing while in the car, shooting out the rear window.

But the wrong guy got killed. Mr Flores had no criminal history and was just visiting a family birthday party.

The Zeta commander for Nuevo Laredo – Miguel Treviño Morales, a fugitive wanted on five state warrants for murder, kidnapping, and organized crime – was believed to have ordered a hit on Mike Lopez, Mr Flores' step-brother. Mr Treviño was angry at Mr Lopez for dating a woman he was interested in. A month after the Flores murder, on Feb. 26, 2007, another group of Zeta gunmen killed Mr Lopez, according to Laredo police.

Cells on retainer
Much of the specifics of the inner workings of Zeta operations in Laredo came out during testimony of prosecution witness David Martinez, a former Zeta gunman serving a federal sentence for weapons violations. He provided details on how the cartel set up three cells, composed of three people each, who were on retainer at $500 a week, just to wait for instructions. Sometimes they were called on to buy cars for gang use. Other times, to perform killings.

Marquez read through the middle section of the article detailing testimony at the trial, and then stopped on the last piece.

The Zetas' reach into Dallas
The trial of Rosalio Reta offered a glimpse into the shadowy workings of the Zetas, the enforcement arm of Mexico's Gulf Cartel, and the inroads of cartel violence into Laredo. Below is a look at some cases in the Dallas area that were linked by police to the cartel or to the Zetas . . .

He left a message for Anderson late that afternoon and listened once more to the CALTIP message he'd heard at Fish and Game headquarters. The young woman who left the tip hadn't called back yet and he tried her again now.

This time she answered her cell phone. Her name was Terri Delgado.

'I live in Los Angeles and I don't want to say exactly where, if I don't have to.'

'You don't.'

'I met this older guy at a cocktail party in Brentwood and we talked a lot out by the pool. He told me he was going to hunt bighorn sheep on Mount Williamson in the eastern Sierra.'

She sounded unfamiliar with hunting, but she didn't sound naïve or as if she had exaggerated a party conversation into something more.

'He wanted me to meet him in Bishop after the hunt, and then I was supposed to go to Las Vegas with him for the weekend. But you know what that sounds like, so I changed

my mind and called him the next day.' She added with a wry
note in a slower voice that made him smile, 'That was after
I was sober and my best friend lectured me.'

'Did he say why he was going to shoot bighorn?'

'Yes, and that's probably why I called the hotline. He said,
and this is an exact quote, because he didn't have a California
bighorn yet. It was disgusting.'

'Where was this party where you met him?'

'At a producer's house, but he's a friend, I want to keep
him out of this. I probably shouldn't have called.'

'No, you did a good thing. It's OK, keep your friend out
of it.'

Marquez wanted to know. He wanted the name off a guest
list. That would make it a lot easier to warn the guy off and
track him down, but she sounded too skittish. He decided to
try her again on it later.

'Talk to me about the hunter. Give me a description if you
can and tell me when the hunt is supposed to happen.'

'I don't know for sure. When I called him to tell him I
wasn't going, he made it sound like his plans had changed
also. I don't know if they did or he just wanted me to think
that, but at the party he mentioned a place called Anvil Camp.
I remember the name because it's so old school.'

'What did he say about it?'

'That the trail up to it is really steep, like straight up. He's
like early sixties or around that age, but he's in really good
shape, and I think he told me about Anvil Camp to impress
me.'

Marquez jotted down everything she said. The man had
black eyes with gold flecks in them. He was friends with the
producer, but he wasn't in the movie business. She thought
he'd invested money in movies and that's why he was there.
He had a really funny line about the movies, but she couldn't
remember what it was.

'He's really intense, but I like men who are.'

This man, Patrick Maitland, had houses all over the world.
When she had called him to back out, she tried to talk him
out of hunting bighorn.

'Did you threaten to report it?'

'Not really, but I did say I thought it was really bad karma
and he shouldn't do it.'

'There is a place called Anvil Camp. Describe anything else you remember about his physical characteristics, height and weight, for example.'

'He's a little over six feet and about a hundred and ninety pounds. I already said he's very fit. But his face is lined. I mean, he is older. From his clothes and watch and stuff, I'm pretty sure he is rich. You know that way you can kind of tell. And I'm a pretty good judge of men's bodies. I worked for a year helping pick male models for clothing ads, underwear and everything – that was a great job. He's got a really good body, especially for someone his age. And there's only one thing that's sort of weird, and that's his hands. I don't know if it's from a disease or some congenital thing, but it's like the bones going out to his fingers are thicker than normal. When he closes his fists they stand out.' She added, 'It's not that big of a deal.'

'Not enough to keep you from going to Vegas.'

'Not that night. You know, I got introduced to him and then we were just out by the pool talking and I think I said I wanted to travel all over the world and he jumped on that and started talking about his houses. I mean, I knew what he wanted. It's not really any different than most people I go out with. He talked about a place in Argentina, but I can't remember the name of it. I think it started with a B. I'm sorry I can't remember.'

'If you do remember, call me, OK?'

'Sure.'

'And thanks for calling it in to CALTIP. A lot of times the tips make a big difference.'

She giggled and said, 'Now you sound like an ad.'

If the SOU wasn't standing down, he'd pick up the phone now and relay all this to the warden out of Bishop, Adrian Muller. Instead, he debated driving down there. The tip sounded legitimate. The hunt sounded like it might happen.

Sheryl Javits called before he made a decision.

'We got through Holsing's code. It turns out they're GPS coordinates with some bogus numbers and letters thrown in. The coordinates correspond to addresses. From the addresses we got owners. Then we started digging into the owners.

'We came up with a few unlikely coincidences and I want to run some names by you, but with only initials for the first names because one of them works for a local DA's office. So just tell me if you recognize any of these other names.'

'OK, go for it.'

'There are nine names. Here's the first one. F. Garcia.'

'I once knew a Frank Garcia.'

'Frank is wrong, and don't mess with me. This might be bad and it might affect your team. P. Aldred?'

'No.'

'O. Castle.'

'No.'

She read the rest and Marquez didn't recognize any. Then she asked, 'Did you talk to Anderson?'

'I did.'

'And?'

'He says don't get anywhere near Stoval. Stay away from any FBI task force offers.'

'And what about the leak?'

'Not much.'

'Not much to me either.'

When he hung up with Sheryl he made two calls, the first to Anderson. He wasn't surprised to get him. Sheryl told him that ever since computers came on, the word from headquarters was Anderson never left his desk except in the summer when he went to baseball games.

'I've got a question for you, Kerry. You said Stoval has made several trips into the States in recent years.'

'That's right.'

'What's he doing on those trips?'

'I don't know. He's hard to track once he's here. I know he was in Texas twice. And he's been in California.'

'Where in California?'

'He flew into LAX.'

'Does he still trophy hunt?'

'Yes, definitely.'

'Then I've got an off-the-wall question for you. We got a tip to our Fish and Game hotline about a trophy hunter planning an illegal bighorn hunt in the southern Sierra, and I know this is highly improbable, but there's a physical description that sounds like Stoval. Similar height, general build, age, and black eyes with gold flecks – this is coming from a young woman who sounds like she paid close attention to his face. This was at a producer's party in LA. Our tipster believes this individual is planning to hunt bighorn. He also made comments to her about having houses around the world.'

'It's possible. I mean, it really is. Like you, the eye description grabs me. If he's putting money into movies, that's news to me, but, sure, it's possible.'

Marquez called Muller, the warden in Bishop. Muller listened and then jumped in.

'I got a call from a biologist monitoring the radio collars on bighorn sheep in the zoological preserve on Mount Williamson,' Muller said. 'Two collars haven't moved for a couple of days. He wanted to know if I'd heard anything from anybody coming off Williamson.'

'Can he pinpoint the locations of the collars?'

'He can get close.'

Marquez thought about that a moment. He had time available he wouldn't otherwise have.

'If I drive down there, do you want to hike up there tomorrow with me?'

'Let me check what I've got going on, but I think I can do that.'

After hanging up, Marquez made another call, this one to Ted Desault.

'I heard about your warden, so I understood why you didn't call back,' Desault said. 'I'd still like to meet with you.'

'I'm driving to the southern Sierra in very early morning.'

'I'm in Reno. Which way are you driving down?'

'Do you know Lee Vining?'

'Sure, the little town just before the road up to Yosemite.'

'Meet me there at 8:00.'

'Are you going to get there that early?'

'I'll get there, and there's a place near the center of town called the Latte Da. See you there.'

THIRTY-TWO

Desault's dark blue Bureau car was parked up against a chain link fence on a side street half a block from the Latte Da. He sat upright in his seat, but his eyes were closed and after watching him a few moments Marquez realized he was asleep. He read the fatigue on Desault's face, dark slashes under his eyes, the sag in his cheeks. Etched lines marked his mouth. We're all older, he thought, and then rapped lightly on the glass.

They bought coffee drinks at the Latte Da and drove across the highway to the Mono Lake Visitors' Center in Marquez's truck. There they walked out through the gray soil and sage to a rock overlooking the lake. Gulls wheeled through a blue sky above the tufa islands in the lake. The water was topaz-colored, the snowless mountains to the east pale. The wind smelled of sage and it struck him that neither he nor Desault could have ever imagined that here was where they would meet and measure each other again.

'I was too much of a hard charger in those days,' Desault said. 'I was full of ambition to make a mark and I made a mistake with your DEA group. I still owe you an apology I'll make now. I'm sorry. I made a mistake. I used to think you get information out of people by being tough. It took me another decade to learn it's the opposite, but then I'm not a fast learner.'

'Neither am I. I wouldn't be here if I was.'

'You're here because you have to be. You haven't forgotten what he did.'

'So make your pitch.'

'All right, let's get to it. What I'm doing with the task force is taking a shotgun approach to bringing down Emrahain Stoval. We're going to try every angle and one of those is an animal angle, the illegal trophy hunting, the trafficking in animals and animal parts. That's how your name came up. I'd like to bring you on and make you a TFO, a Task Force Officer. Deputize you for a year and give you a Bureau badge. I'll also run you by the US Marshal's office and get you deputized there, so you'd be cleared for both articles twenty-one and eighteen. We give it a shot for a year and when it's over you go back to Fish and Game, or maybe you'll like being a Fed again. Maybe that's the big circle for you and you become the animal guy for the Department of Justice.'

Desault took a sip of coffee and continued.

'I'm talking about giving you a license to chase Stoval around the world. You'd be the one and only for the Bureau, the James Bond of wildlife enforcement.'

'James Bond.'

'Sure, why not? The Department of Justice needs a wildlife agent, so it really could grow into something. I'm told you still talk to Kerry Anderson of the DEA. That says you haven't forgotten, and this is a funded opportunity, Marquez. We're going to use terrorist dollars and get him. All we have to do is prove he smuggles mixed contraband into the US and leave a few question marks about the contents of the contraband and we'll be funded.'

'OK, so I'm James Bond with fur and chasing him around, with what goal?'

'Build a wildlife trafficking case or help bring him down for poaching a black rhino in Africa. If it's in the right place, the locals will help.'

'No one will hold him. He'll pay and go.'

'I think we can slow him down and if he shoots the wrong animal or traffics in animals and you can prove it, I think we can lean on police in some of these countries to hold him. If he pays and goes and gets tried in absentia, that's still a score for the good guys. At that point he's a fugitive. That's how we're going to get him. We'll bleed him out one small cut at a time. But, look, we've studied him. Hunting is a passion for Stoval. He's less careful there and he'll make mistakes you'll be able to work with. I've got the money, Marquez. I can send you anyplace he hunts or traffics in animals.'

Even after all this time it reached Marquez. He went years looking to the day he caught up with Stoval. He looked down at the wind-riffled water of Mono as Desault continued.

'I want your expertise, your grit, your ability to get it done. No one else has your resume. I'll pay for translators, guides, vehicles, equipment, whatever you need. Anywhere the US flag flies you've got jurisdiction. In most foreign countries we'll have to work through the State Department, but once things are in place I can bring agents in to back you up. That's a sketch but you'll have all the latitude you want. I'm looking to you to figure it out. I'm your backstop. I'm resource when you need it. I'll get you new creds and a passport, and you'll travel on behalf of the US Department of Justice. You'll go anywhere in the world you think it's going to help us take him down.'

'You've said that. I get it. I'm just wondering if it could work.'

'Look, I've got people trying to unravel bank accounts, people tracing the arms trading, drugs, counterfeiting, money laundering, you name it. I've got an army trying to smoke this guy's operations and I tell my guys all the time, we are not as bright as Stoval, but we can wear him down.' His voice rose a notch. 'We can bring this guy down, Marquez. We can finally bring him down. I'm giving you a chance to go after a major player in the black market for animal parts who killed friends of yours.'

'No, it's like you said, you're looking for a new angle for your task force and when you started looking at poaching, my name made the list.'

Desault shook his head. 'Shit, I thought you'd jump at this.' Marquez didn't answer that and Desault misread his silence.

'All right, at least I offered it to you.'

'Hey, thanks for thinking of me.'

That was everything about the Bureau and task forces Marquez didn't like. Look around for who would be useful and call them up and tell them how lucky they are to be chosen. He poured his coffee into the gray sand and said, 'I'll take you back to your car.'

After they crossed the highway and Desault got out, he didn't shut the passenger door, instead held on to it and leaned in to talk at Marquez.

'Not everybody agrees with me, Marquez, but I think the same person who got him the Fifty-twos he gave you in the bull ring is still active. They went dormant for a long time and then started up quietly again. In the last year they've been very active. Information is going out and some of it is getting sold to the wrong people. There's so much suspicion my task force isn't even in the real loop. That's what this is about. We're back to the wall with this guy. That's why we're looking for any legal means, including animal trafficking and his bullshit trophy hunting. I talked with a couple of US Fish and Wildlife agents before you. I wasn't eager to dig up the past with you, anymore than you were eager to see me. But, you know what, those guys over at Fish and Wildlife do a lot of administrative stuff. They sit in on too many meetings and I started thinking that if I send one of them after Stoval, I may as well send them out with body bags so they can be mailed home.

'Then I really began to ask around and that's when your name kept coming up. So now I'm saying to you, tell me what you need and I'll get whatever it is you want. You'll have autonomy. We'll work together, but you're the animal guy.'

Marquez reached around and grabbed his logbook. He opened it to a blank page and handed the book to Desault.

'Give me the best numbers to reach you at and several more days and I'll call you.'

He watched him write and fold the book shut and lay it on the passenger seat. He leaned in before shutting the door and said, 'Call my cell. I don't care what time of day. I keep my phone with me always. I'll be waiting for your call. I've got a feeling about this. We need you.'

'Enough.'

Desault pointed a finger and said, 'Call me.' Then he let the door fall shut.

THIRTY-THREE

Adrian Muller kept his head buzzed and stood about six foot, two hundred pounds with little fat. He ran every other day and cycled or mountain-biked in between. After three tours in Iraq he also flinched at a car door slamming and had a jumpy restlessness that the mountains might eventually take care of. Or it might stay with him for life, hard to say. Marquez knew several Vietnam vets who never got over it.

Muller returned home to Bishop in the Owens Valley within sight of the high peaks of the Sierra Nevada. He'd gone through warden school in Santa Rosa a couple of years ago. He was new to warden work but not to the mountains. He was ambitious, smart, and confident. His wife, Jen, was a minor celebrity as a climber, and moved here for the rock before Muller met her. Eight months ago, barely a year and change into being a warden, Muller had applied to join the SOU and Marquez had met him then. He left it with Muller that he needed to work as an area warden longer first. That was not the answer Muller wanted, so there was some tension this morning as they shook hands.

The Fish and Game office was on West Line Street in a building that looked like a converted motel. A sign on a window read *California Department of Fish and Game*. Out front was a small lawn, hedges, and a place to park Marquez's truck. They drove south toward Independence in Muller's Fish and Game rig.

'It's going to be a steep climb up to Anvil Camp,' Muller said. 'How are you with altitude?'

'I'm usually fine.'

'If you think it's a problem at all, I don't mind going up alone.'

Marquez smiled.

'I think they spent a night there,' Muller said. 'I found a backpacker who may have seen them.'

'You found a backpacker after you talked to me?'

'I called a friend who works at the ranger station in Lone Pine and she checked permits for me. Three backcountry permits got pulled for Anvil Camp, none in the name you gave me. What is it again?'

'Maitland. Patrick Maitland.'

'Right, and there aren't any in that name, but I've got names and numbers on the other backpackers. Do you want them?'

Marquez copied those numbers down as they drove. In Independence they went west toward the mountains on Onion Valley Road until they reached the dirt track that broke off toward the Mount Williamson trailhead. Few peaks in the lower forty-eight were bigger than Williamson. Only Whitney and White Mountain Peak were taller. California bighorn summered above ten thousand feet and in the winter, if mountain lion didn't force them to stay high, they dropped out of the preserve to around five thousand feet for better grazing. Right now, after the unusually light winter's snow, they were moving back into the high country. But Muller and Marquez weren't chasing the bighorn. They shouldered backpacks and hiked toward the stationary radio collars.

The trail followed Symmes Creek, crossing it several times before making a long switchbacking climb up through trees and rock, rising twenty-four hundred feet to a saddle that looked across at the big granite face of Mount Williamson.

Many of the chutes had already melted off and the rock was dark. It was the earliest melt Marquez could remember, but he was glad it was as warm as it was this morning and after the climb up from Symmes Creek, it felt good to sit in the sun and take a break.

They slept at Anvil Camp that night and at first light Muller spread a topo map and marked the route he thought they should follow. Half a mile along that route they stowed their gear and hiked five miles through loose talus and the occasional stand of limber pine, both climbing and descending as they followed sheep trails. On the steep talus slopes they sent loose rock sliding with each footstep as Muller worked off a hand-held GPS unit and they moved toward the coordinates the biologist had given.

When they got closer they smelled the carcasses. It happened just as they crossed under a small outcropping of rock. The wind carried up the mountain and on it the dead. Then it was easy to find them, two male bighorn, both decapitated, and not just horns but the heads gone as well. Not easy to carry a head out from here and Marquez stopped and thought about that. The body of one lay with its hind legs in the flow of a small snowmelt stream, the other in the sparse brush. Coyote and birds had fed on both.

'Let's look around for the heads,' Marquez said.

'They took them.'

'Let's look anyway.'

As they searched they found the radio collars lying side-by-side on a flat piece of granite and as Muller reached to pick one up, Marquez stopped him.

'Let's videotape first.'

The collars weren't thrown down; they were displayed on the rock. Someone making a statement. They videotaped and then collected the collars before returning to the carcasses and studying the bullet wounds that had killed them and decapitating cuts that must have been made with a surgical saw. They were that clean.

Terri Delgado warned of a trophy hunt, but Marquez hadn't accepted that. These horns sold for fifty to sixty thousand a pair on the black market, yet the fact that the shooter or shooters may have carried the heavy heads out suggested Delgado's tip was right.

He took a last long look before leaving. Bighorn herds had once roamed much of the west. He remembered reading an account by John Muir of bighorn following each other one after another off a one hundred fifty foot cliff, skipping off tiny ledges to slow their fall, and then bounding away. That they existed or didn't hardly mattered anymore. That fluidity and grace Muir witnessed had no context in our urban world. At best they that might make an entertaining YouTube to forward to friends. But they once had been common in the American west. But that was before they were ever described as elusive and shy. That was before they had run into us.

On the hike out they pushed hard, Marquez and a young man half his age who was determined to upbraid Marquez for not recommending him for the SOU. They came fast down a trail together in the late afternoon, and if you were coming up you might not have heard them coming, but your instinct would have been to step out of their way as they passed, though going by you they wouldn't have made much noise.

When they got back to Bishop they had a beer together and Muller said, 'I had sniper training before my first tour. I learned enough. I'll hike back up there and try to figure out where they shot from.'

'Good. Call me if you learn anything.'

Muller nodded and asked, 'What's going on with the SOU?'

'There's an investigation under way.'

They walked outside, shook hands, and Marquez got in his truck. He lowered the window and asked, 'If the guide was a local, do you have anyone in mind?'

'I might.'

They left it there and that night Marquez stayed in Bishop. He checked into the Creekside Best Western and called home before remembering that Katherine was in a meeting in San Francisco until later tonight. He turned the TV in the motel room on but the conversation with Desault weighed on him and he couldn't relax. The room felt too small.

After clearing his messages he walked out to his truck and drove up the long grade from Bishop to Lake Sabrina where it was empty and the sky bright with stars and the white arch of the Milky Way. He took an old metal thermos cup and a half pint of Scotch over to a rock and sat down. It was cold and his body was tired from the hike. He zipped his coat, turned the collar up, but the cold seemed to come from inside until he poured half an inch and drank it down. Across the valley above the desert floor was the black silhouette of the White Mountains. He looked at the lights of Bishop below and the dark road falling as things that happened eighteen years ago returned to him. He heard the voices of the dead, Brian Hidalgo talking about street food in Saigon and the panic in the last days as the US left. He saw Billy Takado standing drinking a beer at a fish taco stand near the concrete plant in Ensenada, and then flashed on Jim Osiers' body in the truck and thought about the article on the Zetas and Stoval and Sheryl's warning.

Desault was right. He was made for this offer, but at what cost? Taking Desault up on the offer would leave Katherine angry and sad, and it was in many ways a betrayal of a future they had many times talked about. He poured another drink into the metal cup. Going after Stoval wasn't just going after an animal trafficker or illegal trophy hunter. It was wading back into the violence. It meant becoming a Fed again. It meant things he thought he'd left behind forever.

He stood and walked back to the truck. In fifteen minutes he'd be in the motel room. At dawn he'd meet Muller. Tomorrow, he should call Desault and tell him no, but he knew he wouldn't. The book was still open. It was about honor and a promise made the dead and tonight under these stars in this mountain there was no line between living and dead. He saw their faces so clearly they might as well be here with him.

THIRTY-FOUR

Anderson sounded like a brittle academic lecturer as he said, 'Stoval prefers to buy, coerce, or use law enforcement officers. He avoids killing law enforcement whenever he can. That's not to say he won't. He may have bought or blackmailed his way into the FBI task force.'

'I don't believe it.'

That agitated Anderson. He didn't like that and his voice quickened as he continued.

'I've got other information on my desk this morning that can only be explained by internal leaks. Not at the FBI but within Federal agencies, including my own. I can't give you specifics but it's all about Stoval and his influence or possible influence.'

'You're making him bigger than life.'

'He is bigger than life. He's very dangerous. The cartels did twenty-four billion in business in the US last year. Stoval is continually funding some fraction of that. He has interests to protect. Buying into our law enforcement agencies is a fact of life. The phone intercept with Stoval mentioning you can only be explained that way.'

'I'm not on the Stoval task force.'

'Just your name triggered a response. You can read it as respect for you. Maybe you got closer to him years ago than you thought, or it's because of what happened with Kline.'

'You told me five years ago that he wanted Kline dead, that he'd had a falling out with him.'

'John, I'm just trying to give you answers. I do analysis of actions. I keep track of roughly a hundred truly bad guys who are out there operating as we speak. For the right price half of that one hundred would help a terrorist group smuggle nuclear weapons into US cities.'

'Let's keep the conversation on Emrahain Stoval.'

There was quiet on the other end and then Anderson said, 'I have to go. I'm late. I'm sorry.'

'Before you hang up on me, I want to ask you to send me an updated photo of Stoval. Can you scan me something I can carry?'

'I don't know when.'

'I need it, Kerry. Do this for me.'

After hanging up Marquez didn't know whether Anderson would send anything or not. He laid his phone down and thought it all over. A few minutes later he took a call from Chief Blakely.

'I want to read you something I found on the Internet,' she said. 'It's an old *LA Times* article.'

'Do you want to forward it to me?'

'No, I want to read this. It'll only take a minute. Here goes, "California is responsible for more than a third of the cannabis harvest in the US." That's one stat and then this, "In California, the state's Campaign Against Marijuana Planting seized nearly one point seven million plants this year – triple the haul in 2005 – with an estimated street value of more than six point seven billion dollars. Based on the seizure rate over the last three years, the study estimates that California grew more than twenty-one million marijuana plants in 2006 – with a production value nearly triple the next closest state, Tennessee." It also says there were more marijuana plants grown last year than there are citizens in California. This is going to be a continuing problem for wardens. We're going to need a field policy. I want your help crafting a policy.'

'You don't want me to write policy.'

'We're going to need an active policy to deal with this.'

'Probably so.'

But it's not going to be a role for me. He realized that Blakely was trying to deal with her feelings about Brad's murder, her own sense of responsibility, and she was also trying to come up with a job for him. She knew what was going to happen.

'You still there?' she asked.

'I'm here.'

'I want to say something else to you today that I've been meaning to say to you for awhile. I want you to stay at Fish and Game. I don't want you to resign no matter how this comes out. Did the FBI make you an offer?'

'Yes.'

Blakely had gone up the ladder and he'd stayed a patrol lieutenant, but they understood each other. He'd always felt that. There'd been other chiefs he'd argued with, and then Blakely. He collaborated with her. He trusted her. She'd worked as a warden. She knew the field.

'But you haven't accepted, have you?'

'Where I'm at is I haven't talked to Katherine yet. But you and I both know I'm going to have to step down from the SOU and I may join their task force for six months.'

'You could do six months on a leave of absence. We can work that out.'

'Melinda Roberts should take over as patrol lieutenant and I've been working with a warden out of Bishop who wants to be and probably ought to be SOU.'

'Adrian Muller.'

'Yes.'

'Muller is doing a good job in Bishop and knows the area. I don't know who we would replace him with.'

'That's not his problem.'

'No, you're right, it isn't.' She paused. 'Don't do anything yet, John. Call me tomorrow.'

He briefed her on the bighorn investigation and hung up. That night Maria came to dinner bringing a bottle of red wine with her and an effusiveness that felt forced. She told funny stories about work but her eyes never rested anywhere very long. They fried small peppers in olive oil and salt and ate them with a glass of wine before dinner. These were favorites of Maria's but tonight she picked at them with a nervous intensity and hurried through dinner, then asked, 'Who really believes anymore that America stands for individual freedom and human rights? Everybody at the top of our government is either rich already or gets rich on the other side.'

Neither Katherine nor he touched it and Maria stood abruptly. She moved into the kitchen and started cleaning up. She moved in a way that didn't leave any room for anyone to help, but Katherine got up anyway. She suggested to Maria, 'Why don't we get together later this week? Can you do that?'

'I don't think so, Mom. There's just too much going on.'

'Even for a cup of coffee? I'll come down to where you work.'

'It's just really a weird time.' She looked at Marquez. 'I didn't mean to get angry or bring my problems here. I'm sorry about that, too. Bye. I love you both.'

Katherine walked out to her car with her and when she got back, she said, 'This is about her breakup with her boyfriend. She'll get over it. He treated her badly.'

'I don't know anything about that.'

'You're right, you don't. You're not around enough to know. What is the FBI offering you?'

'A position on a task force to go after Emrahain Stoval.'

She bowed her head and covered her eyes with her right hand and Marquez sat down and put an arm around her shoulders. He didn't try to sell her. He didn't say anything and Katherine said very quietly without looking up, 'If you chase that monster, you'll bring him into our lives. How can you do that to us? I don't get it. I don't understand.'

THIRTY-FIVE

The next morning Marquez met up with one of his team, Carol Shauf, to visit a concrete contractor they videotaped buying sturgeon roe from Holsing. The contractor was on the phone in his office telling a joke that they could hear from the reception area as if he was standing next to them. When he hung up and his secretary led them into his office they saw walls festooned with fishing gear and photos of him standing near his varying catches, a bluefin caught off Cabo San Lucas, a marlin in Antibes, a huge silver salmon hooked on the Copper River, and then his favorite, a sturgeon taken right here in the delta.

'Do you wish you were Hemingway?' Shauf asked as she studied a photo of him with the fishing pole and the beard.

'Excuse me?'

'Do you wish you were Hemingway in Cuba instead of a guy poaching sturgeon in Antioch?'

He looked puzzled then scared as he studied their cards, but managed to muster, 'What can I do this morning for the Department of Fish and Game?'

'Confess,' Shauf said, 'and we'll hook you up and take you to jail. But I'd like to get a photo of you first so I can hang it on my wall.'

Marquez stepped in.

'We're here about sturgeon poaching as part of an ongoing investigation. We'd like to ask you some questions about Jeff Holsing.'

'I'm not sure I know who that is.'

'If I showed you photos of the two of you together would you remember him?'

Shauf had the photos and was delighted to show them. Then they sat with him for an hour and a half and decided he really didn't know much about Holsing's operation, though he did admit to buying illegal roe. His forehead dampened with sweat as Shauf brought up Judge Randall, a judge who liked to fish but never caught anything and blamed it on poachers. In northern California no one handed out tougher sentences. Shauf had a signed picture of the judge in his black robe holding a fishing pole. It was the first thing you saw when you came in the door of her house, but, in truth, nothing would happen to this contractor for buying illegal roe. An assistant DA would look at what they had and say, you've got to be kidding, so the only question was whether the concrete contractor could point them to another lead. He didn't.

And so the day went, working links to Holsing. They let one fishmonger know he was likely to be charged. The surprise of being confronted with photos and wardens' notes turned several denials into apologies and the fishmonger and another suspect agreed to make statements. At dusk, before calling it a day, he and Shauf bought sandwiches, chips, a six-pack of beer, and took it all down to the river. They sat on top of a picnic table, the beer between them.

'So you,' she asked, 'what's going to happen?'

'They'll conclude Brad was inadequately supervised and the team was spread too thin. They'll recommend a reorg and I'll be out.'

She took a pull of beer. This wasn't news to her. She'd already come to the same conclusion and he didn't doubt the team had talked it out. She reached for the potato chips and looked out over the river, saying, 'If you go, I may go.'

'Go where?'

'DBEEP.'

They often worked with the Delta Bay Enhanced Enforcement Patrol and Shauf liked being on the rivers. He could see her doing that. Having offered that, she wanted an answer from him.

'What will you do, John?'

He laid it out for her now. He told her about the FBI offer. Shauf took a pull from her beer and said nothing. There was sunlight on the river and seals out on the red buoys. Shore reeds moved in the wind but it was warm, and for a few minutes that was enough and then she said, 'You're going to do it, aren't you?'

'I'm talking with Katherine.'

'But you're going to do it.'

Shauf reached for the bottle opener. She opened one, then

a second beer and handed him a full bottle. She raised her bottle and touched it against his in a toast.

'We were good,' she said. 'We were the best and we had a long run.' She clicked her bottle harder against his and toasted the river. 'To the SOU.'

THIRTY-SIX

'I hiked back up there and found shell casings and I talked to the backpacker again,' Muller said. 'He said he talked to you yesterday also.'

'Yeah, I called him.'

Finding shell casings up there must have been next to impossible and he turned the dark thought that Muller, after applying and failing to get into the SOU last year, came up with the idea of shooting a couple of bighorn, and then orchestrating an investigation that he would later solve. After all, he grew up in the area. He knew these mountains. He had sniper training and got someone to play the tipster, Terri Delgado. He listened now as Muller described finding 30.06 shell casings in country so big it had no problem swallowing the wreckage of small planes. He listened and then discarded the idea Muller planned this.

'There's a flat slab of granite I think he shot from. And something else.'

'What?'

'They built a rock cairn like you see as a trail marker. Built it on the rock and maybe that was so they could find it again or else like the radio collars, but that would be spooky.'

'The rock cairn was where you found the shell casings?'

'Yeah, they built it for us, I guess.'

The backpacker Marquez had talked to remembered two guys who came into Anvil Camp near dusk. The backpacker had an old Primus gas stove he was trying to light so was distracted, but remembered an older man who was taller with dark hair that had gone white at the temples. He was probably late fifties, early sixties. He walked like he was used to walking in the mountains.

Marquez had asked, 'Could it have been a father and son?'

'Could have, but I didn't get that impression. The younger man was short and thick, sort of stocky. He was maybe five foot seven, one eighty, and the older man was six foot one or in that area and kind of rangy. I might have gone over and said hello after I made dinner, but I got a weird vibe from the older guy so I just left them alone. It felt like he was studying me and not in a friendly way. As if I was in their space or something, and I shouldn't be there. But they were gone in the morning. That's all I know.'

'No shared whiskey, no compadre with a fellow hiker after a long climb into the mountains?'

The backpacker, who had turned out to be an attorney in Fresno, laughed.

'Nothing like that.'

After hanging up, Marquez entertained the idea he'd danced around since first hearing the description of the older man from Terri Delgado and then quizzing Anderson – that the hunter was Stoval. There were only so many places to hunt bighorn in the States, so it wasn't as unlikely as it sounded. His instinct said the older man would be the shooter, the younger stocky one the guide. He talked with Muller about who among the local guides would fit and the next morning Muller and Marquez drove out to talk to a watercolor artist named Alice Durrell who lived in the Round Valley.

Alice Durrell painted landscapes that sold through a gallery in Bishop. Yesterday was her day to bring work into the gallery and when she did she read about two bighorn poached up on Mount Williamson. She finished reading and folded the *Inyo County Register* in half, and then carried the newspaper with her as she walked through town to the Department of Fish and Game office to tell her story. When she found the office locked she left a note.

As they parked an Australian shepherd raced toward them snarling. Marquez calmed the dog down and the artist came out of a converted garage that was probably her studio. A thick head of snow white hair cascaded down her back and was tied off near her hips with a bright blue rubber band. In a face weathered like desert sandstone her blue eyes were strikingly clear. She wore a blue long-sleeved man's shirt rolled up to her elbows and she led them into her studio where she'd drawn a charcoal sketch of two men standing near the back of a vehicle that to Marquez looked like a new Range Rover.

'What color was it?' Marquez asked.

'Black. They were out on the Onion Valley Road about two miles west of Independence. I wanted to paint the sunset over the mountains. A friend had dropped me off and I planned to walk back into Independence.'

Muller had described her as a local eccentric who for decades could be seen walking along roads in the desert with her easel strapped to her back. Marquez read her as sincere and concerned about what she had found. She also seemed clearheaded. In the sketch the taller of the two had black hair and a ball cap. She touched her sketch.

'The shorter man I recognized. The other man I made a second sketch of because he frightened me. It's around here somewhere, though I don't know what I did with it. I probably turned it so his face wouldn't look out. I'm superstitious that way.'

She told her story now of sitting quietly on her folding stool out in rocks in the high desert and watching the short stocky man lug something out into the sage and cheat grass as his companion stayed near the Range Rover. She'd sketched the other man standing alone near the vehicle. After they drove away she walked over and found the head of a bighorn sheep with the horns cut off. She turned to Muller.

'Did you find it?'

'I haven't looked yet.'

Muller had gotten the story from her late yesterday afternoon over the phone after finding her note, but it was seventy miles from Bishop to Independence and he hadn't had time to go out there yet. It was Marquez's idea to talk to her first or he would have gone out this morning. Marquez studied the sketch and then helped her move canvasses around as she searched for a second drawing.

Before she found it she said of the shorter man, 'His mother was half Paiute and they lived out toward Benton. I've tried to think of his name, but I don't have the memory I once had.'

'Nate Thompson,' Muller said quietly as soon as he heard that.

'Yes, that's right, one of the Thompson boys. He should

have been the one to notice me but it was the other, and it was when he had his back to me. He just sensed me.' She looked at Marquez. 'You're like that too.'

When she found the sketch there were no facial details, but the stance, the look, the posture was right. It was the way the man held his head as he seemed to stare at her.

'Do you recognize him?' she asked Marquez.

'I might.'

Muller cut in, asking, 'Alice, if we took you down to Independence with us, would you be able to take us to the head?'

'I don't think you should be warden for the area if you can't find a bighorn head lying in a field.'

Marquez couldn't help smiling though Muller looked offended.

'The Thompson boy got in trouble for something like this fifteen years ago,' she said. She stared at Marquez. 'He shot a bear.'

'I remember,' Muller answered, and Marquez said, 'I've got a photo that I'd like to bring back and show you. Can we stop back by this afternoon?'

'I'll be here.'

Marquez didn't have Anderson's recent photo of Stoval, but Katherine said an image of a man faxed through last night late. It woke her up. By now, he figured, Kath had faxed it to the Fish and Game office in town. He and Muller stopped there before driving out to Thompson's house.

Turned out Thompson lived out in the desert near Benton. The asbestos-shingled house couldn't offer much protection from the cold winds sweeping this gap in the winter. A couple of vehicles, a Chevy pickup with a high wheel base and an old Volkswagen Jetta, sat in the front yard. The Jetta's tires had rotted and the car had settled on to the rims. Inside the house was a new flat screen TV, an ancient couch, and a dining table someone had carved their initials in. A big Mackinaw trout and two deer heads were mounted on the wall. Marquez looked through the window and across the highway where the long alluvial plain rose toward the White Mountains. When he looked back, Thompson stood as he had in the sketch, a bandy-legged man with a barrel chest. He folded his arms now as Marquez dropped it on him.

'Someone ID'ed you dumping a bighorn head out in the sage a couple of miles from Independence.'

'You've got the wrong guy. I haven't been to Independence in months.'

'You thought you were alone when you dumped the bighorn head, but a local recognized you. That's why we're here.'

'Who saw me?'

'I'm not going to give you a name yet, but we are going to give you a choice. You've got the choice of talking to us about your client and the hunt, or trying to bluff us. If you help us, it'll probably go a lot better for you, because we've got everything, the black Range Rover, the carcasses of the bighorn, everything. You made a very real mistake and now the question is whether you want it to get worse.'

Thompson rubbed the back of his neck and frowned at Marquez.

'You've got the wrong man.'

'Are you sure?'

'I'm telling you the truth, warden.'

'Then we'll take your word.'

Marquez shook his hand and glanced at Muller. Muller didn't get it. His eyes showed his confusion, but he rolled with it, hid his feelings and they walked out.

THIRTY-SEVEN

'He's scared,' Marquez said as soon as they were outside. 'Give me binoculars and drop me as soon as we're out of sight of his house.'

'What do you think is going to happen?'

'If he's got something to hide he'll do it as soon as we're gone.'

Marquez took binoculars with him. Thompson should be patient, watch the road and give them time to get back to Bishop, but no way he was buying the handshake and sorry we bothered you. At least that's what Marquez was betting as he got out of Muller's truck.

Near Thompson's house there was little cover, sage, desert

grasses, a scattering of other houses and buildings, a shack behind the next door neighbor's house that Marquez hid behind now. He settled in. He called Muller and let him know where he was. Half an hour later Thompson came out of the house and walked to the Volkswagen Jetta settling into the side yard. He looked around before unlocking the trunk. A hinge squeaked as the trunk lid went up and Marquez saw Thompson cradling something reasonably heavy and wrapped in a blue blanket. He carried it over to his truck and put it on the floor behind the driver's seat as Marquez called Muller.

'OK, he's moved something wrapped in a blanket from the trunk of the Jetta over to his truck. Close in, let's do this. It looks like he's getting ready to leave.'

If Thompson left he could be in Nevada in minutes and Marquez doubted he'd get okayed to follow. Not without knowing what Thompson had in the truck. And even if they did get it, they'd be in Muller's Fish and Game rig, so that was a bust.

'On my way,' Muller said.

'Come in slow and park so he can't back out. Get out with your camcorder in your hand and we'll try to bluff him. I'm walking down now.'

Marquez threaded through the sage. He walked up as Thompson's back was to him and Thompson lifted a small suitcase over on to the passenger seat.

'Planning a trip?' Marquez asked, and Thompson jumped then quickly recovered and said matter-of-factly, 'This is private property, warden.'

'Yeah, and that's a zoological preserve up on Mount Williamson.'

Muller pulled up now and eased up behind Thompson's bumper. He got out with one hand holding his camcorder and the other resting on his gun holster.

'Game over, Nate,' Marquez said. 'We videotaped you getting the horns out of the trunk.'

Thompson looked from Marquez to Muller. His face said Marquez was right. His plea was to Muller.

'Warden, you know that my sister died of cancer last winter. It's her boy I've got to raise. Everyone knows that.'

'Then, if you care at all about the boy,' Marquez said, 'get the horns out right now.'

If not for his nephew, Marquez doubted Thompson would
have done it. He unfolded the blanket on his truck hood.

'I was going to sell them and put the money in a college
account for the boy.'

They were white-yellow with the half-moon curve and
striations of bighorn. Marquez ran his finger along the horn.
'What did you cut them off with?'

'A battery-powered surgical saw he had. It's for amputating
in wars.'

'Who is he, your client?'

'Yes, sir.'

Marquez turned one of the horns in his hands. He felt the
weight of it. Thompson confessed that his plan was to take
the horns to Los Angeles where he knew a broker who could
sell them. But neither the horns nor his confession got them
any closer to identifying Thompson's client, and it soon became
obvious that Thompson wasn't just trying to protect the man.

'He didn't tell me anything,' Thompson said. 'I was just a
mule to him.'

'When he left here where did he go?'

Thompson pointed toward Nevada. 'Drove off that way.'

'I'm going to show you an old photo,' Marquez said, and
then borrowed Muller's keys and retrieved the charcoal sketch
the Round Valley artist made and the faxed photo Anderson
had sent. He studied the photo again and felt heat rise to his
face and saw Billy Takado in the late afternoon in the bull
ring. If Thompson recognized the photo his decision to join
Desault's task force would be made.

'Where did you get that?' Thompson asked after picking it
up and squinting at it.

'Is that him?'

Thompson nodded. He stared at Marquez.

'Oh, yeah, that's Maitland.'

When they left Thompson they drove back to Alice Durrell's
house. They found her in the studio. She didn't look at the
photo for more than a second before saying, 'That's him, and
you're better off not looking for him.'

'Don't worry, Alice, we can handle him,' Muller said.

'Of course, you can.'

She studied Marquez's eyes, smiled a sad smile, touched
his arm, and then turned back to her studio.

THIRTY-EIGHT

Marquez pulled off on to the road shoulder near Mammoth Lakes Airport. He called Desault.

'Stoval was here and he may be in Vegas now. It's worth checking.'

'Why Vegas?'

Marquez recounted Terri Delgado's story of being invited along on the hunt that would end with a long weekend in Las Vegas. He went slowly through the chain of events with Desault.

'Where are you?' Desault asked.

'North of Bishop at Mammoth Lakes. I'm on my way home. Stoval is traveling under an alias. Patrick Maitland. M-A-I-T-L-A-N-D.'

'OK, I got it.'

'He hired a local guide down here named Nate Thompson and shot two bighorn sheep on the Mount Williamson Zoological Preserve. He used the name Patrick Maitland with both the guide and the woman that tipped us. Anderson faxed me a photo I showed them and both ID'ed him.'

'If he's traveling under an alias I can hold him. If I can prove it, I can keep him out of the country. How do I reach the woman with the Vegas story?'

Marquez pulled his logbook and then read off Delgado's cell number.

'When he left Thompson's house he had a bighorn head with him. I've called Nevada's Department of Wildlife as well as US Fish and Wildlife, so they're looking for him, too.'

'I wish you hadn't done that.'

'Well, Ted, this is about wildlife. I don't know what plans he has for the head, but he can't carry it around indefinitely and there are only a handful of taxidermists in that area, so between Nevada's and Fish and Wildlife they should know where to look. Let me give you the names and numbers of who I talked to in those departments.'

He heard Desault's pen scratching. Then a question came.

'What made you show this guide a photo of Stoval?'

'A bunch of small things I'll run through with you later. If Nevada Wildlife can tie him to the horns then they can make an arrest and the guide here will testify against him.'

'I'll call the Field Office in Vegas and talk to you later.'

When he hung up with Desault he pulled back on to the road and started to believe they had a real chance to take Stoval down. He drove north up 395 and then over Monitor Pass and on into the Tahoe Basin. After he was out of the mountains and just a couple of hours from home, Muller called and said, 'I found it. Coyote dragged it away from where Alice saw them dump it, but it's bighorn. There's something else that's bizarre and with it. I'll have to drive back out and ask Alice Durrell about it.'

'What's that?'

'A postcard with a skewer through it, like a shish kebab skewer. When I look at the drag marks I can tell it was near where they dropped the head. The postcard was skewered into the ground between two sage bushes. I haven't touched it yet and I've got an evidence bag in my truck. I'll get it and bring it back.'

'You're saying it was stuck in the ground near where the head was before the coyotes got it?'

'That's right.'

'OK, what's on the postcard?'

'You want me to handle it? I bagged it as evidence.'

'Go ahead and take a look at it.'

Marquez listened as Muller opened the plastic evidence bag. He could tell Muller was holding his cell to his ear with his shoulder.

'The picture is mountains, ocean, and boats. It's torn though.' He laughed. 'Looks like one of the coyotes bit through it.'

Marquez heard him muttering to himself and then wind gusting was loud and made Muller hard to hear as he said, 'It's a town in Alaska. I thought it was Alaska. What do you make of that, a bighorn head and a postcard from Seward, Alaska?'

'I don't make anything of it yet, but my sister lives there.'

'Then you ought to see this. It's a weird thing.'

'Has your cell phone got a camera?'

'You want me to email a photo?'

'Yeah.'

'I'll do it right now.'

Marquez emailed the photo to Desault and got ready to call him. He punched in Desault's number, then erased it and called Darcey instead.

THIRTY-NINE

The next day Marquez drove to Sacramento so they didn't have to do it over the phone. The morning was already hot and the lawns around the capitol building humid as he and Chief Blakely walked to a place on J Street she liked. They took an outdoor table in the shade of a plane tree and the chief ordered a mineral water, Marquez black coffee.

'They're calling it a failure at the supervisory level,' she said, 'but it's not as bad as it sounds. They acknowledge that you were pulled away by an ongoing operation, and that Brad disobeyed a standing order that would have kept him from crossing the slope without backup in place.'

'What's the bottom line?'

'That I want you to remain as head of the SOU, the director wants you replaced, and the legislators who fund the budget feel you have to be replaced or we're going to run into trouble this year. Personally, I don't believe that.'

'Director Morgan wants me replaced.'

'Yes, but he understands what happened. There's not going to be any disciplinary action and they understand how stretched the SOU gets. No one has any illusions about that.'

If the Director of Fish and Game wanted him out of the SOU, then it was done. Nothing Chief Blakely could do would change that and he got it about the legislature. Every year it was a battle to prove the money for the undercover team was well spent. If he remained in place after a finding of supervisory negligence it would create an opening for those who wanted to cut the budget.

His coffee and the chief's mineral water arrived, and suddenly coffee was the last thing he needed. Even knowing this was coming, it was very hard.

'When does all this come out?'

'Monday.'

'So everybody would like to get clear this week?' When she didn't answer that he said, 'I'll step aside today.'

She shook her head and he read real emotion there and it touched him.

'I'm going to talk to the press about you and tell them what you've done for California, and I'm going to say again to you, don't leave the department.'

'What would I do here, Janet?'

'You're not leaving.'

'Even after I'm gone I'll keep working with the team to make sure the cases go in whole. I think Melinda Roberts should step in for me.'

She looked pained and older and answered, 'You've already told me that.'

The chief didn't refuse to accept that his long run was over, but Marquez continued talking about the open cases, the court appearances he'd have to make, time he should spend with Roberts or whoever got the nod to replace him. He looked across the table at his old friend. It felt strange to work so many years and have it end as simply as this. But he didn't know what else to do other than talk about the open cases, the things that would need taking care of.

He talked with Katherine the whole drive home and she said, 'I can't change you. I know that, and that's how it is, but, John, there are always going to be people like Stoval. That'll never end and I feel like you're being used. Seems to me the FBI is starting to outsource and you fit what they're looking for. I'm not going to get all emotional right now, but I wish you weren't going to do this, though I know you are.'

'I am about to call Desault.'

He didn't get a call back from Darcey yesterday, but he got one now.

'John, I'm not worried about it and I've got a gun that I know how to use.'

Seward wasn't a big town. There was fishing, tourism, and the jump-off point for Kenai Fjords National Park. Her restaurant and bar was right there in the small boat harbor and anyone coming into town would only have to ask, 'Where do I find Darcey Marquez?'

'What can I do about it anyway?' she asked.

'Watch for anything unusual. Call me and I'll get on the next flight.'

'Come on, John, in what movie? And what does that mean anyway? Watch for anything unusual. Everyone around here is unusual. This place attracts unusual. And I don't have time to watch out for it, let alone avoid it. Do you know what I'm doing right now? I'm deep frying halibut and French fries. I've got five orders for fish and chips, two for halibut sand-wiches, and one grilled salmon. I don't have any vegetables prepped yet, or anyone to do it. I've got a half-ass bartender who got fired off a fishing boat last week and is out there over-pouring for his friends right now. I've got my cell phone in my left hand. What am I going to do, watch out the window or just keep an eye on the people who come in?'

He called Desault after he hung up with Darcey.

'How long will it take you to get the creds, the passport, and the rest?'

'Not long at all.'

'All right, I'm in.'

'That's great news. I mean, that's great news. The Department of Justice just got itself wildlife enforcement. Let's meet here tomorrow. Welcome aboard, no, welcome home, welcome back to the Feds. This really makes me happy, John. This is a good decision.'

If it made Desault happy, it made Katherine sad and his promises to her sounded hollow. He stayed in Sacramento, stalled until late afternoon, and then he parked outside the Water Resources building and rode the elevator up to Fish and Game headquarters. Chief Blakely wasn't in her office, but her assistant let him in and he put the six green logbooks on her desk. He stacked them one on top of the other, the oldest on the bottom. He laid his resignation letter next to the books, started to leave the room, and then walked back from the door to the green logbooks and rested his hand on the warm cover of the top one. He kept his hand there for several minutes, standing alone in the late sunlight in the chief's office, emotion coursing through him as he let go.

III
Angel of the Wild

FORTY

They flew low and fast, skimming the tundra, hoping to startle a bear. It was Stoval who spotted a big grizzly feeding on a caribou carcass. He shouted to the pilot, 'Right side, three o'clock.'

The pilot banked hard as the bear ran and now willows bent under the rotor wash as the helicopter settled lower and Xian Liu, rifle raised, waited for the helicopter noise to flush the bear out of the willows. When it did, the pilot held the copter steady and Liu's shot caught the bear in the hindquarters. But the bear hardly slowed.

A half mile later they hovered close enough again, though the bear was only partially visible under another stand of stubby low trees. Stoval had the pilot bring the helicopter down fifty feet. He wasn't sure Liu could make the shot and turned to him and asked, 'Want us to put you on the ground?'

'No, he'll come out.'

'He's done moving for now. You hit something with that first shot. He bled a lot.'

'He'll come out.'

'We'll put you down and he might come at you, but you'll get a shot.'

Liu wasn't going to do that, but Stoval stayed with it until they all understood that Liu was too cowardly to leave the safety of the helicopter. Liu took another shot and a tree branch dropped. He fired four more times before striking the bear. When it left the willows, it moved more slowly. Stoval found the new wound with binoculars, a lucky shot that had caught the bear near the right front shoulder, and it was easy to stay with the bear now. The pilot nosed lower, pulled in front of the big grizzly, and turned so that Liu's next two shots were straight on. Both hit the bear but neither killed it. A fist-sized hole bled from its left side and still it kept moving. The big head swung looking for a foe on the ground that wasn't there.

The next shot dropped the bear and after they landed Liu still didn't want to get out of the helicopter. So it was Stoval who made sure the bear was dead, walking up to it unarmed with Liu watching him. Then he left Liu alone with his Chinese medical myths and ate a sandwich and drank a beer, talking to the pilot as Liu carved out the gall bladder he imagined would save his mistress from terminal cancer. She was already as good as dead, but Stoval still needed Liu a little longer so he'd set up the hunt.

Steam rose from the bear's carcass as Liu lifted the gall bladder out. He slid it into a large Ziploc bag and the bag went in the cooler with the cold drinks and salmon sandwiches the pilot had packed for them. The other thousand pounds of bear they left to the wolves.

Liu's jet was in Anchorage waiting, and all that really mattered here was that Liu's gratitude for the hunt got Liu past any remaining worries he had about retribution from the Taiwanese government. Sooner or later, the Taiwanese would track things back to Liu and Liu was afraid the Americans with their paranoia over terrorism would then come for him. He was getting fat and fearful. Liu was not the man Stoval had first worked with. He was distracted by his mistress and had become cautious and self-important.

Stoval carried the cooler on to the jet. He rarely carried anything for anyone, but did this as a gesture Liu couldn't mistake. They embraced and he watched Liu's plane take off before driving to Seward. In the two hours it took to make the drive he decided he would do this last deal and not go any farther with Liu. After this deal he would throw his business to Liu's rival and then prove his intentions to the rival by working to destroy Liu. It was time.

In Seward he found Darcey Marquez's restaurant within minutes. Inside, he went upstairs to the bar. A large window looked out over the small boat harbor, allowing drinkers to enjoy the dismal gray clouds and cold water. A woman in a red flannel shirt and jeans cleaned glasses behind the bar and Stoval knew immediately she was Darcey Marquez. He smiled as he slid on to a stool. He picked up a menu. He made small talk, got her name and told her it was a pretty sounding name, but really it was a name typical of the new American peasant.

'What kind of local beer should I order?'

'You choose.'

'Don't you want to recommend something?'

It offended him slightly that she didn't. Her offhand rejection irritated him and he ignored her joking now as he ordered a whiskey rather than a beer. He studied her legs in the tight jeans. There was always something sexual in this, but he didn't desire this woman. He drank the whiskey and ordered a halibut sandwich and beer and watched her put the order in, then go retrieve it. After she returned and was behind the bar again she was watchful. He made her nervous and she was so right to be scared because he was studying her now as he did an animal he was hunting. When she turned to meet his gaze directly he smiled and imagined how she would look when they found her.

FORTY-ONE

'**D**ad, where are you now?'
          'Crossing the Golden Gate on my way to the FBI Field Office to get sworn in. I start working with the task force in a couple of days.'

'Did you hear about the condo fire in Arizona yesterday?'
'Sure.'

It was all over the news and the FBI was calling it ecoterrorism. The fire burned seventy-two condos under construction in an Arizona canyon and now was burning through drought-weakened, beetle-infested national forest.

'I might know something about it,' Maria said.

'What do you mean? How?'

Marquez slowed. He adjusted his ear piece so he could hear her better.

'I overheard something in July when I was still going out with Jack that I want to talk to you about. When I heard about the fire last night on TV it all clicked. Jack was talking to a friend of his, Ben Marsten, the guy that founded 1+1Earth. But I don't want to tell you over the phone, and I have to tell the FBI, but I want to talk to you first.'

Marquez remembered the name Jack Gant, but he didn't have a face to go with the name. He knew that earlier in the summer Katherine had believed Maria was falling in love with

Gant, but the relationship had ended abruptly and it really hadn't lasted that long.

'I'm on my way to the FBI Field Office in San Francisco to get sworn in. I become a Federal officer again today and you could—'

'Oh, that's right, Mom told me, congrats.'

'Do you want to meet me there?'

'No.'

'OK, but tell me a little more. Where did you overhear this?'

'In Los Angeles at the W Hotel in Westwood in mid July, the same day we broke up. July fourteenth.'

As she talked Marquez crossed the Golden Gate Bridge. Out of habit he reached for a pen and wrote the name of the founder of 1+1Earth, Ben Marsten, on a pad, Jack Gant's name underneath it. Ahead of him, the traffic was solid going into the toll booths, and he was late. The Special Agent-in-Charge, the SAC at the San Francisco FBI Field Office had a tight schedule today. The swear-in was slotted for 11:45 to noon.

'I'll tell you the rest when I see you.'

'All right, I'll call you as soon as I finish at the FBI. It'll probably be a couple of hours from now.'

He was going to say one thing more, but Maria was gone.

FORTY-TWO

Marquez did the new passport photo and filled out the Federal form, the FD871. Desault ran the criminal check, and then with the help of Desault's boss, the SAC, Mark Gutierrez, he'd pushed it through. Marquez knew the way he was dressed this morning made Desault uncomfortable, but he wanted to communicate with jeans and a fleece coat with a torn sleeve that, yes, he was signing on as a Fed agent, but only temporarily and he wasn't here to conform and blend in. He was here for one specific thing and he didn't mean to throw off attitude or come off as an asshole, but he did want to set a boundary. He was signing on as a Task Force Officer, a TFO, good for a year, a concession made to Desault as originally Marquez had wanted to hold it to six months.

When they walked into Gutierrez's office, Gutierrez was on his feet on his cell phone, a conversation he ended abruptly. He offered his hand to Marquez.

'You look like you're ready to hike into the woods.'

'I don't want to forget where I'm coming from.'

'The question is, do you know where you are right now?'

'I do, and if I didn't think this had a chance of working I wouldn't be here.'

Marquez knew Gutierrez had read his file and knew the circumstances of how he'd left the DEA. He probably wondered if he was bringing in trouble. But he was also onboard with bringing him in and was curious about the bighorn poaching. His questions about that now proved he'd read the Fish and Game file Marquez had copied for Desault. Gutierrez asked questions and then in the same quick manner he'd ended the phone conversation earlier, he said, 'OK, let's get this done,' as in let's get you sworn in.

'Let's wait,' Marquez said. 'There may be a complication. I got a call from my daughter on the way here. She may have a lead on the condo fire in Arizona yesterday.'

Desault looked stunned and Gutierrez surprised, though immediately right on it.

'What does she know?'

'She overheard a conversation in a hotel, her ex-boyfriend talking to somebody. She put it together last night and called me as I was on my way here this morning. She's not involved in any way. This is just something she overheard and I'll bring her in today, but if it's real and it sounds like it might be, who knows where it could go.'

Desault frowned and Gutierrez got it. Gutierrez saw Maria as a person of interest now and saw what Marquez saw, the Bureau embarrassed as the media discovered her father was on an FBI task force.

'You believe we should talk to your daughter first?' he asked.

'Yeah, but listen to me, I'm saying my daughter is coming forward with something she overheard and was worried enough about to call me. My daughter broke up with this Jack Gant weeks ago. She's not a link to him anymore. She's not involved in any plot.'

'We appreciate her coming forward.'

'I want to be there when she's questioned.'

Gutierrez said nothing and Desault stepped in now and revealed what Gutierrez might not have.

'We're already looking for Jack Gant. We've got an agent named Jane Hosfleter who heads the ecoterrorism squad. She brought up Gant's name this morning. They're looking at a Bay Area angle on the Arizona fire. Hosfleter will want to talk to your daughter as soon as you can get her here. Do you want to call Maria, right now, and you and I can go pick her up?'

'I'll get Maria here.'

It turned out Hosfleter wasn't going to be back in the Field Office until mid afternoon and Maria wasn't at work. Marquez left a message on her cell phone, told her he'd done what she and he agreed earlier. 'Call me as soon as you get this.'

He hung up and Desault said, 'OK, well, we're waiting anyway so let's go get lunch. I was going to take you to lunch.'

They walked to a Japanese restaurant Desault liked. It was cool and dark inside and there were slender tall aquariums with tropical fish. They took seats at the bar where CNN played on a big flat screen above them. Anderson Cooper was in Iraq talking about aging military equipment. An old Sherpa plane used for ferrying men and materials in Iraq showed on the screen and Desault read the caption aloud, *Workhorse of the Desert*.

'I once flew into a drug bust in one of those,' Marquez said. 'We busted the pilot and cut a deal with him to pretend he was still bringing in the load.'

The report went on about the aging fleet of C-23 Sherpas, the complex procurement process, and the need to revamp after five years of war. Cooper returned to a final shot of the Sherpa and said, 'No other aircraft in the Iraq war has carried more.'

CNN switched to the Arizona condo fire and footage of the fire line showed. A reporter questioned a tree ecologist about what he thought the prolonged drought had done to Arizona trees, and then they cut to an FBI spokesman out of the Phoenix office who appealed to the public for help. An aerial view from a helicopter looked down on the remains of the condos and the burned cottonwoods along the canyon floor, and as the obligatory shot of a plane dropping fire retardant appeared on the screen Marquez and Desault ordered lunch.

Desault ate a bowl of donburi, explaining that he liked the chicken and egg version they did here. 'At home my wife badgers me about my cholesterol, but here I sneak eggs. Man, I love eggs.' When Desault finished eating he pushed the empty donburi bowl away and said, 'Here, I've got something for you.'

He pulled out Marquez's new creds, badge, and passport. Marquez checked out the maroon passport that back when Marquez was a Fed agent had been called a redback. He picked it up and then the black wallet holding the creds. The feel, the shape, the weight was still very familiar.

'A couple of details about traveling that you need to know, John. When you get there you go straight to the airline counter and get your tickets. You won't have a gun, so there's no issue there, but you've got to wait through security like everyone else. When the transportation security guys see your badge they'll wave you through. Since 9/11 more of these flights have Federal Air Marshals or FAMs onboard, and if you don't meet them or other law enforcement officers ahead of time, hold your boarding pass and creds like this.'

Desault held the cred and boarding pass together so you could make out both.

'Don't wave it, but hold it so that if there's a FAM seated already or another LEO, they should acknowledge you. But good chance you'll be the only one on the plane.

'You'll fly business class. You'll always be seated forward. That way you can sacrifice your life when the time comes. You need the leg room anyway. You've got a knee, right?'

'Yeah, but it doesn't bother me much.'

'It has to, because I wrote that you can't ever fly coach because of the knee.'

Marquez smiled and Desault's phone rang. Desault scooped up the creds and the passport and said, 'I hope to turn these over to you later today.' He pointed at the TV. 'I've got to take this outside where I can hear.'

Marquez paid for lunch and walked out into the sunlight. He watched Desault on the phone and waited. After Desault hung up, he said, 'That was Jane Hosfleter, the agent I told you about who runs the ecoterrorism squad. She and another agent were at your stepdaughter's workplace half an hour ago. Hosfleter wants a call from you right now. Let me give you her number.'

'Tell Hosfleter I'll bring her in by three, and that I won't be calling her.'

Marquez started to say more, but instead turned and walked away.

FORTY-THREE

After Maria chained her bike to a rack near the Ferry Building they walked south along the Embarcadero waterfront toward the ballpark. Wind carried fog and the fog stripped the brightness from the afternoon.

'They're already on to Gant, Maria. There's an agent named Jane Hosfleter who heads an ecoterrorism squad out of the Field Office here. She's been looking locally for Gant after getting a tip he was planning an arson fire that would dwarf anything the Earth Liberation Front has ever done.'

'Did they come looking for me because they think I'm involved?'

'You're going to meet this Agent Hosfleter and you can ask her what she thinks.'

Maria was shocked that Hosfleter and another agent had visited where she worked. She was shocked and Marquez was angry.

'Dad, you know there's nothing wrong with 1+1Earth. You know that, right? There are two million members. Every time someone new joins that's one more and eventually the goal is to have everybody, so one earth, one voice. It might sound dorky, but it's about people working toward sustainability.'

'Sure, but right now let's stay on Gant. Tell me everything you can before we go to the FBI.'

'OK, we went to Los Angeles for the weekend and it was supposed to be our big getaway, except that we got in a bad fight right after we got there Friday night. The next morning

I went out to get us coffee and forgot my money, so went back for it. But the truth is I forgot it on purpose because I was jealous. Jack said he had to make some business calls and asked me to get us coffee and something to eat, but I thought that was because he wanted to call a woman named Lisa who lives in LA. I was starting to suspect things. I probably knew it was over between us, but I couldn't accept it yet, so I faked the thing about forgetting my money because I wanted to catch him talking to her.'

She folded her arms.

'This is a little embarrassing.'

'I understand, but it's human, Maria, and everyone at the table will get it.'

Maria looked out at the water. She looked worried and still shaken that the FBI showed up where she worked.

'Jack travels a lot and I think he was hooking up with this Lisa whenever he was in LA. Anyway, when I went back to the hotel room to get money I came in quietly. He was on the phone. He was in the bathroom and pretty quickly I figured out that it was Ben Marsten, the founder of 1+1Earth. I could tell from the words he used. It's a kind of a shorthand way they talk to each other. Jack was talking about a condo project in a canyon in Arizona. He called it Wonder. He talked about being "at Wonder" four days ago, and that made total sense because he disappeared the week before and I couldn't get a hold of him. It was how our Friday night fight started. He wouldn't tell me where he'd been. On the phone to Marsten he said things like, the grade in the canyon is perfect and the wind funnels through there, so if the wind is blowing hard nothing will stop it. So last night when I was watching TV news and heard the name of the condominium complex it was obvious.'

'And what did you think that morning?'

'That they were just talking about something they thought shouldn't have been built and predicting what was going to happen to it. I've heard them sit around and do that before. Anyway, I could tell the call was going to end, so I freed the hotel door and let it shut, and then called his name like I'd just come back for my money. He didn't come out of the bathroom right away. Maybe he wondered if I overheard him. Maybe he realized I was already in the room and was debating what to do. But I didn't wait for him to come out and see my face. I left and got the lattes, and when I came back he said, "Let's just go home."'

'Like that?'

'Yes, like that, let's go home, as in forget about the rest of the weekend and everything else.'

'So he probably knew, right?'

'Yeah, Dad, he probably knew, and there's something else he said another time that I've thought about this morning. Remember how you used to take me up to the delta on the sturgeon stuff?'

'Sure.'

'I wanted to show Jack how beautiful it can be there. He borrowed a boat and we motored around looking for an island to picnic on. This was in June and it was windy like this today and we didn't end up stopping anywhere, but we went past this one with a rotting dock and he said that it was Ben's island.'

'Ben Marsten?'

'Yes, and I asked why would Ben have an island in the delta and he looked at me and said, so we can change things. I thought he meant organic farming or something, but when I asked him he said no, it was a big idea. But he wouldn't tell me what the idea was and that was sort of weird and when I asked him again on the ride home he got angry. In this real authoritarian voice, like a command or some way of talking he learned when he was in the military, he said, forget that I said anything and don't ask me again. Then he got all moody. Should I tell the FBI about the island?'

'Tell them everything and they'll sort out what's useful.'

She turned and brushed hair back from her face.

'OK, let's go, Dad, I'm ready. I'll leave my bike here. Let's just go in your truck.'

FORTY-FOUR

Now Maria was in an interview room sitting across from Jane Hosfleter and two other agents. Hosfleter had blonde hair cut short and a Nordic cast to her cheekbones and nose. She had fair skin, blue eyes, and a take-charge confidence. Marquez was in the room despite her objections. She glanced his way occasionally, her eyes dead to him, her tone with Maria varying. She was a good interrogator. She came on hard, turned soft, backed away, and came in another direction. The agent sitting alongside her said nothing and didn't need to. It was Hosfleter's show and Hosfleter moved the conversation from the W Hotel in Westwood and Maria's relationship with Jack Gant to politics and civil disobedience, as if she was just shuffling cards and not really even engaged yet. She kept reassuring Maria, but Maria like her mom was a born skeptic.

'I'm not going to bait you, Maria, or try to trick you. And I'm not questioning anything you've told us. You saw the fire on TV last night and everything clicked. I get it. But what I want to do now is ask some questions about your views to see if we can learn something about him. Is that OK?'

'Go ahead.'

'All right, here's a question, would you say global warming is the biggest threat facing our country?'

'It might be.'

'Bigger than terrorism?'

'Is that a serious question?'

'Yes.'

Maria put on a perplexed face and said, 'Global warming will affect the whole earth.'

'Then why aren't we dealing with it?'

'Because it'll mean we have to change how we live. It could affect our lifestyles.'

'And we're too selfish to do that?'

'Maybe.'

Hosfleter nodded as though something had just been revealed to her that made a great deal of sense. She paused before saying slowly, 'You believe global warming has to be dealt with. There's no choice. So is anything we do to stop it from happening justified as long as it doesn't hurt people?'

'I thought you weren't going to bait me.'

'Maria, I'm not trying to bait you. I'm just thinking this through. I'm sorry.'

'Why don't we talk about Jack Gant? That's why I'm here.'

'I really want to know what you think we the people should do about global warming. It doesn't have to be a long answer.'

'OK, we should vote out those who pretend the science isn't in yet, so they can drive their big SUVs and justify what they're doing to their children. And then elect some realists. How's that for an answer? I like realists. I like people who make things happen.'

'Jack Gant may believe burning down a controversial condominium project is making things happen.'

'What do you want me to say?'

'Well, here's another way of looking at it. What do we do when a rich developer, who doesn't care about anything but making himself money, builds a condo project in a canyon with a fragile ecosystem in an area already running out of water anyway? I guess I'm asking if there are circumstances where setting a fire and burning a project is justified because it protects the earth?'

'OK, but I'm not in favor of setting arson fires.'

'You were Jack Gant's girlfriend. What did he see in you? What did you have in common? I'm trying to get at how he thinks. I'm not saying he influenced you. I'm trying to better see him through you. Does that make sense?'

'Not at all.'

The agent alongside Hosfleter chuckled and Hosfleter turned and glared at Marquez. She was looking at Marquez when she asked, 'What would he do if he knew you were here?'

'I don't think I want to know.'

'Does that mean you believe he's capable of violence?'

'I don't know.'

'I assume you know he was a Navy Seal and highly trained.'

'He didn't like to talk about it.'

'But you knew?'

'Yes.'

'Do you know he was in the first wave that went to Afghanistan? He was part of the hunt for Bin Laden at Tora Bora. He re-upped and after that he quit. His senior officers said he became disillusioned. He didn't believe we should have gone into Iraq. Have I said anything you don't already know?'

'I didn't know any of that. The times I asked he didn't want to talk about it. He didn't like to talk about his past.'

'Did he like to talk about the US government? How would you characterize his feelings toward the US government?'

'Angry.'

'Maria, we have information that leads us to believe he set the fire in Arizona. Did he ever talk to you about stopping developers by burning their projects?'

'No.'

'You need to be really sure about that. If it came out later that you knew something more, you could get charged. And I don't mean taking part in a plot, I mean knowing of its existence and not coming forward.'

'I've told you everything I know.'

Hosfleter tapped her pencil lightly on the table. She took time to choose her next words.

'We all send conscious and unconscious signals. We do it all the time. We're very social creatures at heart. That Jack said what he did to you about the island says to me that he felt he could confide in you. He may have communicated other plans consciously or unconsciously, and this is where I need you to really dig down and try to remember everything he said, or confided to you. But, I want to say first that I agree with you about global warming. It is our worst problem and the Arizona condominiums were very controversial because people felt they weren't environmentally responsible. There were lawsuits and many people today may be secretly thinking it's good that they burned. You might be thinking that. Your stepfather might. But the Arizona fire is probably sending up more gasses that cause global warming than the condos would have in a thousand years. You know, twenty per cent of the gasses contributing to global warming come from fires, clearing land, and forest fires.'

She leaned forward. She stopped lecturing and spoke as if Maria was the only other person in the room.

'I admire you for coming forward. If all I had was an overheard conversation and an offhand comment made on a boat, I don't know if I would put myself through this.'

She waved a self-deprecating hand at herself and the agent alongside.

'You may also have been in love and afraid now you're being unfair to him and blowing things out of proportion, but you're not. He set that fire, Maria. He's planning other operations and we're racing the clock. I need you to help me, right now, here in this room. We don't have a lot of time and you could save lives. Who else should we talk to? Give me some other names.'

Maria didn't have any other names. Hosfleter thanked her, but later that night after Gant's face showed on national news and the FBI announced a fugitive warrant naming him as wanted in connection with the fire bombing of the Wonder Rock Condominiums, Maria's name got leaked as a former girlfriend questioned today. It sounded as if she'd been picked up and brought in. It was unfair and a decision to sweat Maria, despite Maria having come forward. Marquez listened to the TV report and then called Carol Shauf.

'I'll meet you there tomorrow,' Shauf said. 'I'll borrow a DBEEP boat. See you around noon. Do you really think we can find this island?'

'I don't know, but I think we've got a better chance than anyone else.'

'You might have a short comeback as a Fed if you go poking into someone else's investigation.'

'They're coming after Maria.'

'See you tomorrow. Look for a DBEEP boat.'

FORTY-FIVE

The next morning as Marquez drove toward the delta he talked to his sister. Darcey asked, 'Do you remember when we were out of money and living in Berkeley in that trailer on that lot next to Mom's friend's house?'

'Sure, on Blake Street, it's hard to forget.'

'Mom's friend let us use that bathroom in the basement, only there was no shower so we had to wash in the sink or else go up to that lake in the park. What was the name of that lake?'

'Lake Anza. Good times.'

'Yeah, good times. It's why I've never had kids. Something happened last night that made me think about that summer and helping Dad sell dope on Telegraph Avenue. Mom had that little colored tape for the baggies and you and me and Dad would go up there after dark and he'd find clients and then send us to get the money and deliver the dope because we were still minors.'

'We were good at it.'

She laughed and said, 'No, we were great, especially you. But remember that night that weird guy led us down the street to his van. We were carrying the baggies and he was going to pay us at his van.'

'Durant Street toward the parking lot; there's a building there now.'

'We both knew that man was going to try to do something. Remember that feeling?'

'What brings this back?'

'Last night I started to go to my car after I locked up, and I just felt something was wrong, I don't know what. I park my car where I can see it from my office, and we don't have many problems like that here, but when I'm locking up late I'm more careful. I got that same feeling as that night in Berkeley, so I went back inside and sat up in the office with the lights out. I sat in my chair where I can look out the window and after awhile I fell asleep. When I woke up, I decided I was crazy. But when I looked outside, there was a man standing back behind the right rear of my car. It was like he stood up to stretch his legs. He must have been crouched down between a truck and my car.'

Her voice slowed now. She wanted him to register and remember what she was going to say next.

'He stood for a minute or two and then crouched down again and I called the state troopers. Before they got there he took off in a Jeep Cherokee, so I called the troopers back and told them he was leaving Seward. They pulled him over in Moose and he had two guns in the car with suppressors. Turns out he's wanted for a double murder in Georgia and the FBI agents up here think he's a hit man.'

'Have you got the agents' names?'

She had their cards and read off their names and phone numbers.

'I'll call them. Is there somebody who wants your restaurant?'

'You mean, like my partner hiring someone to kill me?'

'Yes.'

'Jesus, John, this is Seward, Alaska.'

She didn't have the fishing boat anymore and she'd never remarried, but she had a partner in the bar/restaurant and they

were doing enough business to get by and he had never heard
her talk about any strife with the partner. What he was going
to ask now was unfair to Darcey, but even after being sworn
in only yesterday, it was possible. Unlikely, but with a leak
with the Bureau, it was possible.

'Do you have some place outside of Seward where you
could stay?'

'Who would run the restaurant and bar?'

'Your partner.'

'John, I've got my dogs.'

'Take them with you.'

'You say it like it's easy. John, all I have for money is this
business.'

'I'll send you some money.'

'You'll send me some money? What are you talking about?
I'm supposed to go hide? Until when? Is it because of what
you're getting into?'

'It could be, Darcey, and I'm very sorry.'

'What does that mean, that you're sorry? You're crazy if
you think I can just pick up and go. Come on, John, is there
really somebody out there who would come all the way here
to hurt me because of something you're doing? I don't believe
that. People like that don't exist.'

'There is somebody and the task force I've joined is targeting
him.'

'OK, then I'll just leave everything and wait for you to tell
me when I can come back. When are you going to tell me that?'

He didn't have a good answer and he drove thinking about
what to do. The Sacramento River was off to his right, green
and smooth in the morning sun and he remembered Captain
Viguerra saying that there are a few men that you should never
go after unless you are prepared to give up everything you
love. Some will take it all from you to stop you. Viguerra had
brought his hands together slowly to demonstrate Miguel
Salazar crushing the skulls of his enemies, then said, 'But the
ones to fear will kill you from the inside out. They will find
out what you love and take it away. You will be alive still but
dead inside. These you can only fight if you have nothing to
lose.'

FORTY-SIX

Maria remembered the island as close to the Antioch Bridge, so he and Shauf worked slowly away from the bridge, island to island. They circled several and returned a third time to one. Shauf dropped him at a rotting dock and Marquez climbed up to a levee road where he found a fishing rod and a tin bucket with anchovies, but no fisherman. He walked the road looking down to his left at the island and watching on the other side in the trees and brush near the water for the fisherman. He figured it was someone was looking for catfish in the tules.

On the island side of the levee was an ancient apple orchard and falling-down sheds with corrugated metal siding. Even from here he could see someone had walked through the dry rye grass between the trees in the orchard to one of the sheds, and momentarily he considered hiking down, but they'd already been on the river four and a half hours and Shauf was ready to call it an afternoon. She needed to get the boat back. He studied the sheds out across the orchard, and then walked back to the rotted dock and Shauf's DBEEP boat.

On the way home he called Hosfleter and gave her the co-ordinates of three islands. Then he made another call and a stop in the town of El Cerrito where Alicia Guayas and her son, James, lived in an apartment just off the freeway. Maybe he stopped today because he felt the past returning. Alicia handed him a mug of rich Mexican hot chocolate with *canela* and frothed milk. A Telenova soap opera played on TV. She turned that off and their conversation turned first, as it always did, to family.

Alicia named James after his father, Jim Osiers, and he was like any other American kid that had grown up here. He sounded and acted like a typical American teenager, and Alicia expressed her worry that she was still illegal and that everything could come crashing down for James. Years ago, Marquez wrote letters for her to try to help her get legal status, but he didn't think she ever did anything with them. She was either afraid of being deported or blew it off.

On his last trip to Loreto in 1990 Marquez discovered that Alicia had gone north with the baby and crossed the border. It took him two more years to track her down in California and longer to get her to understand he didn't mean her any harm. He helped her out financially and she paid him back. She always insisted on paying him back. She worked two jobs and had never remarried. Her focus now was on James going to community college next year.

Beautiful Loreto with its sand and Sea of Cortez was just a tourism poster on her kitchen wall now. Sitting at her kitchen table he could hear the trucks going by on the freeway. The hot chocolate mug vibrated on the table when he set it down and stood to leave. He had asked new questions about Jim Osiers and after walking him to the door she said, 'For me, I just want to be here with my son. For you, the past is still alive, isn't it?'

When he got back on the road Katherine called and reported factually, but sounded very disturbed as she said, 'We got broken into today. When I got home the slider to the deck was open.'

'Where are you now?'

'In my car waiting for the police to get here. I didn't go in. Where are you?'

'Leaving El Cerrito. I stopped to talk to Alicia Guayas and I'm stuck in traffic now. It's going to take me forty minutes.'

'Here come the police.'

'Call me after you walk through.'

Katherine walked through with two police officers and couldn't find anything missing except a photo of Maria. The photo had been stripped from its frame and the frame dropped on the hardwood floor.

'Why would anybody do that? Who would do this? It can't be about getting her picture. They can get that from Facebook. So who is it, John? Who would do that?'

FORTY-SEVEN

Katherine loaded a carry-on suitcase with all the photos in the house of Maria. That included Maria's baby book. She locked those in her car trunk and then sat trembling on the front steps.

'I can't stay here tonight,' she said, and though he doubted the burglar would return and had already put the sliding door back in its track, Marquez said, 'We'll get a room.'

They didn't drive far, checking into the Best Western in Corte Madera, and then walked across the road to the Il Fornaio restaurant where they found an open table on a small patio off the bar. They ordered drinks and as they waited a waiter brought breadsticks.

'This happened tonight because you've joined this task force.'

'It could be anybody. It may have been some nut who saw Maria's face on TV last night as Gant's former girlfriend.'

'Then how did they find our house?'

Marquez didn't have an answer or any real theory yet. He shrugged. He poured his beer into the glass and thought Katherine was overreacting. He looked at her thinking he should cancel the motel room and they should head home.

'Are you going to say anything? Are you going to answer me or are you practicing your spy craft so you can trap Stoval?'

'Easy, Kath.'

'For years I've looked forward to the day when we wouldn't have to think about people trying to get even with you. I've looked forward to a normal life like other people have. But instead of that, now you're going to go after a monster. You haven't even really started yet, but already things are happening. Stoval knows he's a target and the FBI knows how dangerous he is, so they're not sending their agents. They're putting you out there like some hunting dog.'

'I was brought on to a task force. There are six others who've been working nothing but Stoval for almost a year.'

'Then why do they need you? And when exactly are we

going to have this normal life you've promised me and that I've waited for? Is that going to be when you're done locking up all of the people wiping out wildlife? What year should I look forward to, 2025, 2040? Or do I have to wait until the last wildlife is wiped out?'

She lowered her voice to a rushed whisper.

'You could disappear out there, just vanish because you've followed him into some jungle and he knows you're there. Then what, I sit by the phone and wait and your new FBI boss comes by and holds my hand and reassures me everything is going to be fine, that they're going to find you? I can hear him saying they've got forty agents looking for you. They're always looking for somebody and they don't find half of them.'

Her eyes glistened with tears and she formed a fist and hit the table.

'I'm so angry at you. This isn't some conniving diver up on the north coast trying to poach abalone. This is a monster and you know it. You left the DEA and got away from this type of person a long time ago. Now you're bringing the worst of the worst of human beings into our lives. How can you do that to us?'

'We're down to the wire with a lot of animal species—'

'Oh, please, spare me. I'm not going to listen to this tired speech. Get over it. The animals are all going away. The earth is going to be wall to wall with humans. It's already wall to wall and there are what, maybe three thousand wild tigers left? You do the math. Any idiot can see what's going to happen. On top of that the seas are going to rise a meter and an area the size of West Virginia is going to vanish from the United States, not to mention what's going to vanish from the rest of the world. This is about you and me and our lives. We don't have forever and you can't stop what's happening. They're raping places like the Galapagos Islands now for shark fin, so what chance do unprotected places have?' She stood up. 'I can't do this. I can't listen to you talk this way.'

Katherine pushed her chair back and left, and not through the front door, instead walked through the hedge surrounding the patio. He watched as she crossed the street and went into the motel. He stared out across the parking lot. When the waiter came back he ordered another beer.

'Is your wife coming back?'

'Not tonight.'

The waiter cleared her wine and left. He returned with the new beer and Marquez sat and listened to the freeway. He knew the odds were that Katherine was right. In the end there wouldn't be anything left. All the real complexity and mysterious beauty of earth would be gone and replaced by the things we made. He was pushing his marriage into a bad place. She vented tonight, but she was trying to reach him. She meant everything to him and yet he was willing to do this to her. What did that say about him? Nothing good.

Yet he held her close that night and early the next morning they went home. Katherine drove into San Francisco for an early meeting as he tinkered with the slider, opening and shutting it, checking the lock, and then walking out on to the deck. Boards creaked underfoot, but it was otherwise quiet. He smelled the trees and brush downslope wet from the fog and went down the stairs and walked along the house to the corner, looking for footprints there and in the redwoods leading out to the street. He didn't find any.

Marriage is a promise made to another and in Katherine's anger was a plea for fairness. He heard that. He understood her frustration. He locked up the house, drove down off the mountain, and was still thinking about Katherine as he crossed into San Francisco. He was on Van Ness Street when he learned about it by turning on the radio.

Two out of three Californians depended on water from the Sacramento/San Joaquin Delta. So much depended on the delta pumps that damage estimates were already running in the tens of billions. The rivers feeding the delta would run to sea again until this was repaired. The judge, who two years ago ordered the pumps shut down as fish counts plummeted, wouldn't need to issue another ruling anytime soon, and a small band of environmentalists had formed an impromptu parade down Market Street in San Francisco.

A local reporter was on the scene at the pumping stations near Tracy and she was doing her best with the information she had so far, but it was sketchy and confused and the early information got repeated and repeated. Still, you could hear in her voice that this was the big story of her career and she knew it.

'Significant pieces of two major pumps supplying water to

southern and central California have been severely damaged this morning in explosions that may be terrorist related.'

The report was live and as he worked through the different stations word seemed to be getting out that the FBI had some prior knowledge, though no one at the Bureau was commenting yet. Marquez clicked the radio back to the first station.

'Patty, are the pumps shut down?'

'Yes, and I'm hearing that the damage is extensive, but they don't know how extensive yet.'

'Was anyone hurt?'

'Bob, we're not hearing any reports of any injuries.'

'Is the FBI calling this a terrorist act? Does this mean Al-Qaeda?'

'It could mean that, Bob. We don't know yet. We're waiting for more information now, and at this point we can only say that whoever is behind it is endangering thousands if not millions of people.'

'Thank you, Patty, and we'll stay with this live throughout the day. For those of you who haven't heard yet, terrorism reached California this morning . . .'

Marquez clicked the radio off, took the call from Desault.

'Where are you?'

'On my way in, I just heard the news.'

'Jane Hosfleter is looking for you. You got the right island.'

'I gave her three islands.'

'Well, it's the one with the apple orchards that you emphasized and she's there now. They found a shed where he assembled what they think were very sophisticated self-propelled mines. Think missile underwater with onboard GPS guidance. The first mines blew the grills over the pumping stations and the follow-up mines blew the pumps. The Navy disarmed one that didn't detonate and they've pulled it out of the water.'

Marquez called and left a message for Hosfleter. She called back fifteen minutes later and he learned more about the unexploded mine. She wanted to meet with him and she wanted to talk to Maria immediately.

'How do I reach her?'

'Let me see if I can get her for you. I'll call her right now.'

Maria picked up on the first ring. 'Jack did it,' she said. 'I bet they have other things planned.'

'Did he talk about anything else?'

'No.'

'Call Hosfleter.'

'OK, I will.'

Governor Schwarzenegger was on his way to the pumping stations, as was an elite Navy team of divers and dozens more FBI agents. In the San Francisco Field Office agents watched CNN in the conference room, but Marquez and Desault moved to where they could talk.

'The design for these torpedoes probably came off the Net,' Desault said. 'Nowadays, you buy everything like this online. Our friend Stoval has sold US military blueprints to several countries. Through a wealthy Chinese businessman he employs a team of hackers in central Asia and another in Taiwan. You hack into the right computer and you'll find plenty of buyers out there. Plans for the current US military helicopters got hacked into and forwarded to Taiwan, and then probably on to China. Shit is flying all around the world over the Internet.'

He shook his head.

'This is a sophisticated terrorist event. What they found on the island is forward-thinking prototype stuff the military couldn't figure out how to get into production. This isn't two guys with bad teeth mixing fertilizer and diesel out back in the barn. This is money, connections, skill, training, the whole ball of wax.'

Marquez left for the delta a few minutes later. He was nowhere near a TV when the website went up. He was with Hosfleter. They heard it on a car radio, sat in the car and listened together.

FORTY-EIGHT

'*T*wo hundred thirty-four years ago in Boston a tea party got thrown for a government that wouldn't listen to the people. We claim and accept responsibility for the fire at the Wonder Rock Condominium Complex and for the Tracy Pumping Station bombing. We will continue acts of violence against property aimed at bringing down those who*

have turned America into a country whose morals are based
on economics. This is a revolution of values. This is a start
of the Second American Revolution.

  'The entrenched powers will label us terrorists, but our goal
is to return the United States to the principles on which it was
founded. We believe in the Founders. We believe the issues
confronting the United States of America are so significant
they can no longer be left to politicians and those who stand
to profit from the status quo. We believe it is urgent to combat
global warming. We believe it is urgent that America move
away from further military-industrialization and relentless
conspicuous consumption. We believe if the People act the
government will follow. We believe the time of debate has
passed and the time of action has arrived.'

All major media had simultaneously received the same
email with the website address. In minutes it bounced around
the world, but it carried a personal immediacy for Marquez
and Hosfleter. He walked the island with her, showed her the
rotting dock where he and Shauf pulled in with the DBEEP
boat and where he'd found the bucket of bait and the fishing
pole. From the top of the levee he saw all the vehicles parked
in the apple orchard and the crime tape perimeter around the
shed. The trail through the dry rye grass had long since been
trampled.

'Is this water running free a good thing for the delta?'
Hosfleter asked. 'Is it good for the river systems, the wildlife,
the fish, all that?'

'Sure.'

'Are you secretly glad nature has been liberated?'

'Do you really want to do this?'

'I'm just asking.' She held out her hands. 'It's done. There's
nothing we can do and now the rivers will all run to the sea
again and all that crap. Excuse me, the water will flush out
the delta and save the midget fish whose name I can't remember
and the salmon which I do remember because I love to eat
them. I'm just asking what you really feel, coming over from
Fish and Game, and all.'

'You're not asking anything, you're making a statement.'

Gutierrez had sworn him in this morning with Desault
standing behind him. It took less than five minutes. His new
creds and passport were with him and Hosfleter probably

knew that. Maybe it made her angry. Maybe she believed
Maria knew more and he was coaching her. Or she was
frustrated to get to the island too late and blamed him. Either
way, she had crossed a line.

'I am coming over from Fish and Game, and it's tempo-
rary, but what you might not know is that I was a Federal
agent once before, right about the time you were lying in bed
hoping you'd get the third grade teacher you wanted. My
career has been in law enforcement and one thing I swore I'd
never do is be a Fed again. But here I am.' He offered his
hand. 'Good luck. I'm not sure we'll be meeting up again.'

'Marquez, wait, don't go yet, and I apologize, I'm sorry.
I'm frustrated. The National Security Agency came close to
tracking our tipster's email, but it turns out he has very sophisticated computer defenses that detected the probes and he's
gone quiet. He's gone, probably forever, and I don't know
where to look for Gant next.'

None of what she'd just said made much sense to him. He
knew someone tipped the FBI to a San Francisco link that
included Gant, but that was about it.

She continued.

'Gant scares me. Truly scares me. Come look at what's in
these sheds. Let me show you why we need to find this guy
and now. I know Maria is not involved. I do know. But come
look at why I'm leaning on her for help, and don't get me
wrong about you. I've got nothing but respect for you signing
on with the task force. Please come look.' She paused. 'I'm
really asking because I need help. I don't know where they're
going to hit next.'

FORTY-NINE

'Ever think about Jim Osiers anymore?' Sheryl Javits
asked when she called him that night. She sounded like
she'd been drinking. He was reading Stoval files and
stepped away from them to talk with her. Desault's idea of
taking Stoval down on animal trafficking charges or illegal
trophy hunting had gotten a tepid response from the rest of

the task force and skepticism from himself initially, but the
more he learned the more it seemed possible. Katherine was
in San Francisco at dinner with Maria so he'd read into the
night and he was seeing patterns in Stoval's habits. He felt
the first thread of excitement and got how Desault came up
with the animal angle.

There were gaps in the reports, but also stretches where
they knew where Stoval hunted grizzly in Siberia and Canada,
and a recent entry suggesting he might have been in Alaska
with a Chinese businessman named Xian Liu. The files had
sketchy info on legal boar hunts in Italy in September, repeated
visits to a bird market in Mexico City, details on a trawler
owned and sailed under a Liberian flag and working off the
north coast of Africa catching illegal tuna to feed the EU
markets, and a lot of wing hunting of the kind Billy Takado
had talked about.

Stoval owned thousands of acres south of Bariloche. He
had residences in Argentina, Capri, Barcelona, London, Hong
Kong, Zurich, and Cape Town. He had pieces of hotels and
of hunting preserves in Africa, Chile, and Poland. He was
building a new residence in Mexico on the Baja peninsula.
But if there was a pattern it was that every month or so he
got himself out in open country and hunted.

Sheryl's call disrupted his concentration and he talked
reluctantly at first. Then, as she revealed more, he listened
closely.

'I should have told you before now. I don't know why I
didn't, except that I thought it would all go away. I'm being
investigated by Internal Affairs. Jim Osiers' oldest son, Daren,
persuaded them to reopen the investigation. Daren went to
work for the DEA five or six years ago. He's out of San Diego.
He's got a theory going where the La Paz bank account was
mine and that I framed Jim.'

'You're kidding.'

'No, really, he got his SAC to persuade Internal Affairs to
reopen an investigation and Internal Affairs up here has interviewed me three times this week. The agent in charge is a
woman named Beth Murkowski. You may hear from her as
early as tomorrow. She's got a story Rayman fed Daren Osiers
about me taking bribe money to pass information to the
Salazars. He claims he helped feed information to the Mex

Feds and frame Jim Osiers and now with the Salazar brothers dead he's free to tell the truth.'

She exhaled and muttered something he couldn't hear.

'Another thing you don't know is that I went to several of Rayman's parole hearings after he'd served most of his sentence for the KZ Nuts deal. He was a model prisoner and they were thinking of letting him out early, but I fought it because I always thought he had something to do with Jim getting killed. I wanted him to do his full sentence.'

'Did he?'

'Yes, I made sure. So he's got it out for me.'

That last didn't quite ring true and Marquez sat down. He jotted *Beth Murkowski* on the pad where he'd made Stoval notes. He wrote *Rayman* underneath it.

Marquez remembered the three Osiers boys at the funeral. The oldest, Daren, had looked the most like Jim and was dressed in a black suit too small for him. Unlike the other two boys he'd held his grief inside. It was Daren that Marquez had given the letter and flowers to at the Osiers' front door. Clea, Jim's wife, hadn't come to the door, and later Marquez learned that Clea believed that he and the rest of Group 5 had known about Jim's girlfriend in Loreto and that he'd assigned Jim there so he could be with her. She wouldn't talk to him at the memorial service and he understood. He tried six months later and there was no response, but he would never hold that against her.

'Supposedly, I used Jim's face and a fake ID and the banker did what he was told to do by the Salazars. I was the woman behind the fake man. Funds went from the La Paz bank account to a fictitious corporation called ALCRON that was really me in an offshore account.'

'A-L-C-R-O-N?'

'That's right.'

'Sounds like an insecticide.'

She drew a deep breath and from her voice he knew there was something else, another reason why she was calling tonight.

'I got grilled a couple of days ago on how I afforded the down payment on my house in San Francisco. I told them the truth; I got the money from my ex-husband when we divorced. I got it from Pete. It has nothing to do with Group Five, the DEA, or anything that happened eighteen years ago.'

'How much money?'

'Two hundred thousand dollars.'

'They must have asked Pete Phelps. He's not denying he gave you the money, is he?'

'He is and he signed an affidavit. He lied.'

Sheryl did something he'd never heard her do. She choked up and wept, wracking sobs that the phone carried easily.

'I married him,' she eventually got out. 'I've made such a mess of my life. I've made such a mess. I'll call you tomorrow.'

She hung up.

FIFTY

Sheryl called the next morning and Beth Murkowski, the agent from DEA Internal Affairs that Sheryl called Murky, showed up with another DEA agent in tow. Murkowski didn't come to his house. She came instead to the FBI San Francisco Field Office. That she came here surprised Marquez and made him wonder if the DEA had a tail on him, or a phone tap in anticipation of Sheryl's arrest.

Murkowski stood about six foot two with pale blue eyes and a hard face. The male agent's name Marquez didn't catch and didn't need to. He was there to carry her briefcase. In a conference room Murkowski laid it out for him in a very deliberate voice.

'The Mexican Federal Judicial Police have turned over previously withheld documents to the US State Department. Copies of those documents are in my possession. I'm going to show them to you. I don't have any problem showing them to you, but I'd like to record your answers if that's all right with you.'

'That's fine.'

The male agent placed a tape recorder on the table.

'We're going back to 1989 to the bull ring.' She watched his eyes as she said that. 'This is the testimony of a Tijuana police officer who was in the bull ring when you were there.'

She slid it over and as Marquez picked up the Mex Fed document it felt for a moment as if he was in the Cadillac again, rolling through the dusty lot with Billy sitting next to him.

'There's a translated copy underneath the one on top.'

'I can read this one.'

'Agents at the San Diego Field Office discovered that your former SAC, Jay Holsten, suppressed information that the Mexican Federal Judicial Police had provided the DEA. He buried it or destroyed it, but the Mexicans kept their own records. This is a copy they made from their records. Agent Marquez, if this account is accurate you made a choice in the bull ring about your future.'

'You're right, it was a big day, and a sad one.'

'It's going to get sadder, I think, but you may feel better when it's over.'

Marquez didn't answer that and read the Spanish account rather than the translated. When he finished he laid it down and asked, 'Where do you want to start?'

'With Sheryl Javits, ALCRON, the money in the La Paz bank account, and how Jim Osiers got framed. If you help us, I can pretty well guarantee you'll get a deal.'

'I don't need any deal,' he said quietly, 'and I've made plenty of mistakes myself in investigations. I have to tell you you're making one now.'

Marquez had been part of operations where a few early conclusions cascaded into a series of mistakes. He'd been in her shoes. He knew how it could go. You get going the wrong way and everything seems to fit and you get more and more pumped up as you build to a confrontation like this.

They went through his version now, the bull ring, the drive back with Billy's body, the copies of the Fed form, the 52s, and Jim Osiers' murder. She slid him another document, a signed statement by the same Tijuana cop, as well as one from a Mex Fed who had witnessed Marquez meet Miguel Salazar outside a restaurant in Tijuana.

'It wasn't a meeting and it cost me my career. You could check that with my former SAC, Jay Holsten.'

'Your former SAC is in a nursing home with Alzheimer's. He can't remember his name or how to use a toilet.'

Now she handed him her final document, or at least the last of what she'd brought with her. This one got his interest, a single page with all lines blacked-out except for a lone paragraph at the bottom. Someone had written the word *Stoval* in blue ink at the top of the page. Marquez's guess was that this page was a CIA document passed to her through the State Department. That could mean someone wanted her to have it. Maybe Kerry Anderson could explain that to him. The paragraph at the bottom recounted a bull ring meeting between Miguel Salazar and the DEA agent the Salazars paid to deliver Billy Takado to them.

'Emrahain Stoval gave that account to a CIA officer eight years ago. I know you're on a Stoval task force and I'm very clear who Stoval is, but as you also know, he has a relationship with the CIA. Regardless of what anyone thinks about that relationship, it exists. What you're holding in your hand is his testimony. Tell me why he would lie.'

'Tell me why he wouldn't.'

She didn't really like the look of the document any more than he did and he doubted she believed in it because as soon as he laid the document down she switched abruptly to talking about Jim Osiers. Still, the blacked-out page lay on the table as another layer. It troubled him.

'You went to Loreto in 1990 looking for Alicia Guayas.'

'That's true, I did, but I didn't find her and I learned later she'd gone north and crossed the border.'

'We have reason to believe you murdered Alicia Guayas and dumped her body in the Sea of Cortez in May 1990.'

'You don't stop, do you?' Marquez turned and looked at the other agent. 'You two came here believing I murdered Alicia?'

'You went back to Loreto and you found her.'

'I went back but I didn't find her. I found her in California later and she's not dead. She lives here in the Bay Area and I still see her about once a month. Her son lives with her.'

'Where? Give me an address.'

'She's not legal. She never took the steps. I'm not ready to give you an address.'

Murkowski had to think awhile on that one. She had several options including going to the SAC here and requesting that he get Alicia Guayas' address from Marquez. Instead, she demanded, 'Are you in a relationship with her?'

'As in an affair, no, and my wife knows her. Alicia and her son have been to our house for dinner.'

'Why?'

Marquez understood what she was asking. 'It's complicated, but let's say I have always believed that Jim Osiers may have been innocent. I saw his body. I made the identification. Miguel Salazar tortured him.'

The agent next to her snorted and said, 'You knew ahead of time he was in the truck outside the Field Office.'

Marquez glanced at him, but spoke to Murkowski after reaching and tapping the first document she'd slid at him.

'There were two cartel guards in the bull ring, both with AK-47s. One was a Tijuana cop Billy recognized.' He held her eye and acknowledged her work. 'I see how you got there.'

He did see it. She stepped out of the room now with her assistant and Marquez picked up his cell and scrolled down to the address book. He found Alicia's phone number. Murkowski walked back in just as Alicia answered. An hour later Murkowski stood in Alicia's apartment looking at a photo of Alicia retrieved from her bedroom. In the photo she was young and Osiers looked trim and fit standing alongside her. Behind them was the Sea of Cortez. Osiers was smiling. He was a month from dying. Alicia cradled the framed photo as Murkowski studied it.

Marquez watched her change as she talked to Alicia. They were there two hours and outside she allowed she'd made mistakes, but took a parting shot before getting in her car.

'If you interfere at all with my investigation of Sheryl Javits, you're going to end up with an obstruction charge. I'll give you my word on that. Is that clear enough?'

FIFTY-ONE

Early the next morning Marquez flew into LAX and then drove to Venice. He walked into the Rose Café a little after 9:00 and told the hostess, 'I'm looking for a friend.' Without missing a beat, she answered, 'So am I.'

They both laughed and she led him to a table outside under a covered area where Raymond Mendoza aka Rayman sat alone with an omelet and a plate of toast. He wore a leather cowboy hat, a long-sleeved black T-shirt, jeans, and sandals. He looked like an artist.

'Rayman.'

'Hey man, what's going on, long time.'

There were no handshakes, smiles or pretense of liking each other, no pretending that they were both just living their lives doing their thing. Marquez slid one of the plastic chairs back and sat down. Rayman took another bite of omelet and spread jelly on a piece of toast. Sheryl didn't know whether Rayman knew yet about Holsing, but said use the information with Rayman if you need to, and Marquez dropped it right on him now.

'They found Holsing's body last night.'

Rayman briefly put his toast down, then reconsidered and took another bite as Marquez guessed he already knew Holsing was dead.

'Do you want to know where he was found and how he died?'

Rayman, mouth full of toast, shook his head, no.

'I need you to pass a message to Stoval for me. It's personal.'

Rayman's face had filled out and his eyes sat back in it, coal black, watchful, the student who studied economics in college still back there somewhere, the guy who did a ten spot in prison watching him.

'The message is that if anything happens to anyone in my family I'm going to quit my job and hunt Stoval until I find him. The message is this time I won't stop. Pass it up the chain. It'll get there.'

'I'm not in the biz anymore. I did ten years in prison.'

'From what I know about him he wouldn't want you to sit on the message. But that's your decision to make. Do you want me to try somebody else and tell them I tried you and you refused to pass the message on?'

'You don't want to send that message, man.'

Rayman ate some more and then got agitated. He pushed the plate away and waved the waitress off as she tried to refill his coffee. He pulled his wallet out to pay as Marquez asked, 'After you made that phone call eighteen years ago and gave Sheryl the tip that the Salazars were going to rip off a load, who did you call next?'

'Miguel.'

'Miguel Salazar?'

'Yeah, man, Miguel Salazar. Who else would I call?' He belched and laid a twenty dollar bill on the table. 'I was working for him.'

'Jim Osiers got set up.'

Now Rayman smiled. 'The bitch is in trouble, isn't she? It's why you're here. She came to my parole hearings and fucked with me and now she's going to get hers. I'm talking to the DEA, I'm out with it, man. I've told them how the Salazars made me lie.'

'Who else did you call that night?'

'No one.'

'Yeah, you called Miguel and you made at least one other call, didn't you? Then you figured it was a done deal. You disappeared back across the California border. But it didn't end there and it was still waiting for you when you walked out of prison. It's waiting for you now.'

'I don't know what you're talking about. I can't follow your crap.'

'What happened has to be answered for. Pass that on to Stoval. Tell him I said it's not over for him either.'

'You're like a prophet, man. You're like this crazy dude who lives down the street from me and dresses like Jesus. He knows all about the future because he reads the Bible. Is that what you read?' Rayman leaned forward, his bloated face hovering over the table. 'Fuck you, Marquez.'

Marquez stood. He tucked the chair back in.

'Pass the message on, Rayman.'

FIFTY-TWO

'Stoval is in Indonesia,' Desault said. 'Have you ever heard of the Pramuka Market in East Jakarta?'

Marquez looked through the slider out toward the dark of the ocean and knew this was the call.

'I've been there,' he said. 'I once rode along on a raid there, but it was all a big joke. Everyone was in on it but me. They set up these raids for illegal trade in endangered animals and

I learned later they tip off the traders first, so the traders either don't show up or leave the illegal animals at home. We were zeroing in on four people in LA who were bringing in orangutans and selling them for thirty thousand dollars each. They'd buy them for nothing and then ship a half dozen babies hoping one or two would survive the trip.'

'Stoval got there last night. His jet is in Jakarta. If he flies out of Jakarta we'll get some help tracking the flight, but you could be landing and taking off again. You could be coming right back home.'

'I get it.'

And that's what happened. Stoval flew out when Marquez was still in the air. Marquez got the word when he landed, but still went out to see the Pramuka Market, see if anything had changed. Not much had. It was still about the size of a football field and packed with animals that were terrified and for the most part marked for death. He walked through aisles with a pair of men trailing him as he took photos without buying. But no one bothered him and he spent a day there before returning to Jakarta. When he flew home Katherine gave this first run her appraisal.

'The Airborne Agent returns,' she said and handed him coffee. She sat down across from him. As she did her robe fell open and she asked, 'Did you miss me?'

'I always miss you.'

'How was your trip?'

'It was a long flight.'

'Was it worth it?'

'No.'

'Who gets the airline miles?'

'We do.'

'You and the Feds, or you and me?'

'When I say we, I always mean you and me.'

'I've been wondering about that.' More of her robe slid open. 'Did you see any new sights?'

'I went to the animal market in Pramuka. If anything, it's a little bigger.'

'Long way to go to look at a market, isn't it?'

'It was.'

'Do you know what I think?'

She was going to tell him either way. The belt holding her

robe at the waist came undone and on one side her robe fell open. Her nipples were a dark brown-red, her breasts a creamy white. He looked at the curve of her belly as she looked at him and then reached and touched smooth skin. He ran his fingers along the curve of her and then took a drink of coffee with the sound of the plane's engines still in his head.

'You're never going to stop doing this, not until you retire. That's what I think.'

She sat down on his thighs, robe sweeping open, legs straddling him. He kissed the breast nearest him. Some hard things had gotten said in the past week and more probably would, but they were talking and both knew if they kept talking there was a way through. He reached and drew her close, and they made love and fell asleep.

When they woke they took a walk up on Mount Tamalpais out a trail that cut across an open slope of grass brown and dry with fall. Earlier there was fog, but the fog was gone and blue sky was laced with strands of cirrus clouds. It was warm on the sun-hard trail with the smells of the dry grass and oak and the salt in the wind off the ocean. They left the trail, went down to a nearly flat spot between the trees where long ago after separating and nearly divorcing they had sat and talked their way through.

The conversation today was nothing like that day, but it was right to come here. From this spot you could look north to Point Reyes and down at the curving sand of Stinson Beach and trace that crescent to Bolinas and the tide running out of the lagoon. Katherine's warm hand touched his and he took her hand in his and the certainty and anger dimmed a little. This choice of his had hurt her. There was no getting away from that.

'It's about everything I've ever done,' he said.

'That's the sort of drama I'm afraid will get you killed. If you do get killed I'll be angry at you for the rest of my life. I'll flush your ashes down a toilet. I want to have fun with you. I want to have time together. We've gone a lot of years with too much time apart and if the new deal is running around the world chasing bad guys and calling me from unpronounceable places, then it's hard to see when we're going to get that time. I know why you're doing it and I know I'll never love anyone like I love you, but I need you to answer something for me, and I don't want the answer today. This is my question. What is it in you that lets you risk everything we have? Not today, not here, but I need to know. I need you to tell me.'

FIFTY-THREE

'Well, so that was our first round,' Desault said, as they talked on the phone. 'There's going to be some of that, and I'm sure you've thought about it.'

This was cheerleading. This was having a direct supervisor, but that was part of the deal and he was getting a feel for Desault. He liked Desault's candor and that he wasn't afraid to take a chance. They talked over the Indonesia trip and how much the world had shrunk since they both had started in law enforcement. Marquez had thought plenty about that on the ride home. A decade ago he chased poachers into Oregon or Nevada or tried to cut off poached abalone coming in from Mexico, but now they talked in terms of shipping points and global routes.

As Desault revisited Stoval's bighorn hunt and the failure to apprehend him in Vegas, Marquez's thoughts floated back to the nineteenth century when skin hunters in the US slaughtered the great herds of buffalo, antelope, and bighorn. A naturalist named Ernest Thompson Seton recorded it. He watched species that once had no fear of man taken to near extinction, but he couldn't do anything to slow it. It took the Lacey Act of 1900 to do that. Seton wrote that the bighorn had no fear of man in those days. He wrote that we have to acknowledge that animals have rights. He meant the right to exist and have habitat. He wrote stories about animals to try to make his point, to try to bridge the disconnect. He wrote about an angel of the wild, a guardian that watched over the wild creatures, and if they ever needed one it was now as we crossed another threshold of extinctions with more or less the same excuses, the same fear that giving animals space risks necessary economic development of increasingly scarce resources. In truth, it risked something more threatening than that. It risked changing our view of how we inhabit the world.

On the flight home from Indonesia Marquez turned off the overhead light and around him most in the half-full business section were sleeping. Many had their window shades down. The engines thrummed, but the cabin was still. The long trip was a failure, yet he had made something of it by going to the Pramuka Market and taking in the scale again, the systematic marketing of life, the stacked cages.

It was an opportunity Desault had given him. It was a small window barely open, an idea forming. He felt in his coat for the maroon passport, took it out and held it in his hand for several minutes, gripping it like a ticket not to be dropped, and in some new way it was. Desault used the old-school slang name, redback, for the passport, and like him, Desault was long into a law enforcement career and trying to adapt to a changing world where criminals had gone global. This passport symbolized a new opportunity, one Marquez knew wouldn't come for him again.

He had to make everything of the moment. Some inward fire relit in him as he walked the Pramuka Market. He did not see the way yet, but he knew this was his last best chance to make a difference.

'We scoured Vegas looking for Stoval,' Desault said. 'We put effort into it. We ran that alias, Patrick Maitland, through everything and everybody.'

And they did the same in Alaska and believed they had a bush pilot with a sideline helicopter scenic tour business, who had yet another sideline that was bear hunting from the copter. In Phoenix there was a credit card used in the name of Patrick Maitland, and again in Houston, and from informants there, whispers of Stoval meeting with Zetas in Texas.

'He may have come back through California and he may have returned to California again recently. We had a call this morning that he's here, right now.'

'That's where you're going with this?'

'Yes. I'm wondering if there's a hunting reason he'd return to California. He wouldn't be after more bighorn, would he?'

'No.'

'You can't think of anything?'

'Not offhand.'

'Are you on your way in?'

'Yeah, I'll see you soon, and I've got to tell you something,

Ted. I passed a message through Rayman yesterday. I want Stoval to know that if anything happens to anyone in my family, I'll turn in my badge and then I'll be coming for him.'

'You told that to Raymond Mendoza?'

'I asked him to pass it on.'

Desault muttered something he couldn't hear and hung up.

FIFTY-FOUR

S toval knew of Rayman. He knew what Raymond Mendoza looked like and could name nearly everyone he had ever met. He'd never met this man, Rayman, who worked clubs in LA for the Salazar brothers and was now part of the reorg and new network. Mendoza was responsible for overseeing the management and harvest of a handful of grow fields in California. He was in charge of the field where the game warden was shot. He was smart, but not bright, and had it been his decision, after the game warden Stoval would have made Mendoza disappear. But though he was heavily invested the low level management decisions were not his call. Mendoza wasn't his to worry about, at least not until now.

Raymond Mendoza was the man John Marquez chose to deliver a message and for that reason Stoval chose to meet with him. He needed to know why Marquez chose him, but now having sat with Mendoza for twenty minutes he was convinced there was nothing special about this man. They were along the coast highway coming through Malibu in Rayman's black Hummer, a vehicle that was large for the road and drew unnecessary attention. He listened to Mendoza's patter, the false earnestness about wanting to do more and move up in the organization, and then cut him off.

'I don't make those decisions and want you to stop talking about yourself. Tell me where you first met John Marquez.'

'In Baja.'

'Where and when in Baja?'

The man shouldn't be running anything, Stoval thought. He was a self-absorbed idiot.

'I met him in Loreto. I was the contact with the DEA for the Salazars. He was the one in charge when Miguel killed the DEA agent.'

'Marquez trusts you.'

'No, man, no, he is afraid of me. He hates me, but he thought I would be able to know how to reach you. He thought I could get the message to you.'

'But you hadn't ever met me.'

'No, I know, I told him.'

'Listen to me and then repeat back what I say to you.'

'OK.'

'You passed the message on to the people you work for and that's all you know. You didn't meet with me today.'

'Oh, OK, that's what I tell Marquez?'

'You've never seen me.'

'Right.'

'Repeat what I just said.' Stoval listened and then said, 'Pull over, here. I'm going to borrow your vehicle.'

'What do you mean, man?'

'I'm borrowing your vehicle.'

Mendoza was slow. It took him another several seconds to pull over. Then he stalled leaving.

'When will I get my Hummer back?'

'I don't know yet.'

Stoval smiled at him and adjusted the seat as Mendoza blinked in the sunlight on the road shoulder. Like a stray dog he'd have to be careful crossing the highway. Stoval pulled back on to the highway. In his rear view mirror he saw Mendoza run across the road and smiled as a pickup nearly hit him. Mendoza was worried about losing his Hummer, but soon enough he'd wish he'd never owned it.

FIFTY-FIVE

Sheryl ordered two glasses of red wine, Marquez a Corona. The waitress looked puzzled and asked Sheryl, 'Two glasses?'

Sheryl held up two fingers and as the waitress left, said,

'They've gone to my bank, the credit card companies, my neighbors, and not only are they prying into my life in any way they can, they expect me to remember every day I was ever in Mexico. They want me to remember in detail things that happened eighteen years ago. I can't remember to get milk at the grocery store unless I write it on a Post-it and stick it on my dashboard. How am I going to remember what happened in Baja in 1989?'

She looked away from him before adding, 'I'm about to get put on paid leave. My DEA career is over and I don't have anything else to go to. What am I going to do?'

By the time the wine arrived Sheryl's hands were shaking and her face had paled. The last week had visibly aged her. He watched her take a sip of wine and could hear Desault saying, 'John, there's a possibility she links to Stoval.'

'It's what I told you the other night, they went back to Pete. He showed them the checks written as part of the divorce settlement, and then agreed to sign an affidavit swearing there was no other money. But there was other money. He paid me the rest of the divorce settlement on the side. The settlement was as fucked-up as our marriage.'

'So that money was the money you used for your house down payment here.'

'Yes.'

'You never declared the money?'

She didn't want to say it aloud. She nodded. Marquez got it now. Murkowski alleged that Sheryl's down payment on the house came from bribe money.

'When does Murkowski think you got this bribe money?'

'She goes all the way back to the Salazar Cartel or Stoval paying me via deposits made into the La Paz bank that Jim Osiers got tagged with. Then I hid the money offshore in that ALCRON account she told you about.'

'You hid it for years until you bought the house?'

'That's right.'

'OK, back to Phelps, where did a guy with an ATF agent's salary get four hundred thousand dollars he could split with you?'

'From a real estate deal he did with his brother and two sisters after their parents died. I don't know any of the details of the deal, so don't ask me.'

'Come on, Sheryl, don't say that. Don't tell me you took it without knowing where it came from. Tell me some rich uncle died and was sleeping on a mattress stuffed with hundred dollar bills, and taxes were paid on it fifty years ago. But don't tell me the Phelps I knew gave you a big chunk of cash and you don't really know the details of where it came from, other than it was some real estate deal with siblings. That's just not good enough.'

'That's what happened. The real estate was before me, before we married. It wasn't money I was entitled to, but he bragged about it for too long and I was that angry. I wanted him to hurt. I wanted half and I told him I'd hire private investigators if he didn't come across. I told him I'd go to the IRS and give them a statement.'

'What statement could you give them if you didn't know anything about the real estate deal?'

'I knew enough about it and I knew about him and his crooked siblings. I knew he'd split it with me if I pushed him hard enough. And that's what happened. We met at a bar on the marina one night when our divorce lawyers were still going at it, and he brought his shitty old gym bag filled with money.'

'Cash?'

'Yes.'

'What kind of real estate deal did that come from?'

'A back door deal in property the siblings inherited. They swapped property with some Chinese guy and part of the deal was cash so they could dodge capital gains. The Chinese guy ended up with some site he had to clean benzene out of. They screwed him.'

He paid you because he knew if you took it, you were in, Marquez thought. You wouldn't have any way to back out later. Marquez looked at her and knew he'd always wondered how she pulled off the San Francisco house. She was a saver and he'd figured she had finally saved enough. Everything he was hearing now disappointed him and suddenly he was unsure what to believe.

'This might sound crazy, John, but I was thinking I'd been married to him for two and a half years and that was worth something. I remember sitting with a calculator dividing thirty months into two hundred thousand dollars. I still remember

the number because it's like the mark of the devil or something
– six thousand six hundred sixty-six dollars and sixty-six cents
per month of marriage. I did it over and over because I kept
thinking that's not enough money for what I went through.
Not for cleaning up after him and sleeping with him, and
the whole thing with his lies. He was such a scuzzball that
finally I thought just do it, make him hurt, make him split
his secret stash, then call it a divorce and walk away. I promised to take myself on a great vacation and I did. I went to
Hawaii for ten days. That's another thing they're looking
into now. Murky was here yesterday asking who I met with
in Hawaii.'

Marquez absorbed that for a moment and then his phone
buzzed again. It was Desault calling for the third time in five
minutes.

'I'm going to have to take this.' But he didn't answer the
phone yet. He asked, 'So it's just your word against Pete
Phelps?'

'Yes, and he's already denied that it ever happened.'

'Where's he living?'

'He remarried. He's in San Diego selling real estate.'

'Do you have an address?'

'In my briefcase in the car.'

'If you get it for me, I'll go see him.'

She left to get it and he called Desault back.

'Jack Gant got recognized at a convenience store by a clerk
in South Lake Tahoe. The clerk didn't put it together until
after he left so doesn't know what direction he drove, but
we've got a make and model on a pickup and video from the
store. It's confirmed. It was Gant.'

'When was this?'

'About two hours ago. Didn't you say your daughter is in
the mountains?'

'She is, but well south of Tahoe. She's in Yosemite hiking
with friends.'

'Can you get ahold of her?'

'I'll try.'

'Find out where she is and we'll get agents to her. For all
we know, Gant is after her.'

He hung up with Desault as Sheryl returned with Phelps'
address and phone numbers written on a piece of lined paper.

She handed it to him and said, 'I am so sorry and so ashamed, but you have to believe me. Everything I told you is true.'

FIFTY-SIX

That night a Mill Valley police officer knocked on the door and explained to Katherine that the mother of a teenager who lived down the street had found the stolen photo of Maria in her boy's room. It was not the kid's first break-in. He had psychological issues and his mother was suspicious enough after she heard about the burglary that she searched his room. That news came as a great relief to Katherine.

Then Maria returned Marquez's calls. The bounce was back in her voice, but the phone reception wasn't good so it was hard to follow her, and she was in a little bit of a rush. She and her friends were in the Yosemite Valley. Though they were camping they were also splurging on a good dinner at the Ahwahnee Hotel.

'That's where I am, right now,' she said. 'I just wanted to tell you that we hiked up to Olmstead Point from the valley today. I didn't even know about that trail. It was really steep with a lot of switchbacks, but we went early in the morning and it was beautiful climbing up as the sun was first on Half Dome. I wanted to tell you also that I'm over everything else. I don't blame the FBI, but why were you calling me, Dad?'

'Jack Gant bought food at a convenience store in South Lake Tahoe this morning. The FBI has all kinds of people looking for him and they'd like to know where you are to protect you.'

She was quiet so long he thought the connection broke.

'I'm not going to call them. We're camping. Jack doesn't know where I am. Tell them I'm not going to call and I'm turning my phone off. I'm going to leave it in the car. I'll call you when we're on our way home.'

She hung up and less than an hour later Desault called.

'John, it's getting complicated with Gant. He checked in

under a false name at the Tioga Lodge which is near the eastern Yosemite entrance.'

'I know where it is.'

'The pickup he had in Tahoe was parked there and it looks like he used the shower. Some grocery bags were found inside, but we haven't found him. There are agents there waiting for him to come back, but at the same time the search has extended to Yosemite. An employee in the café at the Tioga Lodge believes Gant may have gotten a ride into the park. Where is Maria in Yosemite? We need to get to her.'

'She called an hour ago from the Ahwahnee Hotel where she and her friends were having dinner, but I don't know what campsite they're at and she told me she was turning her phone off and would leave it in the car. Are there agents on the valley floor?'

'There are and they can be at the Ahwahnee in minutes. How about the names of the friends she's with and the make and model of the car?'

'Hold on, Katherine knows more than I do about them.'

He handed Katherine the phone and she gave Desault the names of two friends of Maria's and another who wasn't with them that would have phone numbers or be on Facebook. Desault said it wouldn't take long to get phone numbers. It didn't and they got to Maria through a friend she was with. Two agents met with her at the Ahwahnee and Maria told them she had walked from the campsite. She wouldn't tell them where that was or what vehicle she and her friends had driven to Yosemite in. They told her that what Gant had pulled off so far suggested he wasn't working alone. They worried that Gant perceived her as a threat and was in communication with someone who'd tailed her to Yosemite, and Maria dismissed that idea. She refused protection and was evasive.

'She told them she wanted to be left alone,' Desault said.

'But they know where she's camped.'

'John, your daughter left the hotel on foot and walked away on a trail. She may have been picked up by one of her friends, but that's not confirmed yet. It seems they've got two cars but only one make and license plate was written down on the camping permit. The other car was parked outside the park gate and we haven't located that car yet. We believe Maria is in it, but we're not sure.'

There was more, but it all added up to Maria with the help of her friends leaving Yosemite and avoiding FBI protection.

'If you hear from her, you need to call immediately.'

She didn't call or answer her phone. But that didn't really worry him or Katherine. It was pretty clear Maria and friends created a ruse to get her out of the valley. Or that's how it seemed that night. The next morning was a nightmare.

FIFTY-SEVEN

In the cool gray light near dawn a deputy sheriff on the eastern slope of the Sierras spotted a late model black Hummer parked off the road under trees up Rock Creek Canyon. After spotting the Hummer the deputy pulled over and put his light on it. He got out with a flashlight and looked inside. When he shined his light through the driver's window he saw a woman slumped against the passenger door and assumed she was sleeping.

Then his flashlight beam caught the wound at her throat. He held the light there a long moment and then moved it down, saw broad dark stains on her shirt, her skirt, the seat. Blood was everywhere, and yet, it still took him a moment to absorb what he was looking at. He leaned over, looking in, and then took his hand off the car roof and stepped back, realizing he shouldn't even touch the vehicle. He shouldn't touch any more than he already had. He walked around to the back, wrote down the license plates and ran them. The registered owner was a Raymond Mendoza with an LA address.

He reported an apparent homicide and within an hour, somewhere, someone connected Raymond 'Rayman' Mendoza to an ongoing DEA investigation and lapped that into the Bureau's widening search for Maria Marquez and Jack Gant. Marquez got the call from Desault. That was at 8:30 in the morning after he'd been trying for hours to reach Maria by cell phone. He found his wallet, keys, creds, and badge as his muscles went weak with fear. His hands shook. Rock Creek was north of Bishop in country he knew well. It would take him five hours to get down there, maybe less if he pushed hard.

'They're moving the victim in the next hour or so, and we're impounding the vehicle. The Bureau is getting involved. There's no identity on the woman yet. She's approximately twenty-five with brown hair, and hazel eyes, and John, this is very hard to say, but from the description we can't rule out Maria. They'll fax me a photo. Why don't you come into San Francisco and wait here with me.'

'It's not her.'

'I'm sure you're right.'

'She's with two friends, but I'll drive there now.'

'You don't need to do that.'

Desault almost said, you don't need to do that *yet*. He barely caught himself. Marquez walked out to his truck, still talking to Desault as he started the engine.

'Raymond Mendoza is who you gave the message for Stoval to, correct?'

'Yes.'

'Mendoza is in custody. We picked him up at home this morning. He claims the Hummer was stolen and that he didn't report it stolen because he was traveling. Or some story like that. A neighbor who hates both the vehicle and Mendoza, and pays attention to his coming and going in it, says Mendoza was home last night and the night before, but not his vehicle.'

Desault tried to talk him into turning around, but he couldn't do that. He drove and tried Maria's cell several times and got through to one of her friends and learned they'd smuggled Maria out of Yosemite last night and she and two others were supposed to be camped at June Lake on the eastern side. Marquez got the names of the friends and the car make and model and called the Mono County Sheriff's Office.

But they didn't find the car in the time it took him to cross the Sierras. By then he had called Katherine at work, though he didn't tell her the homicide victim's physical characteristics were similar enough that the FBI was faxing a photo of Maria. He couldn't do that, and Desault was right; Maria was fine. She and her friends had ditched the FBI last night and were somewhere no one would think to look for them.

When his phone rang next he could barely breathe as he answered. It was Desault calling with the victim's identity.

FIFTY-EIGHT

Years ago, when he and Katherine couldn't get enough of each other and decided to marry, some wealthy friends of Katherine's threw a party for them in St Helena in the Napa Valley. Maria was in a dress with a big blue bow in the front and her hair pulled to one side and with flowers there that she kept touching delicately on the drive up. She had shiny red leather shoes and was very excited about the party, and then in the summer heat and with the adults drinking wine and eating, and the older girl she had been told she'd be playing with being unfriendly to her, she had gotten flustered and overwhelmed.

An acquaintance of Katherine's, a noted winemaker with an odd pale narrow face, watched this and then tried to get Maria to sit on his lap. She pulled away from him and he scooped her up from behind and lifted her high in the air as if imitating some amusement park ride. He made sounds like she was on a ride as he whooshed her along and smiled widely at the people nearby as he set her down. When she burst into tears, he said, 'You must not be old enough for a big party like this.'

Maria ran to their car parked on the crushed gravel beneath an arbor. Katherine followed. The car was unlocked and by the time she reached her Maria had climbed into the backseat. Her face was streaked with tears, the flowers that had been in her hair lying where she had torn them out and thrown them on the gravel. Marquez could see Maria and Katherine in the car and near him the winemaker joked with a small circle that kids hated him and that no matter what he did they cried.

Katherine talked Maria out of the car but she broke free and ran back and an exasperated Katherine said, 'I don't want her in the car out here alone. The car is way too hot anyway. I don't know what she's so upset about. I guess the party is just too much excitement for her.'

'I'll talk to her.'

And that was probably where he first connected with Maria. He got in the car and asked, 'Can I sit with you?'

She didn't answer. She'd had enough of adults and was feeling sorry for herself and very disappointed after all the expectation of what the party would be. She kept her head pressed against the window. Her left hand gripped the hem of her dress and tears still ran down her cheeks, though she didn't make a sound.

He lowered the other windows to cool the car off and kept talking to her. He talked her into getting into the front seat where he knew she was used to sitting with her mom and hadn't been since the three of them started riding together. Her world had been disrupted. The mom she'd had to herself, she didn't have in the same way anymore.

'Let's get out of here for a few minutes,' he said. 'Let's go for a drive.'

Heads turned as he backed out. The hostess looked over reprovingly at this unnecessary indulgence of a little girl who just needed a nap, and this Marquez, this game warden, leaving in the middle of a party that was a nicer event than he'd probably ever been to. With Maria he stopped and got an ice cream. They drove slowly back and looked at vineyards and she told him about starting first grade and the friend she met, and now she was going to be going to a new school and wouldn't know anybody at all.

They weren't gone forty minutes. It didn't affect the party. It didn't affect anyone at it except the hostess, but it was the first real connection with his stepdaughter and the start of a conversation that was still going on today. He knew something of how she thought. He knew she had said she was going to Yosemite to get away and clear from her head the tag of being labeled the former girlfriend of an ecoterrorist. Maria was stubborn, independent, and smart. She went somewhere last night with her friends where no one would find them. Still, his heart pounded and his voice was a croak as he swerved off the road and answered the phone. And his body suffused with an almost chemical relief when he learned from Desault that the victim in Rayman's Hummer was not Maria.

FIFTY-NINE

Marquez took in her face, the widow's peak, dark thick brown hair, dark eyes, and straight nose. The victim was similar in age to Maria. She wasn't much older. The bullet was large caliber to do the damage it did to her throat. Marquez's gaze went from her destroyed trachea to the manicured nails on her left hand and two rings, then back at her young face again. He had just left the victim and stepped away from the county detective when Maria called.

'We're on our way home. I'm really sorry I didn't call back. We were up near the Fourth Recess last night and there was no cell reception. I'm staying with friends the next few days. I won't be at my house, but I'll have my phone.'

He heard her friends in the background. He heard laughing and relief swept over him again, and sadness for the victim. Maria signed off as he took a call from Desault. He told Desault he had just talked with Maria and that he was en route from Bishop to Los Angeles.

'I'll fly down and meet you,' Desault said. 'This may tie to Stoval.'

When Marquez reached the LA Basin it was near dusk. Desault flew in and they ate dinner together. The FBI had picked up on a rumor relayed through the DEA in El Paso that Zeta assassins had been hired to take out the guy who blew the pumps in California. Hired through a third party for big cash, this from a DEA informant considered reliable.

'What do you make of that?' Desault asked.

Marquez didn't make anything of it yet. It was odd. He checked into a motel and the next morning he and Desault sat down with Rayman and his lawyer. When Rayman saw Marquez he said, 'He took my Hummer.'

'Who did?'

'I gave him your message and he took my Hummer, said he was going to borrow it.'

The lawyer tried to shut it down but Rayman kept talking and in twenty minutes they had an account of the meeting with Stoval. Obviously, Stoval knew the police would beeline to Rayman, and so there was some message, some as yet uncovered reason. With the lawyer there he didn't want to question Rayman much about that. The lawyer was no doubt a cartel lawyer, there to listen as well as advise, and Desault had been told there was a tentative ID on the victim, possibly to be confirmed this afternoon.

They left Rayman, and then Marquez left for San Diego.

'This is about Sheryl Javits,' he told Desault. 'I've got to go see a guy I knew as an ATF agent years ago.'

SIXTY

Pete Phelps had a belly he didn't used to have. He had a wife, a big white stucco house in San Diego with a pool, and a couple of little Phelps who looked like they were eight to ten years old. They looked like sweet kids so maybe they had their mother's genes. Marquez watched Phelps leave the house, drop the kids at school, and then stop and pick up coffee before going into the office. It turned out Phelps was a mortgage broker not a real estate broker. He specialized in subprime loans. Business was off lately.

Using binoculars he watched Phelps in his office flirting with his receptionist. Watching him was boring, but toward the end of the afternoon he saw him lean over and give the receptionist a long kiss. He cupped the back of her head with his hand. He held her face to his and glanced outside as he let her go. That wasn't much leverage, probably would get a laugh out of Phelps, but maybe he could work with it. He called the private investigator friend he'd worked for years ago as he was trying to figure out a career post DEA.

'You're anxious to move on this?' his friend asked.

'Yeah, I can't sit in a car in San Diego much longer and watch this guy.'

'He's married, got a wife, two kids in school?'

'Yes.'

'Then he'll have it down to a routine. Give him twenty-four hours more. That's my advice.'

Marquez followed as Phelps picked up the kids and brought them home. His wife arrived and unloaded a Suburban, and it was one of those warm nights where you walk your dog and think you're lucky to live in a place like this. Lights went off in several rooms at around 10:30 and then Phelps left the house and went grocery shopping. Could be that was his deal, shop when the store was quiet. Except that the real estate firm's receptionist pulled into the store lot as he went through the checkout line.

Phelps carried two bags of groceries to his car. Then he followed her out of the lot, talking on his cell phone, probably to her, and Marquez trailed them to the driveway of a house for sale. She pulled in and parked where her minivan didn't show. Phelps parked down the street and walked back. He got in the minivan.

Marquez figured Phelps was working with a window of time and that he wouldn't waste any now. He gave him five minutes and then walked down the driveway and rapped on the door. He pulled out his badge, held it at window level and said, 'FBI, open up.'

He knew it would be Phelps who slid the door open and, from working joint operations with the ATF in Baja, that Phelps wouldn't be intimidated. Not only that, he'd probably recognize the voice. Phelps slid the door open, looked at Marquez and the badge, and then asked with genuine curiosity, 'How did you end up working for those dipshits?'

'Get your shoes on and let's talk.'

Phelps slid the door mostly shut and put his shoes back on and their voices murmured. When Phelps got out she slipped into the driver's seat, but not before Marquez took a few candid photos. That got everybody angry.

As his girlfriend pulled away, Phelps asked, 'Is this Sheryl's bullshit? Is that why you're here?'

'Let's talk in my car.'

'I've got a better idea, how about if you just fuck off.'

'I can talk to you or talk to your wife, it's up to you.'

'When did you turn into a sleaze bag?'

'Look, Phelps, I'm not here because I want to be. But I'll do whatever it takes to get the truth out of you.'

'About what?'

'You're not listening.'

Marquez was back in his car before Phelps came up the sidewalk. When Phelps got in on the passenger side and before the door shut, he told Marquez, 'I showed them canceled checks. I told them her other story was a crock, so what do you want?'

'I believe Sheryl.' He waited a beat and lied to Phelps. 'I don't care where the money came from and she's going to lose her career out of this either way, but if you gave her part of the divorce settlement money at the back door, she shouldn't be going to prison for life.'

'What are you talking about, prison for life?'

'They've built a case against her that says she took bribes and set Jim Osiers up to get killed. She fed information to the Salazar Cartel and they paid her through a bank account in La Paz. Not only that, but over her career she's worked any number of joint operations with the FBI and the theory goes she was leaking information for money paid by Emrahain Stoval. She used the money you gave her as an unexplained payment on her house in San Francisco. That money is the bottom brick in their case and they're searching for the rest. You might hate her, but this isn't right.'

He couldn't see all of Phelps' face, but could see he was very still. When Phelps spoke again his voice was quiet and low.

'That was family money. It was a real estate deal after my dad died. Sheryl wasn't entitled to any of it. I paid her just to back her off.'

'I'll need it in writing tomorrow morning.'

'That's going to get the IRS on my back.'

'It's your call, take on your wife, or take on the IRS. You decide which is worse, but I need to hear from you by nine in the morning.'

He got it in writing at 9:30 the next day and called Beth Murkowski. Then he made two copies and did what she asked, took the original to the San Diego DEA Field Office.

He called Sheryl, talked to her, and then he sat down with a double espresso and thought about it. It came down to timing and who had all the needed information and access. He flipped his phone open and flipped it shut, thought some more and then phoned Kerry Anderson. But it wasn't Anderson who answered. It was a young woman who told him she was Kerry

Anderson's replacement. Anderson's retirement party had happened last Friday. He'd left on a long awaited Caribbean vacation. She had a phone number and he copied that down and then read an email on his Blackberry from Desault.

It read, *'Victim identified. Call me.'*

SIXTY-ONE

'Her name is Terri Delgado and we can't and neither can the DEA connect her to Raymond Mendoza. So far, there's no apparent link. She lived in the LA area, in Brentwood. The family had money and she was trying to break into the film business as a producer. Her parents filed the missing persons report. Does any of this ring any bells with you?'

'I know who she is. I've talked to her. She tipped us to Stoval's bighorn hunt in the eastern Sierra. She met him at a party in LA and he invited her to go to Vegas with him after his hunt. Instead, she called us.'

'Called the DFG hotline?'

'Yes, and it sounds like I got her killed.'

'You can't draw that conclusion. What you've told me about the hunt may have gotten back to Stoval. It's been discussed by everyone on the task force.'

'Yeah, but Raymond's vehicle, the timing.'

'The timing works because he was already here to kill her. He wrapped the meeting with Raymond Mendoza into that and improvised with the Hummer. Probably didn't get the idea to use Mendoza's Hummer until he was sitting in it.'

Marquez called Chief Blakely at Fish and Game and told her. Then he sat in a room in the LA Field Office with the lights off and once more listened to the archived CALTIP recording of Terri Delgado. In Terri Delgado's voice he could hear her youth and a mix of guilt and desire to do the right thing in calling a tip, snitching on a guy who'd invited her to four days in Vegas.

It brought him way down. He couldn't add it up any other way. At Fish and Game they relied on the public, and Marquez

felt protective toward anyone who helped them, and yet he
may have gotten her killed out of concern for his own family.
Stoval would have come for her anyway, Desault claimed, but
Marquez wasn't sure. Rayman gave the message and Stoval
questioned Rayman, then took his Hummer and either had
Delgado kidnapped and delivered to him – most likely that –
or abducted her himself. More likely kidnapped and drugged,
Marquez thought, and maybe in response to his threat to
Stoval. Or as Desault said, he was here to kill her.

Stoval was getting inside his head. First his name in an
intercepted phone call, then a hired gunman sent to Alaska,
and now this exhibition murder of Terri Delgado. He didn't
need to kill Delgado. Nothing more was going to happen with
the bighorn. He wants to get inside my head, Marquez thought.

What happened next was Rayman got kicked loose. There
was no way to hold him, no evidence he had anything to do
with Delgado's murder. Marquez was still in LA and heard
about the killing over the radio. When he drove there firemen
were hosing off the sidewalk in front of two ATM machines
outside a Wells Fargo bank. This was in a mall parking lot
less than a mile from Rayman's stucco house in the hills.

In the bank video Rayman arrived at 3:34 p.m., just hours
after his release. A man wearing a motorcycle helmet with a
dark visor walks up on Rayman's left side. A second man
with a Dodgers cap and sunglasses is to his right and slightly
behind him, but crowding him so may have held a gun to his
back. That man is with him as Rayman withdraws money.
Motorcycle man arrives after Rayman has already punched in
his PIN and withdrawn the money.

The adjacent ATM was in use and a second witness told
the detectives she was walking from her car toward the Wells
ATMs when Rayman's convertible Mercedes pulled up and
double-parked. It annoyed her that they had double-parked
and would get to the ATM ahead of her. Her name was Patti
Wright and she didn't realize at first that a violent crime was
in progress.

*'I didn't know the man who got out of the car with him
had a gun. I knew there was something odd about how he
was moving and staying close, but I just didn't put it together.
The other man on the motorcycle I didn't even see arrive,
though I think I remember hearing the motorcycle. By the*

time I noticed him, he was holding a gun to the other man's head.'

Rayman's lawyer dropped him off at home at approximately 12:30 and Rayman left the house in the convertible Mercedes soon after. He drove to an In-N-Out Burger and returned home at 1:30 according to a DEA surveillance team. The two agents watching mistook the man who showed up at 3:18 p.m. for a friend – it was still possible he was an acquaintance – it was very likely, Marquez thought, that the man they sent did know Rayman. This 'friend' was seen leaving the house via the front door accompanied by Rayman. The 'friend' wore a hooded sweatshirt with a sleeved pocket in front that likely concealed a gun.

Rayman and that man drove from the house to the mall and the Wells Fargo ATM. They double-parked, got out, and then the man on the motorcycle arrived. This was the part Marquez hooked into, executing him in front of a camera. It keyed with something Kerry Anderson had said years ago, and, in fact, he'd jotted down in one of his old logbooks.

The motorcycle rider walked up as Rayman and the unknown first assailant approached the ATM. Rayman slid his ATM card in. He entered his PIN and the bank record showed a two hundred dollar withdrawal. That money was disbursed by the machine, but left there, and if there was some meaning in that Marquez didn't get it.

At this point, motorcycle man was along Rayman's left side, still with his helmet on as he raised a gun. The woman standing in line, Patti Wright, and the teenage boy using the second ATM both reported having heard the command, 'Look straight ahead!'

Rayman started to turn his head and the bank camera captured the spray as the bullet exited the right side of his head just forward of his right ear. Both men fled on the motorcycle. DEA surveillance did not pursue. They called it in and secured the scene. Marquez stood in front of the Wells Fargo ATMs and then flipped open his cell and called Desault as he walked back to his truck.

'Kerry Anderson once told me that Stoval likes or requires photo verification from the Zetas or any other hired gun,' Marquez said.

Marquez called Anderson but didn't reach him. He flew

home to San Francisco late in the afternoon and stopped at
the DEA as he came through San Francisco. Murkowski came
to talk and gloated, her cheeks reddening with the thrill at
being the first to tell him.

'You're too late. She resigned this afternoon.'

'Why did she quit?'

'Well, Agent Marquez, I think it's pretty obvious she doesn't
belong here.'

Marquez knew there was no point to a tit for tat with this
Internal Affairs agent, but he couldn't leave it there.

'You forced out one of the best to ever walk through here,
Murkowski. But you wouldn't know that, and what's more,
you'll never see it. You'll never know the difference. You're
working for the wrong side.'

'That's the most offensive thing anyone has ever said to me.'

'Then never forget it was me that said it. I'll see you later.'

His mood was dark that night. Katherine was gone three
days on a business trip. She had taken Maria with her. He
talked with both, and then sat outside slow drinking under
the stars. The impunity with which Emrahain Stoval moved
and did what he did reached to the core of Marquez. He
didn't feel anything at all for Rayman, but he kept thinking
about the way Terri Delgado's life was discarded.

He couldn't sleep that night. The house creaked and moved.
His phone rang a burred half ring at 4:00 a.m. and when he
checked it was Sheryl. He called her back and there was no
answer. He drove to her house in San Francisco early the next
morning, couldn't find her, and then he got the call from
Desault.

SIXTY-TWO

'Stoval is moving,' Desault said. 'He's in the air headed
to Italy. Last time he went from there to Africa. Do you
want to follow?'

'Yes.'

'Okay, it's your call, but are you sure? There's no lead.
There's no tip he's going to hunt. There's nothing.'

'I'm going to stick with him, and I've been thinking more about the hit squads, his relationship with the Zetas, and what he gets out of it other than he needs them for business. He may get the same thrill out of ordering a hit as bringing down a lion.'

'Where are you getting that from?'

'He didn't have any reason to kill Terri Delgado. Without a bighorn case she wasn't a threat to him.'

'You're having a real hard time with her murder, aren't you?'

'Of course, I am.'

'How much is it affecting you?'

'Don't even go there. I'm fine.'

Some say insight is just pattern recognition at a subconscious level. Marquez guessed that Stoval was due for a hunt. The periodicity, the past frequency, the timing was right. He packed his go bag. When Stoval's pilot diverted to the Bahamas, ostensibly with a mechanical problem, and then filed a flight plan to go from there to Argentina, Marquez called Desault and asked him to book a flight for him to Buenos Aires.

Four hours later he was off the phone with Katherine and on his way to the airport. In Buenos Aires he bought another ticket, this one on Aerolineas for a flight to Bariloche where Stoval owned a hacienda in what the Argentinians called the Lake District. His FBI contact in Buenos Aires, an agent named Jose Verandas, met up with him at the US embassy in BA. Sometimes Stoval stayed in Buenos Aires for several days at the home of an old friend, a retired general named Trocca. He was there now according to Verandas, so they drove out to scout Trocca's house.

'We've got a liaison, an Argentinian military attaché, a colonel, but we're not cleared yet for any active surveillance in Buenos Aires,' Verandas said. 'In Bariloche the rules are a little looser, mostly because there's no one to keep track of us. There's a lot of open country down there. You're a game warden, you'll like it there.'

'I've been there. Tell me about General Trocca.'

'He's a hunting partner for Stoval and was a lieutenant in the Dirty War thirty some odd years ago. There's a scar that runs the length of the left side of his face they say he got throwing someone out of a plane over the ocean. A bad guy, but a survivor who got rich peddling arms to African rebels.'

Marquez thought of Billy Takado's tape, the riff on Argentina and wing hunting. But that was fall hunting and this was the southern hemisphere and early spring, barely spring. Verandas had a photo of Trocca for him. He was tall, thin, and white-haired. He had a large nose, dark eyes, and the unmistakable scar. Trocca accompanied Stoval to the airport the next morning.

The airport in Bariloche was built on a plain with snowy mountains in the distance. Marquez got there ahead of Stoval and Trocca. Cover was sparse, and it was windy and bright in the late morning when he trailed the gray BMW carrying Stoval and Trocca up a road into mountains southwest of Bariloche. Five miles later, he watched a heavy gate swing open and the car disappear up the road to Stoval's hacienda.

Verandas flew down that night. So did a second FBI agent named Taltson, who like Verandas was also working out of the US embassy in Buenos Aires. Late in the afternoon Marquez sat with Verandas in a car in heavily wooded country half a mile from the estate entrance. He felt jet-lagged. He felt weighed down by Terri Delgado's murder, but was glad he'd flown down. That Trocca was a hunting partner ramped up the chance something would happen, and there wasn't any large legal game Stoval could go after. He had the phone number of the local game warden but hadn't called him yet. It was all very loose. They were looking for opportunity based on Stoval's patterns. Verandas and Taltson followed his leads and simultaneously second-guessed him.

Marquez worked out a rolling surveillance plan, and then took the first leg alone. Verandas spelled him just after midnight. When he left Verandas he drove the road around Lago Nahuel Huapi toward the hotel. From the road he looked out over the lake in moonlight. It was cold still and felt like winter. The lake was quite large and in many places fingers of water reached in deep into the shoreline. He remembered a lot more of the country than he thought he would. The big hotel that didn't seem much changed at all. He slept deeply and was standing at the window of the room at dawn looking out over the lake when the call came that Stoval had just driven through the hacienda gates.

'He's coming your way, Marquez.'

SIXTY-THREE

Stoval picked up a man in Bariloche who looked dressed to be out in the raw weather, and now they were north of town in open country running out a dirt road muddy from spring runoff. Marquez waited five minutes before following. The rental car bounced in the potholes. His wheels spun in mud. From a wooden sign Marquez knew the road led to trailhead parking, but he didn't follow them all the way in. He watched the odometer and when he guessed he was a third to a half mile from the trailhead he pulled over. Brush scraped the passenger side as he parked. He gathered his gear and walked the last stretch quietly through the trees.

Stoval and the other man stood outside the Range Rover looking like they were getting ready to hike into the mountains. Marquez focused binoculars on Stoval and saw the hollowing of the cheeks and deep creasing at the corners of the eyes, but in many ways he looked the same. He looked fit and lifted a soft gun case out of the back of the Range Rover, and then unzipped a silver-plated bird gun and dropped shells into the big pocket of his coat.

The other man didn't carry a gun. He slipped a pack on, looked like a local and moved like a guide, a gold-skinned, dark-haired man smiling in anticipation. He wore a red bandana and sunglasses and led Stoval into the cold raw morning and chill in the trees.

After they hiked out, Marquez went back for his car. He drove into the trailhead lot and parked it where it couldn't be missed, then radioed Verandas.

'They hiked in and Stoval is carrying a shotgun. I don't know what he's going after this time of year, but I'm going to follow.'

He pulled on another layer and a windbreaker and ski cap, but once he set out to catch them he warmed up fast. He figured they had twenty-five minutes on him and that it wouldn't take him long to catch up. He doubted they were more than three quarters of a mile ahead of him, and when

that turned out to be true he hung back far enough to make
it unlikely they would spot him.

Neither looked back much. Whatever they were here for
was ahead. The barest first edges of the coming spring showed
as mud and a softening of the snow in the sun between the
trees. In many places were larger snow banks and the trail
moved through forest and then climbed steeply, switchbacking
up, and higher on to exposed rock. The wind blew hard off
the Andes. It scoured away the early clouds and cut through
Marquez's clothes. His boots crunched through snow and slid
on wet rock.

At roughly the five mile mark his radio no longer reached
Verandas. He got only static. Ahead, strands of cirrus whitened the
sky above the high peaks and he watched as Stoval and
the other man rose through a long stand of trees to a saddle.
They walked close together, Stoval carrying his gun with an
easy confidence. They moved higher and into a longer stretch
of trees and he saw only flashes of their clothing, the red
bandana, the back of Stoval's dark blue coat, and beyond them
the dark gray rock of a ridge ahead. When Marquez reached
the saddle he followed their boots' prints through the snow,
saw where they'd tromped through a muddy patch and picked
up the rockbound trail again.

The trail left the trees and climbed a steep rock slope toward
a knife blade of a ridge. It steepened and the snow among the
rocks was windblown with a hard smooth crust that broke under
his weight as he left the trail and worked sideways. He didn't
know if they'd hiked over the ridge and down the other side,
or were on top, so he stayed below the crest. When he climbed
up he was well down the ridge, away from their line of sight,
and edged up. He stayed low and now with binoculars he saw
them easily. They stood behind a granite outcropping and above
them eagles circled raggedly in the cold wind.

Stoval watched the eagles, and as the guide pointed out two
condors flying toward them from out across the deep forested
valley ahead, his attention left the eagles. The condors were
still small at this distance, but their wingspans were striking.
They held a clean line cutting cross to the wind. They looked
thick-shouldered and dark as they neared. Spring melt had
begun and winter-killed carcasses were becoming exposed, so
maybe they were searching for food.

Stoval's right hand left his coat. He broke the shotgun open, loaded, and swung the gun up in a smooth arc. The silver inlay on the stock flashed in the sunlight as the long clean shadows of condor wings swept over ridge rock and Stoval shot the lead condor. The echo of the discharge rolled out over the mountains. Feathers scattered. The condor folded and fell.

He only wounded the second bird and it tried to fly back toward the valley, but it faltered and then tumbled and fell, dark, small, and lost among the trees. The eagles fled with the first shot and as Stoval broke apart his gun and removed the spent shells, the wind-scoured sky above was an empty bright blue.

What do you say about a hunter who kills condor in the age of the last great creatures of the wild? Marquez watched the guide hike across the rocks to the first bird and strip the tail feathers. He bundled them carefully and eased them shaft first into the pack, folding the flap back so it wouldn't damage them on the hike out. The other bird was too far away to go after. It wasn't worth the effort and it didn't matter. They got the one, so it was a successful outing. They rested with their backs against the rock of the outcropping and the guide opened wine and cut dried meat and Marquez read the Malbec label on the wine bottle as it balanced on a rock. He read Stoval's face, content and cheerful, enjoying the moment, gun propped there near him, and the other man talking and smiling.

They hiked out, picking up on his tracks as they did and watchful now. At the trailhead, they studied Marquez's car and another in the lot before loading their gear and leaving. Call it whatever you want, but Marquez waited before going to his car. He radioed Verandas. Verandas could see where the dirt trailhead road intersected the paved road and reported what Marquez had guessed or sensed. The Range Rover was yet to turn on to the paved road.

Almost an hour later, Stoval walked out of the shadows at the curve of the road and into the sunlight near Marquez's rental car. Before driving away from the trailhead Marquez saw him stow his shotgun, but now it was back under the crook of his right arm as he stood jotting down the license plate of the car. Then he looked straight ahead up into the trees. Slowly, his head turned toward the left until he was looking at where Marquez was hidden. There was no way Stoval could see him, but it was strange and disturbing. He stared for several minutes before the Range Rover rounded the corner. Then he climbed in and they drove away. Minutes later, Verandas reported them turning onto the paved road.

SIXTY-FOUR

S omeone had followed them and Stoval ran through the possibilities. He'd found tracks as they hiked out and it could be the local game warden trying to be clever and trailing him in a rental car. Or it could be as simple as a tourist, but that was unlikely with this weather this time of year. It could be an enemy or someone hired by an enemy. That was always possible.

After dropping the guide, Alberto, on a street corner in Bariloche, he called a source in Buenos Aires, recited the license plates and listened to the clipped British accent as it was repeated back to him. Then he drove home. He was in his study when the source called back. Of the two cars, one vehicle belonged to an older local man. Stoval ruled him out and focused on the rental car. The car had been rented in the name of a corporation, not an individual.

'I need the individual's name.'

'I'll get it.'

Within two hours he heard back.

'Rented through an arm of the US State Department, so probably a cover car, but I don't have a name yet. I'm still working on it.'

'Thank you.'

Stoval hung up. So a US government agency was playing. He could deal with that. In truth, it relieved him. He had a Russian mafyia problem that was worrisome and needed resolution. The Russians could be impatient. They might come after him before that was settled and he considered calling and ending the dispute today. He made another call now, this one to a police officer. The Lake District had a number of hotels, but not so many that narrowing it would take any length of time. He gave the officer the make, model, and license plate on the car, and knew the man would be thorough.

'I want an identity. I want to know if there's more than one and if so where they're staying.'

When he hung up, he emailed the Russians and offered to settle. At dusk, he still hadn't heard back from the police officer and called him.

'What did you learn?'

'I found the car, but not the driver yet. But he's male. The car is at the airport and there were two men when it was dropped off. I found someone who saw them. They did not come into the airport building. A man drove the car up, parked it, and another man picked him up. I checked with the rental agency and they say the car has been returned.'

'But the man did not go into the airport?'

'No, they had another vehicle ready and waiting for him. One of the employees brought him out the keys, but she's off work and has gone home.'

'I need a description of him.'

'No one could give me one.'

'Then find the woman who brought the keys to him.'

'I'm looking for her.'

'And get a list of all cars rented from the airport today.'

'That'll take more time. I still have other duties. I have other things expected of me.'

'Then make up an excuse.'

Stoval hung up and he did not get the list until the next morning. Then he saw his feeling was correct. Two more cars had been rented by the corporation; the first one returned with a complaint about its handling, the second with some other excuse and yet under the same corporate name, BestMat Ltd. They suspected he'd check so they swapped out cars. That was fine. He did not have any problem with that and he might even enjoy hunting them down.

Two airlines flew in and out of Bariloche, Aerolineas Argentinas and LAN Airlines. If the men were US government, and he suspected they were, then he could ignore flights to Calafate or Esquel. It would be Buenos Aires. They would come direct. They would hub from there and work in the blunt stupid methods of government agencies. Aerolineas had three Buenos Aires flights a day, four hundred forty-one seats, and

LAN two, three hundred twelve seats. He made the call to the airport at mid morning. He expected a name or names by this evening. After he knew who he was dealing with, he would decide how to deal with them.

SIXTY-FIVE

Marquez got a warning before he called the local game warden. The warning was, 'Chole Joulet is a great warden but he drinks too much, he's combative, and takes it all too personally. Not everyone likes him and he's too tough on hunting guides. He shot and killed three poachers in one firefight and if they hadn't been foreigners he wouldn't have a job anymore. He's a zealot, passionate but half-crazy. He's more muscle than brain. Stay away from him, he's normal one day and the next day he's three hundred miles away chasing someone who was over limit trout fishing. He doesn't have any internal guidance system, if you know what I mean. Can you see yourself chasing people hundreds of miles over a few fish?' There was a pause, a search for a more accurate description – 'Picture a roving gang looking for trouble, that's Joulet. He gets up in the morning, goes out and looks for trouble.'

'How will he react to a shooter taking out a couple of adult condors?'

'That'll punch his ticket. He lives for that shit.'

Marquez met Chole Joulet in a Bariloche bar. He figured to have a couple of beers with him, find out what it was like covering all this open country, and then let him know what he'd witnessed. That meant pushing the boundaries a little and Verandas was against it, but Desault said it's yours to shape, so now after taking in this warden with his black mustache, chiseled cheekbones, and bullfighter build, he bought him another round and ordered another beer for himself. He suggested they take a table.

At the table he showed Chole his creds and said, 'I was a game warden for fourteen years. I'm still a warden but I'm attached to an FBI task force right now. We're chasing a guy who traffics in black market wildlife and hunts anywhere and anything he wants. He lives here. You probably know him. Emrahain Stoval.'

Chole nodded and some of the glitter went out of his eyes. He glanced down at the table, at his hands, at his drink, and then back at Marquez again.

'Dangerous man.' He slid his chair back and pulled his left pant leg up, showed big scars on his left calf. 'Stoval.' He dropped the pant leg without explaining. Chole wore a gray, long-sleeved, waterproof shirt with an insulated shirt underneath. The pants were also part of his gear and what he walked around in when he was off work. Looking at him, Marquez guessed he lived his job.

'Who gave you permission to be in Argentina?'

'It's an agreement between the governments, but we're not here for long.'

'I don't need any help from Americans.'

'I know, no one does anymore, but Stoval just came from the US and he killed a couple of bighorn in my territory a few months ago. I'll follow him wherever he goes.'

Chole liked that. It brightened him right up and he grinned. But the grin didn't last and they were still where the conversation could go either way.

'I saw him shoot two condors here.'

That got immediate interest.

'He collected the tail feathers from one. He goes anywhere he wants in the world and trophy hunts.'

'I've heard what he has.'

Marquez didn't understand what he meant by that. He waited but Chole didn't elaborate.

'I shot videotape of them hiking out with the condor feathers. I'll turn that over to you. Maybe you can do something with it.'

Chole shrugged.

'It's yours anyway.'

The arms unfolded. Chole said, 'What is your name again?'

Marquez reintroduced himself and Chole, who had looked at the FBI creds before and not bothered to read his name, studied them closely. It hadn't mattered to him and now it did, so maybe they were going to get somewhere after all. Marquez put his hand out and said 'John Marquez.' As they shook hands he felt the strength in the big man.

They had more drinks. They talked about wildlife enforcement and he told Chole about the SOU. Then they took it
back to Stoval and sitting at the table across from this warden
who in many ways was not much different from him, he had
an idea.

Chole Joulet looked tough. He looked like he could walk
from here to Buenos Aires and it wouldn't bother him. He
said in the summer he often slept in the mountains. There was
an office in Bariloche, but he never went there. He reached
in a pocket and pulled a cell phone, checked it and slipped it
in his pocket again. He told Marquez now that he used a dirt
bike and a four-wheel drive. He relied on his radio. He had
some alliances with park conservation wardens, but most of
the working day he was on his own. He was used to that and
Marquez understood completely. He said he lived alone in a
house outside of Bariloche and patrolled his territory
constantly. They seemed to like him here in his favorite bar,
so he couldn't be that kind of drunk. But he could be that
kind of experienced, resourceful, hardnosed but smart warden
type Marquez was looking for.

There was a dark light in Chole's eye when Marquez said,
'I'll go anywhere Stoval goes. I'm going to get him.'

But what Marquez was thinking was this. Desault gave me
license. Desault has talked to Bureau headquarters and they're
interested in expanding the wildlife enforcement angle, and
this is how to do it, find the wardens like Chole. Build a new
team. Build an international team. The fight crosses borders
so I'll form a band of wardens from across the world and
they would need to be like this guy, resilient and unafraid.
Like Shauf. Like others he'd known. He thought of a Canadian
warden in BC. Others were out there. He knew a Kenyan
warden. South Africa had an elite unit. They were out there.
They were in India and Australia and New Zealand. He
thought of a Brit named Jameson. He drank from the beer
and thought, an experienced team that can move fast, the
tough ones, and let the Department of Justice or State
Department work out the alliances in the countries where we
go in to help. He'd find the hardened wardens, the ones that
wouldn't quit. He'd know them on sight and if the Feds would
back him he'd take it all to another level. Marquez felt excitement as he turned the idea.

They had a final drink then left the bar. As Chole walked away, Marquez zipped up his coat and turned up the collar. The night was very cold. The night was the start of something and he felt things moving. At midnight he took over from Verandas, and then was alone in the darkness of trees on a dirt road a half mile from Stoval's hacienda gate and a very long way from home.

SIXTY-SIX

The next day they flew in a spotter plane alongside a forested ridge and looked down on Stoval's estate. A black ribbon of road climbed two miles from the gate in the valley to a plateau fringed with fir and pine and bare stands of *lenga*, the local beech. Marquez counted six buildings and took in the plateau with its remarkable view of the Andes. He picked up the spotting scope, turned to the pilot.

'That fenced area down there with the track running to it. That looks like it's on his property. What is it?'

The pilot didn't know and acted like he didn't want to know. With the spotting scope it was easy to follow the dirt track crossing the plateau and dropping into the trees. He saw a stream silvered now in sunlight and the track picking up on the other side. He turned the scope on a fenced area. The fence cut through forest. Trees had been logged so they weren't too close to it and that said animals to Marquez. He tapped the pilot.

'Can we turn around and make another pass? I want to fly lower.'

This time the pilot shook his head no, and in the backseat Verandas smiled. They'd hired four hours of air time and on the ground the pilot had said he could fly them anywhere, even to Tronador, if they wanted to circle the volcano. But once in the air and near Stoval's estate everything changed.

'What if we paid you extra?'

He shook his head again and explained. 'They shot at the plane of a pilot friend of mine. I saw the bullet holes and the police went out there and nothing happened. Two weeks later my friend was gone. They say he moved away, but I don't think so.'

Stoval didn't leave the estate until 10:15 that night. He drove into Bariloche with General Trocca and parked around the corner from a bar. Two hours later, they came out with a couple of young women who carried packs and could only be tourists.

'Can you believe those two guys scored these women?' Verandas asked, and seemed truly incredulous.

'He's got his big house. He probably offered them a place to sleep.'

'Sure, right next to him.'

But now Marquez could see something was wrong. The women acted like they didn't know they were going for a ride. They pointed down the street to where there were other bars open and when Trocca tugged at the blonde and nudged her toward the open door in back, she jerked away, got skittish. Marquez watched a man come out of the shadows, possibly to help the women.

'Where did this guy come from?' Verandas asked.

'I'm not sure. I missed him, but it's good he did or we'd need to get out there and help them. He may have come out of the bar and we were too busy watching them.'

It took Marquez another moment before he said, 'No, wait a minute, I recognize him. That's Chole Joulet, the game warden I was telling you about.'

The women used the moment to get away and Chole moved around to the right rear of the Range Rover with Trocca and Stoval, talking or arguing. Both of the Range Rover doors on that side were open. So was the driver's door where Stoval had gotten out, and the view was blocked.

'Can you see what's going on?' Marquez asked.

'No.'

Marquez started the car and pulled forward a little and what he thought was a confrontation starting had ended and it looked like Chole had gotten in the back of the Range Rover. He didn't actually see him get in, but he had to be in there because he wasn't on the street as the Range Rover pulled away.

'Maybe you made a mistake, Marquez. Maybe this guy is a friend of theirs and he's taking a ride now with Stoval to tell him about you.'

'Can you see him in back?'

'No, the windows are tinted.'

A moment later Verandas hit the dash with his fist.

'Ah, fuck, that's what's going on. Stoval owns him, one more corrupt cop. That's it, we're blown. You moved too fast with the game warden, Marquez. You made a mistake and you may as well book a flight home. He's giving his report to Stoval right now.'

'Not the guy I met last night.'

'Yeah, he is. He's just another good actor.'

They followed as the Range Rover left Bariloche and Stoval drove back to the estate. Verandas radioed Taltson and Taltson turned around on the road and drove toward them and Stoval's Range Rover with his high beams on. He tried to see Chole Joulet in the backseat but didn't see anybody. Marquez turned to Verandas.

'We know he got in that vehicle. So he's lying down. He may be hurt. Either we go up there now, or we get the police.'

'We get the police. We'll call them and give them the minimum, but this warden is on the take like everyone else Stoval touches. He's probably going up to the house with them to lay it all out and identify some photo Stoval has of you. He's up there getting congratulated and paid.'

Marquez listened to that and said, 'We're going to the police. We're not going to call them. We'll be more credible if we show up and explain.'

'We aren't doing that, it'll blow everything.'

'I'm running this and that's how we're going to do it. I got Chole into this. Now we'll get the police up there.'

The police listened, photocopied their badges and sent two officers. Taltson watched the hacienda gate open and the officers drive up. They returned less than a half hour later and radioed in that they had searched and the warden wasn't there. Stoval reported having a brief conversation with the warden out on the street, but because it was cold they hadn't talked long. The warden did not get in the Range Rover. He had no reason to and Stoval did not ask the warden where he was going next. He was sorry not to be of more help.

Marquez couldn't live with that. They drove back to the police station, a bright blue building near the center of town.

He asked them to wake up the chief, who then came in to talk to them. He explained it very patiently to Marquez.

'Chole Joulet and Stoval are enemies. He would not get in a vehicle with him unless it was after arresting him, so I think you made a mistake.'

'Chole's four-wheel is on the street four blocks from the bar. We found it before coming here.'

'His car is often on the street Sunday morning. Women like him, so maybe he went home with somebody and maybe you should go home, too.'

'That doesn't explain it. He got in the Range Rover.'

When they left the police station he said, 'Let's drive back out there. I'll take over for Taltson.'

'You can if you want but this one is blown. We're all headed back to Buenos Aires tomorrow.'

Marquez didn't bother to answer. At dawn he watched the crust of snow on the plateau turn pink. An hour later he watched Stoval and the general leave the house. They came down the long road from the plateau and exhaust from the Range Rover left a cloud in the cold air. He waited until he was sure they were gone. Then he crossed into the woods and started working his way up.

SIXTY-SEVEN

On the plateau he entered a building that was large and rectangular with a high vaulted ceiling thirty feet above a polished concrete floor. Two walls were largely glass, so that as you stood inside you had the sense of being outside. It was a museum or maybe just a big trophy case. Marquez stopped at a stuffed Siberian tiger and read a brass plaque with the date of the kill. He walked past a white rhino and touched a yak shot recently in China, then remembered in the city of Chengdu officials had auctioned permits for hunts that included some rare or endangered animals. Birds of prey hung from the ceiling. He looked up at a bald eagle with an eight-foot span.

The doors to the main house were also open and he didn't

see any signs of an alarm system or cameras, and yet, somehow, that didn't surprise him. Marquez wasn't allowed to bring a gun into Argentina and lacking a gun, he picked up an eight-inch knife in the kitchen. He moved slowly. He moved quietly, and there didn't seem to be anybody here, no servants, nothing, just mechanical noises, the hum of machines, his footsteps creaking on wood stairs as he went up. He checked five bedrooms and looked through a window at what looked like a guest house across the road.

When he came back down he worked methodically through the first floor until he reached the study. The study doors were locked metal French doors with thick reinforced glass. It would take a battering ram to get in. So this was it, this was where he needed to get in. Two computers sat on a glass desk inside. A third sat alone on a separate table. He looked at everything visible and moved on and soon crossed to the guest house.

Inside, the guest house reminded Marquez of a high-end hotel suite. He found Trocca's suitcase and clothes hanging, but didn't touch any of it. He left again as a greater sense of urgency enveloped him, a worry about the time passing and Stoval's return. He was outside working through the outbuildings when he heard the Range Rover coming. He stepped behind a tree and crouched down as it came into view and drove past, Stoval at the wheel, Trocca smiling.

They stopped at the last outbuilding on the plateau, about fifty yards from where he was, close enough to hear their voices. Stoval unlocked a heavy barn door and slid it open. With Trocca's help he dragged out Chole or Chole's body, it was hard to tell if he was alive until they got him to the rear of the Range Rover. There, Trocca kicked him until Chole struggled to his feet. He wore both hand and ankle cuffs and fell several times before they got him loaded in the back. He'd probably been in the cold shed all night, and he was injured. Marquez saw the bruising on his face.

Stoval slammed the rear door shut and they drove out the track across the plateau and dropped down into the trees and were gone from sight. Marquez tried his cell again. He hurried into the main house and tried the phones, but got a busy signal rather than a dial tone and guessed there was a code to call out. He went back outside, looked at the tire tracks running in the dirty snow and started to follow them. At first he walked, and then as he thought more about what they were doing with Chole he started to run.

SIXTY-EIGHT

Twelve foot high chain link gates to the penned enclosure were latched closed, but not locked. Marquez went through and then followed the four-wheel drive track down through Scotch broom and across an icy stream. The road climbed through trees. It reached a clearing and Marquez panted hard as he knelt down. He glimpsed the back of the Range Rover, heard Stoval and Trocca talking. He skirted brush, catching his breath as he caught view of Trocca holding a gun and Stoval leaning over Chole. He could also see the long run of high fence dropping toward a canyon and how trees and brush were cleared away from it, and the electrified strands running at the top. Transistors on the fence hummed and he finally understood.

In the clearing Stoval looped a chain around the cuffs that held Chole's ankles and then ran the chain through an iron hoop staked to the ground. The chain clinked and somewhere in the distance he heard the cry of an animal. Soon after came the low whooping of hyena.

Hyenas wouldn't leave anything behind, not even bones if they were hungry enough, and Stoval probably made sure they got hungry enough. They must be hungry if they were this bold. They were circling, closing. They seemed to frighten General Trocca whose voice carried as he encouraged Stoval to finish and to stop talking to Chole. Stoval bent over Chole, probably describing what was going to happen.

Marquez moved toward the hyenas and a break in the brush. He wanted to get through that opening before the animals spread out more. The opening allowed him to blindside them. Trocca faced the hyenas whooping in the brush straight ahead of them and Stoval's back was to Marquez as he charged into the clearing.

From the look on his face as he wheeled, Trocca expected

a hyena. He got off two shots and missed with both before
Marquez slammed into him, tearing the gun out of his hand
and battering his throat with an elbow. Trocca went down
gagging and Marquez's momentum carried him stumbling on
to Stoval. Stoval pulled a knife. He lunged upward with it and
with luck Marquez blocked it with the rifle. Then he knocked
the knife loose and swept the gun stock across Stoval's face.
He knocked him down, then knocked him out and found the
keys in his coat. He dragged a struggling Trocca over, freed
Chole's legs and hooked up Trocca to the ankle cuffs that had
held Chole.

He got Chole to his feet as Stoval stirred and Marquez
took the chance of getting Chole to the Range Rover before
going back for Stoval. Chole's face was a mess and he was
having trouble breathing. Marquez got him closer to the Range
Rover then had to leave him as Stoval retrieved the knife and
stood. When that happened Marquez quickly picked up the
rifle.

'Drop the knife.'

Stoval didn't answer and then did something Marquez never
saw coming. He moved sideways to Trocca, leaned and slashed
open one side of Trocca's throat. Blood spurted onto Trocca's
face and into the dirt. Trocca's hand rose to his neck and he
spasmed and his body jerked as Stoval ran toward the brush
and Marquez swung the rifle and sighted on Stoval. The shot
was easy, but he didn't pull the trigger. He saw Trocca's blood
sprayed over Stoval's pant legs, and blood dripping off Stoval's
face where the blow from the gun stock had opened his cheek.
He thought about it and let Stoval push into the brush, watched
him disappear.

Trocca bled out before the first hyenas showed themselves.
A big female crept into the clearing as Marquez got a seatbelt on Chole. At his feet as he shut the door and started back
around the Range Rover was a shard of yellow bone that could
be human. He stooped, picked it up, and dropped it in the
Range Rover. He started the engine. Chole needed medical
help and soon. He saw the hyenas reach Trocca's body but
he couldn't do anything about that or go after Stoval yet.
Chole's breath was ragged. His lips were not only split and
swollen, but blue from cold. His nose and front teeth were
broken. He wasn't far from going into shock.

Before Marquez drove away, he locked the gate. The Range Rover rocked as they bounced back down the rough road to the stream. Chole made sounds about needing water and Marquez got him water and then drove on. Several ribs were badly broken and Chole moaned as they bounced through potholes. Up on the plateau, he lost consciousness. He said '*Mi amigo*' and then closed his eyes, and when Marquez reached over and felt for a pulse what was there was erratic.

Now, as he hit the paved road he drove hard. He called Verandas on the way into Bariloche and Verandas met him at the clinic. Two doctors were waiting. They worked on Chole as Marquez and Verandas walked out on to the cold street. The snow on the mountains looked very bright and clean as they talked over what to do next.

'He's not going over the fence,' Marquez said. 'It's electrified.'

'What about the gate?'

'He went the other way, but maybe he knows another way out.'

Marquez doubted there was another way out. He looked over at Verandas and added, 'I heard something in the distance as I was locking the gate. I'm not sure what it was, but not all of the hyenas were with Trocca. We need to get the police chief here to go back out there with us and you've got to get to two computers in a study. There are two steel doors with reinforced glass and when I tapped on the walls there's metal there too. I don't know how you're going to get through, but I think everything is in those computers. None of the buildings were locked. Not a single door except for that study. I'll go down to the pen with the police but you've got to figure a way to reach those computers. Can you do that?'

'I'm more worried about the encryption. This guy has the money for the best.'

The police arrived but didn't want to go anywhere until they had interviewed Chole. It was another hour and a half before Chole was able to say what had happened. He showed the police chief a dart hole in his right side under his ribs. Stoval had shot him there last night and his best guess was that the dart had an animal tranquilizer. He didn't remember the ride or getting to the house. He came to in a shed with his ankles and wrists in cuffs, and Stoval prodding his face with a stick. He'd lost three teeth. He had five broken ribs. Every bone in his left hand was broken.

He looked at Marquez as he told the police chief, 'I told him I was going to arrest him for killing two condors. I told him I had proof.'

'Where did you get it?'

Chole nodded toward Marquez.

They drove back out there in two police vehicles, Marquez and Verandas riding with the chief and another officer. The chief rode in the front seat and the officer drove as they got up on the plateau. As they came alongside the main house the chief turned and said, 'You wait here.'

They went inside after the police disappeared into the trees. A maid had showed up and was working, but she was frightened when Verandas told her she needed to open the study doors. She wouldn't do it, but retrieved a hidden key and let Verandas open them. When he sat down in front of the computers she tried to stop him and Marquez guided her out of the room. Verandas got online and checked in with FBI headquarters in Washington. Within minutes they were running a supercomputer at Stoval's encryption and outside Marquez heard shots fired and then an engine as the police chief and officers returned. The police chief was very direct with Marquez.

'Get in the jeep.'

'Did you find them?'

The chief did not answer the question. Despite the cold he was sweating profusely and though he had ridden in the passenger seat on the way out, he was now driving. He drove down the road and through the water, and as if to compensate for the bouncing ride he went slowly up the other side. He kept talking about the hyenas and looked over at Marquez and shook his head as they pulled into the clearing.

Marquez opened his door and got out. He walked toward the iron hoop and a hyena backed away with a bone. The chief fired into the air and the other hyenas moved into the brush.

'They are disgusting,' the chief said, and Marquez looked down at a stained shred of Trocca's shirt. The ankle cuffs were blood-smeared. There was a shoe, but it was empty and chewed. There were other small pieces of clothing and not

much else, though there was fighting between the hyenas
deeper in the brush. The chief did not want to remain in the
open clearing and they got in the jeep. The police chief turned
to Marquez, as if explaining to him.

'You did what you had to do to free the warden and protect
yourself. Then we came here as fast as we could. We came
straight out.'

'Yes.'

'No time was lost at the hospital.'

'Not much.'

'None at all, nothing was lost.'

'OK, no time was lost, but Stoval went into the brush that
direction. We need to find him.'

'Let me finish,' the chief said. 'They had the conservation
warden chained to the iron hoop. You saw he was badly injured
and when you went to rescue him they tried to shoot you.'

'Trocca fired twice at me.'

'You could not protect Chole and escape without locking
them up first, so you locked up General Trocca and Mr Stoval
escaped.'

'He killed Trocca with a knife before running into the
brush.'

'Why would he do that?'

'My guess is he wanted to draw the hyenas so he could
escape. I'm going to go look for him.'

'That's crazy.'

'Bring your guns and come with me.' Marquez pointed at
the iron hoops. 'There are other bones there. You'll need to
search the site. Chole wouldn't have been the first.'

The chief refused to go but sent his two officers and Marquez
led the way through the trees. He moved toward the sounds.
They were feeding. No question about that and the officers
shot two of the hyenas before they moved away. One of the
hyena dragged what was left of Stoval. It was awful to look
at and an officer shot that hyena and another pulled Stoval's
remains back into the brush. They were that hungry. Marquez
looked at bloodstained shreds of Stoval's jacket and pointed
at the fence.

'He must have fallen,' he said, but neither officer was
listening. Both shot into the trees and brush at targets they
couldn't see. They backed up the trail taking more random

shots and Marquez turned and walked back to the gate alone.

They drove back to the main house and picked up Verandas who looked very happy. An officer searched him to make certain he hadn't taken anything and Verandas protested as he held his arms out wide, but he nodded to Marquez. He'd gotten it all. They rode back in the chief's vehicle and nobody had much to say on the road back to Bariloche.

SIXTY-NINE

In the 1980s when Marquez was still DEA, the Bahamas were known as the cocaine islands. If you got your start in those days then you heard about the opulence, the boats, beachfront palaces, the cars, parties, and beautiful women who arrived when the money did. Marquez located Anderson's house and was unsurprised to learn it wasn't a vacation rental, but that Anderson had recently bought it. It was a nice enough house, a little worn, yet with a wide view of the beach and cay below.

Anderson knew Stoval was dead. He knew the FBI had stripped his computer. And he must have known after years of working with Stoval how meticulous Stoval was. Stoval kept very good records. There were over six hundred photos of the dead dating from 1972 forward. Among them was a recent one of Jack Gant lying on his back out in the desert somewhere. The only clue was two creosote bushes caught in the photo. That narrowed it down to a few hundred thousand square miles.

No one at the FBI could say yet who had ordered the hit on Gant. The client hadn't been identified, but the Gant hit was in Stoval's files. It was nothing personal toward Gant, strictly part of a business enterprise. Stoval trafficked in death on a scale bigger than anyone had ever imagined. In the file on Gant the client was anonymous, but it was recorded that a quarter million dollar fee was paid to a hit team of two men and one woman.

Desault and Hosfleter believed it was Ben Marsten, Gant's

old friend and the wealthy founder of 1+1Earth, who had him
killed to break the link to himself. Hosfleter thought it was
Marsten who'd tipped them. According to Desault, she had a
whole theory about the hit squad making contact with Gant
through Marsten and then convincing Gant to let them help
him escape. Hosfleter believed the hit team moved Gant's
vehicle to Tioga Lodge, and maybe Gant thought he was home
free and on his way to Mexico when they pulled off on a
sandy desert road.

Terri Delgado was the most recent photo. The two Zetas
that killed her were identified by name. Both were arrested
in Dallas later the same day. That was the way Stoval had his
files set up. It was all there so that if he ever went down,
many people would go with him. Or maybe the files were
carefully kept so that if the day ever came and he needed to
trade, he had information.

Marquez had his own theory. He figured Stoval had the files
and photos so anytime he wanted to he could have the pleasure
of revisiting the thrill. He kept files on his hunts and the photos
there were the standard photos of the proud hunter near the
body of an elephant or black rhino or one of the last tigers,
whatever it was he'd shot, the same photos we're used to seeing
mounted on a wall in a bar or bragged about in a club. There
were records also of animal trafficking and Marquez knew he'd
be months unraveling those.

The murder files went back to 1972. The earliest shots
looked like old Polaroids that lately were scanned into
computer files. Among the first were four women, one left
alongside railroad tracks, one in an alley, two on road shoulders. In the San Francisco Field Office everyone wanted to
see the photo of Gant, but Marquez never looked at the Gant
photo. He did study the early photos and especially one of a
woman lying on a road shoulder. There was no notation of
money paid and his guess was that Stoval took the photo
himself.

He remembered from Billy's tapes that her hair was black
and that there was a field of maize behind her body as there
was in this photo. There wasn't a name on this or any of the
earlier killings with women, but he felt sure this was Billy's
wife, Rosalina. She was as beautiful as Billy had claimed.

He found Anderson outside on a deck, sitting on a lounge

chair with a glass pitcher of margaritas sweating on a glass table next to him. Kerry wouldn't look away from the ocean yet, but offered to get Marquez a glass so he could drink with him, and when Marquez didn't take him up on it, said, 'I knew it would be you.'

'No, all along you thought it was going to work, and now it isn't.'

Marquez looked past the coconut trees and the beach to the purples and blues of the Caribbean. He looked back at the tiled deck. Anderson wore red shorts that finished just below his knees. He wore sandals and a Washington Nationals baseball shirt. Near the pitcher of margaritas was a form half filled out for box seats for the Nationals' next season.

'Are you going to look at me, Kerry?'

'I'm going to look at this view as long as I can.'

'That won't be much longer. They're in the air but almost here. Was it all about money?'

'It was about needing something to look forward to. I couldn't have gone on without it.'

'How does it feel now?'

'Terrible.'

'There are some things I need answered before they get here.'

Anderson took another long drink. 'In Washington they called me Mr Information. Go ahead.'

'I want to ask you some questions about Jim Osiers.'

'What would you like to know? When James Gardiner-Osiers was born? That was March 23 1955, and though you worked with him I'll bet you didn't know that for a long time his name was James Gardiner-Osiers. He was raised by his mother who divorced his father because he ran around with other women constantly. In gratitude to his mother, Osiers dropped her name, Gardiner, as soon as he hit eighteen. That's what happened in Loreto. He was just trying to be like the old man. Getting him to fall for the girlfriend was easy. He'd waited his whole life for that. I got everything ready then for later. I left it muddy. I left it so it could be solved when the time came and I was ready to pull the plug. I needed someone because the leaks were going to end when I left.'

'You set him up with Alicia?'

'No, they found her, but she didn't know any better. The

Salazars knew the Americans would back off once they found out about the pregnant girlfriend. I knew he was vulnerable.' He turned and grinned drunkenly. 'I was the analyst. They were right about his tastes and Stoval liked the idea.'

'So why frame Sheryl Javits?'

'The leak needed to be found before I retired. Sooner or later, someone would figure out information wasn't flowing anymore and start looking at me. Her ex-husband took bribe money. We got her through him. He had a story for her. We worked it for a couple of years and when they divorced he gave her the money. By then, she already believed the cover story.'

'Phelps has been arrested and she's out.'

Anderson waved his hand, dismissing that, saying, 'I knew Stoval had records of everything. He was a fascinating man with an incredible memory.' He added with odd pride, 'I made it almost twenty years.'

'But you didn't make it, Kerry.'

Anderson gave another drunken grin, poured himself another drink and lifted a towel on the small glass table to show Marquez a gun.

'You'd better take it away before I use it on myself. How much time do I have?'

'Maybe an hour.'

'I'd like to watch the ocean until then, if I can.'

Marquez picked up the gun and removed the clip. He pictured Anderson in prison a decade from now, small and gray, sitting on his bunk working on a baseball box score.

'You have to answer some questions for me now,' Anderson said. 'How was I listed in his computer?'

'By a code name and number and you're not alone. You're listed under US government employees. It's the bank transfers that are going to nail you. Every date of every payment is in there, along with what he got for it.'

'So why are you here first and they're not here?'

'They're looking at everything and I was looking for what happened to Group Five and this recent thing with Sheryl. You're listed as a Washington Senator, yet you're under law enforcement, US government. I put it together from our baseball conversations over the years. I'm guessing your season tickets came every year from him.'

'Very good.'

'Four FBI agents are on their way. I called when I changed planes in Miami.'

He left Anderson on the deck and figured he'd run into the FBI crew at the airport, but it turned out they passed him on the road around the island before he got there. He called Desault after turning in the rental car and Desault told him he'd scored big with the Anderson hit.

'If you want to keep the wildlife angle going, this is your chance to push it.'

'Yeah, I want to keep it going, but I've got some ideas.'

The flight home took him to Mexico City. He had a layover there and a bad encounter with two Customs officials who detained him and led him to a room. They left him there for fifteen minutes, and then returned and explained that the questioning would not be here, but at a police station. They still wouldn't say what it was about, but asked for his passport and as he got it out, he realized he wasn't going to give it up.

'I'm going to keep this until the police station.' He opened it for them. 'You can take another look, but you can't have it.'

A third man arrived, a big guy who walked behind them as they went outside toward a police van. The van driver was in a *federales* uniform. He was an older guy with a gut, a black mustache, and a vertical scar right down the middle of his nose. Marquez remembered the scar and as the Customs men closed behind him to force him into the van, he pushed his way back on to the sidewalk. The driver was an old Salazar man.

He knocked away the arm of the one who tried to grab him and got back inside the airport with them following, trying to catch him but not drawing their guns. Nor did they yell or call for help. They didn't want to attract attention and that told him all he needed to know. The third man who'd showed up late dropped away as Marquez walked up to the airline counter. He made the connecting flight.

On the plane a stewardess handed him a large manila envelope with his name and seat number on it. Someone wanted to make sure he got it. As the plane taxied toward the runway, he opened the package and pulled out three black and white photos. He guessed he was looking at a dry wash in Baja.

They had dressed Billy Takado in the Hawaiian shirt and the
old cotton slacks he liked so much. They didn't bother with
shoes. The last photo had a handwritten message, *'Nos vemos
pronto.'* We'll see you again, soon. Maybe you will, maybe
you won't, he thought.

He slid the photos back into the manila envelope, tucked
the envelope into the seat pocket in front of him, and as they
flew over Baja, he thought of Billy and his dreams of a beach
cantina, and of Brian Hidalgo haunted by Vietnam and trying
to take it to the cartels. He remembered Sheryl as they walked
the almond orchard in the night so long ago, and a dawn on
the north coast when the sun rose red through fog as the SOU
busted a big ab poaching ring, and how they celebrated later
on a deck above the ocean in the gold light of fall. You fight
the fight even if it's bigger than you, and keep going, and
meet them head-on at the next spot, or outsmart them and buy
time for a grizzly to get away or a herd of bighorn to disappear into the rocks.

The stewardess returned and he ordered a beer. When it
came, he drank slowly. He looked out the window at the line
of the Sierras floating in the distance. Group 5 was gone and
his years running the SOU were over. In the end, it's all gone.
In the end it's what we cared about and how we lived.